❧

The blonde clung to Jon, her lips pasted on his, her hands grabbing his buttocks, clawing at his clothes.

The bags of groceries slid from Kari's hands and the contents nosily spilled out onto the floor. Her gaze slid to the array of foods littering the just washed linoleum.

Kari watched the broken eggs pool into a gooey mess. She needed to watch, aware that when her eyes found Jon her world would never be the same.

THE COLOR
OF TROUBLE

Dyanne Davis

Genesis Press Inc.

Indigo Love Stories

An imprint Genesis Press Publishing

Genesis Press, Inc.
315 Third Avenue North
Columbus, MS 39701

ISBN: 1-58571-096-2
Manufactured in the United States of America

First Edition

Visit us at www.genesis-press.com
or call at 1-888-Indigo-1

Dedicated To

Angelita Fatima Gomez Leatherwood, my surrogate daughter, my friend, and my staunchest supporter: Thanks for believing in me, as I believe in you.

Acknowledgements

First and foremost my thanks go to God.

Many thanks to my husband, Bill, my love, my friend, and my newest critique partner, for always having my back.

My son, Bill Jr. for your encouragement and love.

Brigid Darden, my personal angel and eternal friend, for your unwavering belief, love and support

Elizabeth Rose, for pushing, encouraging and always being there, to talk, console and rejoice. I'm so glad you're in my life, and that we share the same vision on so many levels.

My critique partners, Wendy Byrne, Barbara Deane and Lauren Ford, three extraordinary writers and wonderful friends, Lauren, thank you for never pulling any punches, for being my very first critique partner and for being a perfect fit. Barb, thank you for your gentleness, your ready kind words and your loving manner. Wendy, thanks Missy, for knowing me so well, for having time to come out to play, for setting impossible goals and pushing me to reach them with you. To the three of you, thanks for being my friends.

Beth Spandonidis, Ann banks and Kelle Riley, thanks for always reading my manuscripts and for telling me honestly what you like and don't like.

Genesis Press, especially Nyani Colom, for you vision for Genesis.

My editor Sidney Rickman, Many many thanks, you're wonderful. You managed to take my vision for this book and make it work.

Windy City Chapter of RWA, the most talented, nurturing, supportive group of writers in the world.

Leila Akl, Susan Brown, Joan McGeever, Melanie Agustin, Shelly Olson, Iris Pokosa, Anjum Yousef and Shelly Tracy, thank you all for being there and for your support.

Tim Darden, just for being you, thoughtful, dependable, and a person I love and admire.

Elysa Hendericks, for your help in the title.

Daniel Zorub, You can't read this, but your prayers were felt.

My family and friends, thanks to all of you for your love and encouragement.

Last but not least, my mother, Katherine Whetstone, and my aunt Mattie Beach. I wish you were both here to enjoy this with me.

CHAPTER ONE

Voices drifted to her from behind the thick oak door. Kari straightened, the little hairs on the back of her neck standing at attention. She could feel a tremor of electricity shoot throughout her body, leaving her with a feeling of dread.

Her hand paused in midair, ready to insert the key. Kari took a long look at the heavily laden pecan trees bordering the right side of her rented house. She swung her gaze to the left and stared at the black walnut tree. An involuntary shiver passed through her as she wondered if she would ever get the chance to gather the harvest.

Her glance fell on the wayward nuts lying on the wraparound porch. Resisting the urge to walk the length of the porch and pick them up, thus postponing what waited for her inside, she remained rooted in front of the door. The unnamed fear was building within her.

The voices became louder and the unmistakable thick drawl of a woman overrode every emotion that Kari was feeling. Seeming to watch her own actions in slow motion, she slid the metal key into the lock and turned it, gaining entrance. "Jon." She called his name softly, something telling her to warn him that she was home.

Two steps into the kitchen, the scent of the woman hit her nostrils before her eyes found them.

The blonde clung to Jon, her lips pasted on his, her hands grabbing his buttocks, clawing at his clothes.

The bags of groceries slid from Kari's hands and the contents nosily spilled out onto the floor. Her gaze slid to the array of foods littering the just washed linoleum.

Kari watched the broken eggs pool into a gooey mess. She needed to watch, aware that when her eyes found Jon her world would never be the same.

"Kari."

When she heard the alarm in his voice, dread filled her heart. She closed her eyes, forcing the tears back, picturing the laden trees outside. Stupid. Her life was falling apart and absurdly enough she was mourning the inevitable loss of the trees.

She watched as Jon disentangled himself from the woman's arms and legs. She could see the panic in his face. Panic at being caught.

"Kari," he said, "this is not what it looks like." He took three steps toward her and stopped. "Kari," he called her name more softly, "look at me." But she couldn't. Her gaze was now locked on the woman.

Mute, Kari watched the smiling woman turn toward her. She could feel the tightness in the pit of her stomach, where her stress always started. Her limbs were flaccid. She prayed that she wouldn't fall.

Red lacquered nails disappeared for a moment inside the woman's jacket pocket. For an instant Kari thought the woman was reaching for a gun. In fact, she was hoping that she was. *That's it, a gun.* Kari wanted the woman to produce a gun, pull the trigger and kill her, put her out of her misery.

Instead, she shoved a large brownish envelope toward her. If possible, the woman's cruel smile became even more vicious, filled with the same hatred that Kari had endured since falling in love with Jon.

Trembling, she reached for the envelope. Then suddenly she realized she was holding her breath, she gulped in fresh air as though she were drowning. And in a way she was.

She looked at Jon and felt confused as he stepped toward the woman who less than a minute before he had been embracing. His muscles tensed beneath his shirt and he appeared angry. That confused her even more. Why should he be angry?

Then Jonathan turned toward her. She couldn't believe it, but she saw fear in his eyes. Perhaps the glistening of tears, though she couldn't be sure, because she was looking at him through the haze of her own tears.

"Kari don't! Don't look in the envelope. Let me explain."

He dared a small step toward her and she took a step back.

"Did you really think Jon was going to be satisfied with dark chocolate when he could have me? Correction. *After* he's had me?" the woman mocked. "What's wrong, Jon? Don't you think it's time you told her that you've only been using her?" With a toss of her head, blonde curls bounced around her shoulder. "You never wanted a ni—"

"Don't you dare, Sharon."

Sharon. Kari allowed the name to sink in. How it was possible she hadn't known? Having a name to go with the face made the situation even more surreal.

"Tell her the truth, Jon. You'd never marry her." Sharon turned to smirk at Kari. "Think about it, Kari, you're not a stupid woman. It's been three years. If Jonathan wanted to marry you, he could have done it already. Which of us do you think his parents approve of, you or me?"

"Shut the hell up, Sharon," Jon hissed. "You're lying.

"Jon, unless she's stupid, she'll know I'm telling her the truth. We're lovers, the pictures speak for themselves. If you're going to be ashamed for sleeping with anyone it should be the nig—"

Kari stared at the woman whose name she now knew was Sharon. She wondered if the woman thought calling her that name was going to make her break down. If so, she'd be disappointed.

Kari had heard that name too many times. She blinked and looked at Jon, determined to hide her hurt.

"Kari, it's going to be okay. I promise, just give me a minute to explain." Jon felt panic. Kari appeared ready to fall any moment. He had to get Sharon out of the house. If she said another mean thing to Kari he would not be responsible for his actions.

Teeth clenched, he stood between the two women. One he wanted to strangle, the other he wanted to embrace. He could only pray that Kari would believe her heart, not what she'd seen with her own eyes.

In one easy stride he grabbed Sharon's arm and propelled her out of the room and toward the front door.

"If you want to know the truth, Kari, look at the pictures, all of them." Sharon flung the words over her shoulder at the same time the door closed behind her.

Jon cringed. He needed a chance to explain. He hurried back into the kitchen. Kari would open the pictures. Any woman would. Too late.

Kari's hand shook slightly as her fingers grasped a glossy photograph and pulled it out. She stared at it in shock. Barechested, Jon nuzzled the woman's neck. His hard muscles were cradling her as they had cradled Kari. Sharon's flimsy red silk negligee left no doubt as to the couple's intent, not with the right strap over her elbow and Jon's lips buried in her soft flesh. The photo left no doubt in Kari's mind.

Spasm after spasm racked her body. She felt like a windup toy as she stood shaking uncontrollably, her eyes filling with tears as she watched Jon approach her.

"Get out." Despite herself, her voice trembled slightly and she fought for something to hold onto, anything.

As Kari stared into Jon's glacier blue eyes, she willed ice to form around her heart. She had to shut him out. She could no longer allow herself to love him.

"Please, Jon, don't."

"Kari…" He took another step toward her.

"No, Jon."

Ignoring her he closed the distance and pulled her into his arms, crooning softly. For a moment she allowed herself to settle there, needing his embrace one last time. Closing her eyes, Kari felt an involuntary shudder rip through her and she moaned softly. Jon's hands moved over her, tentatively at first, then bolder as only a lover's would do, gently caressing her skin.

Though her head was burrowed in his chest, her arms still hung limply at her sides. She sucked in air. It was then that the thick musty odor assaulted her nostrils. She gagged and pushed him away, flooded with shame. How could she possibly feel anything for him after all that had happened? "It's over Jon."

"Don't," he began, "Sharon means nothing to me. She was a job, nothing more. I can explain the picture."

The picture… She discovered she was still holding it. She could feel the bones in her spine stiffening as she held it up. "I can see, I don't need an explanation."

Sudden exhaustion pulled at her ebbing strength. If Jon didn't leave soon she might weaken and forgive him for all the lies and hurts. She might forgive him for the three years of her life she had spent loving him.

"Jon, either you leave or I will. I'll go and stay with Jackie." She stood still and watched him, fighting with her heart for control of her life. She was glad she had not gotten around to telling him that, Jackie had moved to Chicago. He wouldn't want her to be alone, he'd worry about her. *Oh God,* she thought, *that was before, he doesn't care. It's over. What will I do without him*? She almost moaned aloud as she imagined her life without him.

"Kari." His voice was ragged, filled with the pain of having hurt her. He couldn't stand the way she was looking at him. What a fool he had been. He had known he would eventually have to explain the incriminating pictures.

Kari flung the picture toward him and for one brief moment he felt relief. That picture he could explain. Now if he could persuade Kari to give him the envelope without looking at the rest of the pictures, they would get through this.

Enduring her glare, he said, "I posed for that picture. We needed the money."

"What's new about our needing money?" she screamed at him. "We've always needed money, Jon." Her eyes went to the envelope in her hand. She was afraid to look at the other photos, afraid of what she'd see. "You should have told me, we could have doubled our income. We could have both posed." She closed her eyes tightly, wanting to hit him, wanting to rip him apart, hurt him as he was hurting her.

"Kari, I didn't have an affair with her."

Kari nodded at the photo on the floor. "Pictures don't lie."

"Kari, Sharon set me up. She pretended she wanted to help me. She came up to me on campus one day and asked if I was a model. I told her no, but she said if I ever wanted to make money, she could get me some modeling jobs."

"And how exactly was that setting you up?"

"That wasn't what she wanted."

"What was it that she wanted, Jon?"

"She wanted me, at least that's what I thought at first." He clenched his hands, then unclenched them, cursing his own stupidity. "When I started posing for the pictures, she began coming on to me. At first I didn't think much of it. I might have been a little flattered, but that's all. I told her about you, that I loved you, that we were getting married. I even told her that we were going to have a baby."

He heard Kari's moan, low and guttural, filled with pain. "Kari, give me the envelope, okay."

"No."

"Then let me explain, please."

"Just tell me this, Jon, if you're not in love with her, why do the things she said make so much sense? Everyone knows how your mother feels about me. Is Sharon right, Jon? Was I crazy to think that you loved me, that you wanted to marry me? She has a point, it's been three years."

"Kari, how can you believe any of this?"

"Because you didn't tell me. If what you say is true, why didn't you tell me?" She was unable to prevent a tiny moan from slipping out. "Why didn't you tell me? And why did I come home and find her in your arms?"

He didn't want to tell her; he would give anything if there were a way out of this mess he'd created. His face twisted in agony and he bit his lips. "Will you hear me out?" She didn't answer; he'd not expected that she would.

"Sharon has been attempting to blackmail me. At first I didn't take it seriously. I thought she'd eventually give up and go away. And for awhile it did seem like I'd gotten rid of her, that she'd finally understood that I would never leave you. Then..."

"Then what?"

"She threatened to go to the police and tell them I'd raped her. She said she could prove it was me, that unless I left you, she'd do it."

"Jon, none of this is making any sense. How would she have proof unless it were true?"

"You don't believe that."

"There were a lot of things I didn't believe before; maybe the things I did believe weren't true. I'll ask you again, why would she say she can prove it, Jon?"

He tried to answer her, he really did, but his mouth refused to work. All he wanted was for her to hand him the rest of the pictures. What she'd looked at so far was bad, but she could get over that one in time. If she saw the one where he— Where Sharon— In his heart, he knew that picture would end everything.

From the first time he'd posed he had known there was more to it, had felt a wrongness in every fiber of his being. But by then he had been determined to do whatever it took to give Kari some of the things she deserved.

"Are you a rapist, Jon?" She was staring at him, listening to the words that were coming out of her mouth, knowing that without a doubt she'd prefer that he was a rapist. She'd prefer to believe anything other than what she knew to be true: He didn't love her.

She looked at the picture, her mother's voice in her head. "I saw that boy in the park, with some white girl, Kari. He was kissing her."

Kari felt the tears coming. God, she didn't want to cry in front of him. She wanted to hurt him, so she asked again. "Are you a rapist, Jon?"

Sharon had been using the pictures to try to blackmail him for weeks. But this, Kari believing him to be a rapist, it was insane.

"Kari, you know that's not true." He reached out for her but was stopped by the look of revulsion on her face. "How could you possibly think that? You've lived with me for three years, you've loved me."

"That's the key thing, isn't it? Loved, past tense. I loved you, Jon. Not anymore."

His voice was thick with pain. "I can explain about the pictures, but this…" He waved his hands expansively. "This is crazy and you know it."

"Why? Because you say it is?" She tilted her chin upward, waiting for an answer. "Is it also crazy that I walk into our home and find you in the arms of another woman?"

For months Jon's whereabouts had been something of a mystery, with him refusing to give her even the tiniest hint of what he was doing. Now she knew why.

"You have to listen to me." He attempted to bridge the gap between them by moving closer but stopped as she moved away.

"Sharon heard you come in the door," he continued. "So did I. It all happened so fast. She threw herself into my arms, then you were here. Watching. She staged the whole thing. She came here with the pictures."

Kari's gaze fell on the envelope still clutched in her hand, felt the bulky weight of the remaining contents.

"Don't look at the others," Jon pleaded with her.

"Why? They can't possibly be more telling."

He took a deep breath. "Sharon was threatening to show them to you, to convince you that we were having an affair."

His voice sounded desperate even to his own ears. He knew what was on the pictures. If the situation were reversed, he didn't know if he would believe what had really happened.

Jon took another step toward Kari and hesitated. He felt tiny pinpricks niggling at his scalp, a sure sign that he was about to lose his temper.

Everything that he had done, he had done for the two of them. Now the one person that he thought would always be there for him was throwing him out.

She should believe me, he thought. *I shouldn't have to explain this, not after all that we've been through*. But he had no time to indulge his anger. He had to make her understand, make her believe him.

Usually when she was angry with him, he had only to hold her and her anger would dissipate. God, how he wished this was one of those times.

He tried once more. "I was in those pictures only to make money. They're staged, you know, for the magazine. That's all there was to it." Jon tried to smile. "I didn't tell you because I wanted to surprise you with a ring. I thought it was time you had one and you know we haven't had the money for it."

He was doing what he could to mask his own hurt and anger. He could only pray that his voice was soothing.

Kari's hand moved slowly upwards toward her face. Her heart was beating faster at his mention of an engagement ring. She gazed at his eyes, warm with what she would have taken the day before as love. Now she trusted nothing.

"Where is the ring, Jon? Let me see it." She looked past him, a small piece of her wanting him to pull a ring from his pocket, but not believing that he could.

"I don't have it, not now. I still don't have all the money for it."

She watched as he tried for another smile. He was trying to charm her as he had done for the past three years. This time he couldn't, not with the stink of another woman on his clothes, in their home.

"Haven't you noticed we haven't been receiving nearly as many calls from bill collectors?"

"No, I haven't noticed." She wanted to slap the smile off his face. *How dare he think he could fix things so easily.*

He sighed, wishing he had chosen to make payments on the ring instead of putting it on layaway. He was losing Kari. She didn't believe him.

"I thought I would have it by now. Just a couple of more jobs would have been all that it would take, but I had to stop posing once I found out what Sharon was trying to do with the pictures." He could feel the desperation clutching at him, closing off his words. "I was set up, Kari."

He watched her eyes. "From the beginning, she only wanted me to pose with her in order to have something to use, something to make you believe I didn't love you. And it wasn't because she wanted me. Someone paid Sharon to break us apart. I don't know who's behind it, Kari, but you can bet someone put her up to this."

"Who, Jon? You're painting a picture of this big conspiracy and all I see is you, you and this woman. I see you've been lying and cheating. Now you want me to believe a mysterious person or persons went to all of this trouble to break us up."

"Is that so hard for you to believe?" He wanted to scream at her to stop it, that she was scaring him with the hate-filled looks she was giving him. *Hell, she probably wants to do some screaming of her own,* he thought.

More rationally, he continued. "Look at all we've been through in the last three years. I don't blame you for being angry, but I swear to you, Kari, that I was pushing her off, not embracing her. It wasn't what you thought."

Jon tried to gauge Kari's reaction. He took a step closer to her. "Kari, I love you."

"Damn you, Jon. Damn you to hell!" Kari pulled at her lips with her teeth, sinking them into the soft flesh. She needed to feel the pain. She was slowly losing her battle to not allow him to see just how much he'd hurt her. She bit down harder, hoping to hang on, if only for a moment longer.

She felt dizzy. She wished now she had eaten. As her body swayed, she screamed out, all her agony in that one sound.

Jon lunged to catch her, but her head hit the corner of the cabinet and she bit her lips hard. Her mouth filled with a salty liquid and she knew it was her blood.

Kari gave herself over entirely to the pain. Not the pain of the fall, but the pain of admitting that the man she loved was a cheat. And if he were a cheat, maybe he really was capable of the crime she was accusing him of. Maybe there really was a sinister side to Jon, a side that she had not heretofore discovered.

As she lifted her hand toward her face, she leveled her eyes on Jon. It was the first time she'd allowed herself to really see him since entering the house. His arms encircled her gently. There was pain in his eyes, yet she was determined to ignore it.

Kari closed her eyes, and shook her head. As her body began a rhythmic rocking back and forth she could feel Jon's arms tightening around her.

She reached out her hand, hooking it under the well worn underside of the chair and pulled herself up from the floor. Pushing aside Jon's hand, she forced herself to take a step backward, away from the confines of the man she loved.

"Keep the house, Jon. I'll leave." With that Kari walked to their bedroom. She glanced around the room wondering what had gone wrong. There was no time to think on that now. She averted her glance from the bed, their bed, the bed they'd shared for over three years.

She shivered as she yanked the closet door open. With Jackie gone she had no choice but to go to her parents' home and that she didn't want to do. She pulled out her luggage from the closet and began ripping her clothes from the hangers, throwing them into the bag.

Her heart was screaming out to her to allow Jonathan a chance to explain, to make it right. But she'd listened to her heart for far too long; now it was time she began listening to her head. Sensing Jon standing behind her, she turned to glare at him. Though a look of pain crossed his face, she could not let it dissuade her. She had to stay focused.

"Are you going to be all right?" His voice was hoarse.

"What?"

He pointed toward her face. "Kari, let me help you. You're still bleeding." He paused, taking a good look at her glazed eyes. "You're scaring the hell out of me."

Anger replaced all other emotions for Kari. She wanted to blame Jon for her falling, for not catching her soon enough, for her biting her lips. She wanted him to hurt the way she was. It didn't matter that her thoughts were irrational. They kept her going.

Her eyes found the phone. Aware that Jon was watching her every move, she inched toward it. "Get out, Jon, and let me pack or I'll call the cops on you myself. I never want to see you again."

"Kari, you love this house." He started toward her and stopped. This couldn't be happening, not after everything they had been through. "You can't really believe I raped anyone. The night she claimed it happened, I was with you. It was the Friday after Valentine's Day. We were together the entire day. Neither of us had classes and for a change we didn't have to work. Remember?"

She looked him up and down. "Yeah, I do remember," she said sarcastically. "We barely talked. I thought you were angry with me about something. I went to bed early. Alone. I fell asleep. You could have left."

"Kari, you know that's not true, the same way you know that I'm not a rapist. And you damn well know I haven't been with you to spite my parents, that's bull. Why the hell would I sleep with you for three years if I didn't love you? That makes no sense."

"I think Sharon said it best. You wanted to hurt your parents so you chose me. What better way to snub your nose at them?"

"Open your eyes, Kari. This thing was set up. I don't know who, but someone was trying to break us apart."

"Tell me who, Jon."

"It could be anyone in this damn town, black or white."

"Why? Why would anyone go to such trouble?"

"Because they hate that we're together. They want to break us apart, Kari! Think. For three years both of our parents have tried everything, using everyone they know to come between us."

Jon ran his hand up the bridge of his nose in contemplation. "Kari, I want you to listen to me very carefully. After this, after what happened today, I believe Sharon will stop at nothing to get what she wants. She's going to give the police my name. If you don't tell the truth, I'll go to jail for something I didn't do."

He stopped talking for a moment before deciding to take a gamble on their love, for his freedom. He knew Kari, knew how much she loved him. Hell yes, she was angry now, but she'd never desert him.

"Kari, if you don't tell the truth, I'll go to jail."

"I have no truth to tell, Jon, unless you want me to tell the police that I don't know where you were. She glared at him. "If Sharon doesn't have proof, Jon, you have nothing to worry about, do you?"

"If you don't believe me, Kari, I don't stand a chance of convincing anyone else."

"Then I'm afraid you're in serious trouble."

Jon took a long look at the woman he loved. Her almond-shaped dark brown eyes were filled with doubt.

"For three years we've fought together against our families and the entire town. You know what we've gone through! Now you want to believe I've been cheating on you?"

There was a catch in his voice. "You can't really believe any of this. You know me. You know I wouldn't cheat on you." In a smaller voice he continued, "You also know I'm not a rapist."

Why hadn't he yielded to Kari's pleading to leave their hometown and start over in some big city? He wondered. He had insisted they stay and fight. Now he had nothing, not even her, not any more.

He had to try again. "Kari, it's not true, any of it. It's all a bunch of lies. Can't you see that? Someone wants to break us apart and you're letting them."

He watched her carefully and saw her lips quiver just the tiniest bit. He knew she wanted to believe him so he pressed harder, confident now that he would win.

Not daring to make any sudden moves toward her, he spoke softly. "Honey, is this really what you want, to throw away everything we've worked so hard for? Tell me, Kari, does our love mean so little to you?"

He paused and allowed the indignation to surface. "When did you stop trusting me?"

"I stopped trusting you when I saw you here in our kitchen with your lover." Kari stopped, her voice choked off by tears. She turned away, not wanting him to see,

not wanting his lies. She couldn't listen to him. He had only used her. Their love had never been real. That thought brought renewed pain. She turned back and her eyes sought his. She threw the packet containing over a dozen more photos of him with Sharon. The pictures flew out and swirled around both of them.

"You never loved me, Jon. Sharon was right. You used me to thumb your nose at your parents and the town. Well, now you're free. Your parents wanted you to have a white woman and apparently so did you. Now you have one." It all made sense to her now. All the calls, all the times he had left her alone, not explaining where he was.

Pain was slicing through her as she lied, "I never loved you either. It was a game for both of us. Now it's over. I'll do the same thing you've done. I'll find someone more suitable, someone my parents approve of." She turned her back to him and refocused her attention on the bag she was packing.

"Why don't you be honest with me for once?"

She stared at him, again surprised by the anger in his voice. *Why?* she wondered. She was the one who had been hurt.

Jon could feel his own anger spiraling out of control. For three years they had skirted around this problem. Now it was time that they named it.

"If you can't be honest with me, for God's sake be honest with yourself. You can't handle the fact that you fell in love with me, a white man. Admit it, Kari."

He moved toward her, then paused, the look of revulsion on her face almost more than he could handle. "Don't you think I ever notice that when we're out in public you pretend that I'm not important to you, that you drop my hand if a black man comes anywhere near us?"

"If I do, its to prevent trouble," she screamed at him. "Not important to me? You're so wrong." She moved to the dresser, Jonathan's words making her even more angry, and dumped the contents of the drawer into her open bag. She was tired of yelling at Jon. The things he was saying were stupid. Not important to her? He was her world. She wanted to tell him that what she'd done, she'd done to keep him from getting his ass kicked by brothers who hated that she was with him. But why bother?

Jonathan felt his heart breaking as he stood helplessly watching Kari toss her clothes into the bag. He had to do something, or she would be gone. He searched frantically for a sign, any hint that she was weakening, remembering how much they loved each other, but it wasn't there.

"Kari, this isn't about Sharon or the pictures. For three years you've been looking for an excuse not to love me. Tell me, Kari, why didn't you cry when you had the miscarriage last month. Or was it really a miscarriage? If you didn't want to love me…" He took in a breath, the effort hurting him as he closed his eyes against the unwanted thought. "It was the same with the baby, wasn't it? You didn't want to love either of us."

He had hoped that his last remark would at least bring denial, but her face was blank. He was getting nowhere with her. He was angrier than he had ever been in his life and at the same time so afraid of losing the woman he loved. This time as he walked toward her he was undaunted by the look on her face.

"For God sakes, stop looking at me as if you're afraid of me." He was masking his hurt with anger. "You sure as hell don't believe I'm a rapist." The muscle in his jaw twitched with anger. "You can stop packing. You don't have to go and stay with Jackie. I'll leave."

A desperate plan took shape in his mind. "Do you want me punished? Would you like to see me in jail for a lie? My only concern in the first place was not wanting you hurt." Once again she didn't answer him.

He sucked in his breath. He was about to take a terrifying gamble. It was all he could think to do to bring Kari to her senses. "I'm not going to submit to blackmail, Kari. You have the key to my cell. When you come for me, I'll know that you believe me and that you love me."

He picked up the phone and dialed. "Sharon, make the call to the cops, give them my name. I'm not leaving Kari."

CHAPTER TWO

News of Jon's arrest spread quickly through the small town as she had known it would. Many of their neighbors watched as Jon sat on the porch waiting for the police car. Kari saw them between the slats of the blinds.

At the sight of the car she felt a coldness that chilled her to the bone. She pressed her head against the wood on the window frame, determined not to give in to the guilt that was weighing down on her. Jon had not raped Sharon. That much she knew.

She watched as two policemen got out of the vehicle. She shuddered as the neighbors watched, curious, as Jon walked toward the car, his shoulders slightly bent. Mr. Johnson, the neighbor to their left, later reported that Jon glanced once at his own front door, then got into the government car.

That last bit of information Kari learned from the Lonett paper. She had finally turned away before Jonathan climbed into the car.

☙

Kari managed to push the occasional guilt aside. *If the police don't have concrete proof they'll release him. Surely,* she thought, *it isn't the lack of my alibi that's keeping him in jail.* That line became her mantra every time she received an angry call or another piece of hate mail.

Within a week it was her empty bed that made her question herself. She wondered if Jon could have been telling her the truth.

She thought about their bills. She hadn't noticed before, but he was right. The frequent calls had ceased. She thought of the pictures Sharon had given her. She'd picked them up after Jon's arrest and shoved them back into the envelope without looking at them. The one she'd seen was enough.

Clutching Jon's pillow, she sniffed for his scent. She missed it and him. He was right. She loved him, and she would not leave him in jail because of a lie. Having made her decision, she dressed quickly before she could change her mind. She wanted Jonathan to explain. This time she'd listen.

She was so eager to be in Jonathan's arms that she missed his mother standing in the lobby of the jail. It wasn't until the woman spoke to her that she saw her.

"What are you doing here? Haven't you caused enough trouble?"

"Mrs. Steele, I didn't do anything."

"You're damn right you didn't do anything, not a damn thing to keep my boy outta jail."

Kari closed her eyes and counted to three. "I'm here now." She ignored the woman and spoke to the officer behind the desk. "I'm here to see Jonathan Steele," she said.

"He doesn't want to see you," the older woman barked at her. Kari ignored her, as she ignored the look the officer gave to Jonathan's mother before he went to the back, toward the cells. When he returned, he told her that Jonathan didn't want to see her.

"I told you he's through with you. You've done enough to hurt him. Why don't you do the decent thing and get outta his life for good? Leave, leave town. No one will miss you."

Kari gave the woman a cold look as the dislike mounted between them. "Jonathan will miss me. He's angry now, but I'll be back. Nothing you can do will ever break us apart. We love each other." She turned again to the officer. "Tell Jonathan that I'll give him a couple of days to cool off. Tell him I'll be back."

Kari walked away from the jail, knowing that when she went again it would be different. Jonathan would see her and she'd forgive him and he'd forgive her. He'd take her in his arms, making things right. She shivered from the vividness of her vision.

Only her vision didn't go as she'd anticipated. When she returned to the jail, prepared to see Jonathan's mother standing guard, she found Sharon with her.

"So, Kari, it looks as if you really are stupid. Did Jonathan's mother tell you that I'm pregnant, that Jonathan and I are getting married?"

"If he raped you, Sharon, why would you want to marry him?"

"To give my baby a name, and because Jon belongs with me, not you. Give it up, he loves me."

"Then have him released from jail, tell the truth. Let him out, then we'll see which of us he loves." Kari saw a look pass from Sharon to Jon's mother. Then Sharon spoke.

"You leave town, I'll recant."

"I'd rather see him in jail than with you," his mother added. "You leave town, leave my boy to me, then I'll get him out. Besides, Sharon's right. Jonathan would never allow a bastard to be brought into this family. He's going to marry Sharon."

Sharon held her hand out and Kari saw the diamond that twinkled at her, the diamond that Jon didn't have enough money to get for her sat on Sharon's finger. She wanted to run out but she wouldn't give them the satisfaction.

They all turned as the door opened again and the minister from Ebeneezer Baptist came in, Pastor Bob. Although they were acquainted, he ignored Kari. He went to Sharon and Mrs. Steele. "Are you two ready?" he asked.

Kari fell backwards against the counter, her head spinning. This couldn't be happening. As the trio was led into the back, she forced herself to walk away. "Leave town, Kari, or Jonathan will rot in jail." The old woman's voice coming from the corridor sounded like a cackle to her.

Kari was numb when she arrived home. She did the only thing she could think to do. She pulled the envelope containing the pictures out of the drawer and looked at them, all of them.

Jonathan had lied to her; he'd cheated on her. Tears ran down her face as she studied the photo of Jonathan's arousal planted firmly in Sharon's mouth.

So, this is why you didn't want me to look at the pictures, Jon. She shoved the pictures away. He could rot in jail for all she cared. She was not leaving town.

CB

Month after month passed slowly and Jon remained in jail. Her financial resources depleted, Kari was forced to make a decision about moving home with her parents or withdrawing from college and finding a second full time job. Even with her grant it took both her and Jon's income to afford the house. Jon, was right; she loved the house. She wanted to keep it as long as possible. She withdrew from school, determined that she would not allow Jonathan's mother to force her out of town. She wasn't the one who'd put Jon in jail, and it wasn't up to her to get him out. *But you could*, a little voice whispered to her.

She thought of Jon and the fact that he too was missing out on his last year of college before he entered law school. She wondered what effect his incarceration would have on his future. *Don't worry about Jon*, she chided herself. *His parents will eventually rescue him now that I'm out of the picture.*

Her parents' offer to allow her to move back home was tempting. Their offer to pay her last year's tuition even more so, but she resisted. Their acceptance for now was enough. She wanted to work hard to regain their respect, a respect she'd lost for three years because of loving Jon.

Kari rubbed at her shoulder, the heavy tray digging into it. She'd been at work for nearly seven hours. She glanced down at her watch, wishing her shift were over. She hated working the day shift. She ignored the fact that she was given more tables and making far less money than the white waitress. After all, this was Lonett, her hometown. What had she expected?

Eventually the last of the customers was gone and she was free to take a much-needed break. She sat with a cup of coffee, almost numb with fatigue from her grueling schedule. Her breaks were the shortest, but again, what could she do? She knew it was unfair but she was grateful for the job. She sighed as she saw Janice sashaying toward her. *No, not again. I don't need this.*

She heard a whooshing sound as the woman's fairly large butt plopped down on the vinyl seat.

"So, how's Jon?"

Kari stared blankly for a moment. *My God, can't the woman think of anything else to say?* She remained silent. Taking another slow sip of her coffee, she counted to ten and waited. Why bother answering questions about Jon when she knew the woman didn't care.

"Sugar, I'm sure glad we became friends. I never thought blacks were all that bad myself. Why there's good and bad in all races, I suppose. I know lots of good black folks. Hell, I suppose I know lots of bad white folks too."

Kari cringed inwardly. *Ignore her. Don't answer, she'll go away.* She took another sip from her cup. The brew now tasted bitter. She watched a smile light up the woman's face. She knew what was coming.

"I have someone for you to meet." Janice paused for a second, no longer. Taking a deep breath she continued, "He's handsome and he has a job."

Here we go again, Kari thought and clicked on her ignore button.

"Well, he's black," Janice continued. "Is that all right?"

Kari didn't answer and Janice appeared not to notice. She was sick of hearing, "Don't you like black men?" And sick of people thinking it was their duty to find her one.

She loved black men. She would be stupid not to. It had just happened that when she fell in love her heart forgot to notice the skin color.

She was also sick of hearing people tell her they had no problem with blacks when she had not asked the question. In her earlier years she had simply responded, "I have no problems with whites either." She'd found that that offended them but they couldn't see that their remarks offended her. They thought they were merely being friendly or honest.

Well, to hell with all of that. Now she no longer had to do that. She wasn't with Jon any longer. She could be herself. Then it really hit her for the first time. She wasn't with Jon.

"You know, Kari, I've never taught my children to dislike you people. I even let them play with blacks. I don't mind from time to time if they invite them over for dinner." Janice flicked at the chipped paint on her nail, deciding whether to divulge her secret for racial peace. She smiled at the pretty young black woman.

"You know, whenever my kids invite you people over, I make sure to make them feel welcome. I always fry up a batch of chicken and cook up a mess of greens from my own garden."

Kari sat her cup on the scarred counter as carefully as if it contained nitroglycerin. She had become lost in thought, familiar with the turn of the conversation. Today was not the day for her to listen and ignore.

"I'm glad to hear that. You know I try to do the same for my white friends. I try hard to think of every tasteless unseasoned dish I've ever eaten and that's what I serve them." Kari watched the woman's face reddened.

"One other thing, Janice, about me and Jon…" Kari stood and smiled. "I'm going to let you in on a little secret. Jon was just an experiment. I love black men. You know that myth they have about black men and white men? Well, it's true. I've discovered it first-hand. From now on it's only black men for me."

Kari's hand disappeared behind her back and she undid the ties of her apron slowly and deliberately. "I think it's time I started hanging with a better class of people. What do you think, Janice?"

Janice was sitting frozen, her face red, not understanding how condescending her entire conversation had been. She was a liberal. How could this woman turn on her? Hell, she'd told her she had nothing against Negroes.

Black, Janice, black. That's what they want to be called now, or is it African American? She felt her cheeks burning hotter as Kari stared at her as though reading her thoughts. *Sweet Jesus, that couldn't be true.*

Kari smiled, then shook her head. Why now was she confronting the woman? She had had this same conversation from the first day she'd begun working at the diner.

Maybe that was the reason. She'd grown tired of listening and smiling, pretending she had been given a compliment by someone acknowledging that maybe she wouldn't personally stab them in their sleep.

Then and there Kari's mind was made up. She would leave her home, not because of anything Jon's mother had said, but because she had nothing holding her here, not any longer.

From far away a little voice whispered in her subconscious ear. *If only we had left together*.

No! At first she thought she had shouted the word out loud. She definitely had to leave before she could continue doubting herself. Now that she knew it all, she had to get away.

Fifteen minutes later Kari had called her mother for a ride, turned in her apron, and walked out the door with her head high, smiling as though she had a million bucks in the bank.

Out in the fresh air, she breathed in the scent of honeysuckle, one of the many things she would miss about home.

Movement across the street in front of the courthouse caught her attention. She didn't know why she remained fixed, not moving toward her mother's car even though she knew that her mother would be annoyed that she'd called for a ride then stood on the curb behaving like a ninny.

Her eyes were transfixed by the government vehicle and its occupant. She no longer smelled the honeysuckle. All the air was being squeezed from her diaphragm. She watched in horror as the officers brought a man from the car. One of them laid his hands on top of the prisoner's head to protect him from bumping it.

Kari heard the rattle of the chains before she actually saw them. In that moment she was frozen in time, willing the man to turn toward her. He did. Her gasp was so loud she was afraid he heard it.

It was Jon, chained, hands and feet. Their eyes connected. The pain and torment in his glance caused her to flinch. *Oh my God, what have I done?*

His blue eyes turned cold and shut her out. Kari shivered once.

She couldn't move. Her eyes remained transfixed, staring at the chains.

Why do they need to have him in chains? Other people were watching also. Someone walked past and spit on the ground near her feet. Kari didn't know how long she would have stayed rooted to the spot if her mother, witnessing everything, had not gotten out of her car and physically removed her, making her get in the car.

"You're not feelin' sorry for him, are you?"

Her mother's voice contained a coldness that Kari recognized. It was the usual tone she used when talking about Jon.

Her mother hated him, hated the fact that he was white. She blamed him for leading her daughter astray, sure that he must have been giving her drugs to make her stay with him.

Kari had tried explaining to her mother on several occasions throughout the years that even though they worked hard, with school and all their expenses they could barely afford food, let alone drugs.

"Kari, I'm talkin' to you. Snap out of it. Now don't you go gettin' no fool notion about gettin' that boy outta jail. You leave him to his folks."

"Mom, I was just surprised to see him in chains."

"Well, it serves him right. He's a damn rapist. I knew he was no good. You shoulda listened."

"Jon didn't rape anyone, Mom."

"That gal wouldn't lie on him, not on one of her own." Her mother glanced at her fiercely. "You'd best be glad you're not in jail for coverin' up for him. You had to know about it. Everybody thinks so." She paused for a brief respite in her tirade.

Kari was sure she was doing it deliberately. She was giving her words a minute to sink in, hoping to put the fear of God into her, no doubt.

"Abetting, that's a serious crime, the sheriff told me." Her mother gave her a smug look before continuing. "I told you months ago I saw that boy kissing that gal in the park." She gave a snort of satisfaction. "You didn't want to listen to me, did you? I bet you never even asked him about it."

Kari was feeling sick to her stomach. She wished for once her mother would just let the conversation drop.

"Well, did you ever ask him?" Her mother was staring at her with furrowed brows, her mouth twisted in disgust.

"No, Mom, I never mentioned it to him."

"For God's sake. Why not? I swear you can be such a fool at times." Her voice and manner spoke of her disgust for her daughter as well as for her lover. "Didn't you wanna know? Any sane person woulda confronted him. Why didn't you?" Her tone demanded an answer.

"I just didn't, Mom, that's all." Kari shut herself away into that dark place in her soul even though she wanted to tell her mother the reason.

She had never mentioned the incident to Jon because for almost three years her parents had shunned her, disowning her and refusing to even speak to her unless it was to call with some insane accusations against Jon.

One day out of the blue, without even inquiring how she was doing, her mother had phoned to say Jon was cheating on her, that she'd seen it with her own eyes. More of the usual accusations designed to break them up.

Oh, yeah, she'd believed that one all right! Besides, the same day her mother called, Jon had returned home from school and work exhausted.

Kari remembered the night vividly. Despite his weary condition he had made love to her so tenderly, so exquisitely, so lovingly, that any doubts her mother's call might have prompted were smashed.

No man made love like that to a woman he didn't love. At least that's what Kari had thought that night. But she would tell her mother none of that. She would suffer through her disgust.

"Honey, you need to worry about yourself and forget about that boy. Good riddance to bad rubbish."

"Yeah, you're right, Mom. Good riddance." She spoke the words despite the almost crippling pain, pain she would not show her mother.

She was the reason for Jon's predicament. His stare, the slight stumbling gait, the chains. She would never forget any of it. It would forever remain imprinted on her soul, as would his betrayal.

She shifted slightly, readying herself to announce her decision. "Mom, I think I'm going to finish school in Chicago. I applied for a loan and the money came through. You remember my friend, Jacqueline Jackson? Well, she moved to Chicago. She said I could stay with her until I find my own apartment."

"Good, the farther you are away from that boy, the better."

For once her mother didn't insist on coming in when she dropped her off. Kari knew the reason. After seeing Jon chained at the courthouse, her mother didn't have to worry that he was hiding in the house. Yes, it was indeed time that she left.

Her decision made, there was no need to malinger. Only one chore remained.

"Mrs. Steele, This is Kari. Don't hang up, please. You told me at the jail that you would help Jon, if I left town. You win, I'm leaving."

"When?" the cold voice demanded.

"As soon as I've packed my things. I should be out by tomorrow."

"Good, the sooner the better. And when you pack, don't take any of my boy's things with you."

"Mrs. Steele, Jon didn't rape Sharon."

"You fool, I know that." Jonathan's mother slammed the phone in Kari's ear. Kari closed her eyes for a moment. She was doing the right thing. Jon would go free.

The call completed, she packed her clothes. The only memento she took of her time with Jon was the packet of damming pictures, in case she softened.

She paid the rent on the house for one extra month, just in case Jon wanted to come back, then locked it up. That, she didn't tell her mother. Penance? She wasn't sure. It wasn't as though she could afford to throw money away. She was puzzled by her own actions.

CHAPTER THREE

Kari Thomas had a new life and she was contented. She refused to dwell on her past. In the seven years that had passed since leaving Lonett, she had successfully put it behind her. Her move to Chicago had been just the kind of clean break she needed.

Now that she was done with that foolishness, as her mother referred to it, she was back in their lives and good graces. No one ever mentioned that for three years they had disowned her.

The other thing no one mentioned was the fact that within three days of Kari's leaving town, Jonathan Steele had been released. Sharon had recanted her story and said that she and Jon had had a lover's quarrel. This she also learned through the newspaper. On reading that, Kari had canceled the subscription to her hometown paper. It was further proof that Jon had cheated on her.

Though Kari had a new life, it took a while for her heart to heal, to accept even the most casual of dates. Her preference when she began dating was very dark-skinned black men. The darker the hue, the better.

She wanted to forget that there had been a time in her life when she had loved a blue-eyed blonde more than life or family, though her parents' visits and their constant questions about her love life had a way of forcing her to relive snatches of her life.

The fact that they were only introduced to black men did nothing to allay their fears of reviving the past. Kari wanted to laugh out loud. Did they really believe she had fallen for Jon's pigment?

☙

Kari shivered. *Stop it*, she scolded herself. *They're going to love Steven. Why not? He's black.*

"Collin, did you hear Kari? Steve's a doctor. Did you see her eyes light up when she spoke of him?"

"Anything would be better than that white boy," Collin Thomas answered his wife.

Bits of her parents' conversation floated to her from the kitchen. She held her hands in front of her body, noticing the slight tremor. *Twenty-eight and my parents still make me tremble.* She sighed heavily.

The ringing of the bell stopped Kari's need for further self-examination. Opening the door for Steve, she smiled automatically.

She kissed him quickly and stepped away, her eyes sweeping over him in appraisal. Her parents would approve. Six foot tall Steve, with muscles the size of melons. Her tongue flicked over her lips as she considered the thought that he looked like a giant Hershey bar. Surely God himself had dipped the man in chocolate. He had the smoothest, creamiest skin she had ever felt on a man and his mouth was filled with straight white teeth. And he was just as sweet as a candy bar. She was lucky to have found him. She thought of her parents. *They're going to love him*, the little voice whispered.

Kari smiled as she introduced him to her parents and saw the look of acceptance pass between them. Then she repeated that he was a doctor. For a moment she actually thought her mother was going to cry.

"I'm so glad to see that you've finally come to your senses." The words were whispered in her ear as she embraced her mother. For a nanosecond Kari was angry.

Why couldn't they forget Jon Steele? She had. How many years would it take for them to forget the biggest mistake of her life? Steven Anderson was her future, her black Adonis.

The conversation flowed easily in the room. Steven had come from a small southern town himself and had much in common with her parents.

"So Steve, I hear you're from a small town yourself."

"Yes, sir. I'm from Cannan, Georgia, about ten miles from Peachtree City. Most folks have never heard of Cannan, so I just tell everyone I'm from Peachtree."

Collin Thomas laughed, causing Kari to glance in his direction. She could tell by his laugh he'd taken an immediate liking to Steve. This was a man he'd be proud to welcome into the family.

"You must be pretty popular with the ladies. Is there anyone besides our Kari that you're seeing?"

Kari couldn't believe her ears. Her father was doing it again. And they wondered why she wasn't married. Hell, they had managed to scare away anyone who might have been seriously interested.

"Don't answer that question, Steven." She rubbed her fingers across his palm, loving the feel of him.

He smiled at her, then gave her fingers a gentle squeeze while turning to answer her father. "Sir, I haven't dated that many women and definitely none like your daughter."

For several seconds the older man was silent. He avoided the glares he knew his daughter would be sending him, then continued with his questioning.

"Surely you have lots of women chasing you. You're a doctor." He paused. "You mean you've never taken a fancy to any of the pretty young nurses you work with?"

Steve laughed out loud. "I know where you're coming from, sir. I don't have roving eyes." He clutched Kari's hand tighter in his own. "I'm in love with your daughter.

Kari was in semi-shock. Sure, she'd known that Steve cared for her but he had never told her he loved her. Now to hear him say the words for the first time and in general conversation...

She wanted to pause, pinch herself, relish the feeling, have him look into her eyes. She wanted him to be a little afraid that she wouldn't return the feelings.

There was a nagging little hurt. She wished he had told her first that he was in love with her instead of announcing it to her father. He was taking her love as a given. It irritated her, however irrational it might be.

The two men sized each other up. It was apparent that Steve's talk of love was to him a subject to be spoken of first to her father.

Kari watched her father's admiration steadily increase for Steve. The older man asked his questions and the younger one responded as the man's due. She didn't know why she should be surprised. They were small town southern men. She'd known after the first date her father would wholly approve of the big city doctor with the country boy hidden inside.

Steve understood her father. Having nothing to hide, he invited his questions. If the situation were reversed, she knew his parents would be putting her through the same type of ordeal.

Despite her dislike of southern traditions, that was one of the reasons Kari had fallen for tall, handsome Steve. He was a man whom her parents would approve of. Their families were the same. They were proud of their heritage. It was important to them to keep it pure, as they called it. In the past, Kari had almost sullied her parents' plans.

She twirled the crystal she wore on a gold chain around her neck, her lucky charm. Maybe they could get through this without moving through the dark patches of her past.

Kari cringed as her father stood and walked toward Steven, feeling a sudden premonition about the next words out of his mouth.

"You know, Steven, a lot of affluent black men, especially the ones in the North, seem to be pairing up with different kinds of women these days. I'm surprised that one hasn't gotten to you yet."

Oh God, Kari wanted to scream. Why couldn't her father mind his own business for once? Why did he always have to travel down the same road, re-visiting the darkness?

Now she knew why her own thoughts had traveled to the past. She had been through the same inquisition more than a dozen times.

The men's eyes locked together and Kari's heart sank. She bit her lips and prayed for Steven to tell her father that while he had no such feelings, it didn't matter to him. She wanted to hear him say that escaping rigid thinking was one of the reasons he'd left home.

"Well, sir, I can't dictate to anyone else how they should live their lives."

Kari let out a small breath and was about to issue a thank you to God when she realized Steve was still talking.

"Sir, if I brought anyone home except one of my own, why, my folks would disown me. As old as I am, my daddy would try to give me a whipping." Steve was grinning broadly. "I'm so glad I met your daughter. My mother will be so pleased. She really worried about me moving up here, thought I would take up with the wrong kind of woman."

He held his hand out to Kari and she took it, cringing inwardly.

A shiver passed through her and she resisted the impulse to run. *Small town southern men. What had she done?*

"Kari and I feel strongly about family," Steve said. "We're both looking for the same thing. I don't believe either of us could ever conceive of going against our families." Steve turned and smiled directly at Kari. "Can I speak frankly, sir?"

How much more frank can you get? The thought flashed like

lightning through Kari's mind. *Stop. Concentrate on what he's saying*, she scolded herself.

"Actually, sir, I asked Kari out because I noticed for months that she only dated in the race." He smiled. "I don't think I would want to marry a woman who had been with anyone other than her own kind."

He shrugged his shoulders and looked directly at Kari. "But since I plan on marrying your daughter, I don't have to worry about that, do I?" He smiled again at Kari, missing the look of revulsion in her eyes.

For several seconds the room was quiet. Then her father's almost frantic, "No, no, nothing to worry about with our Kari," was followed by his booming laugh.

She tried to force the words past her lips but couldn't. It wasn't true. Her father leaned into her, giving her cheek a peck. She heard his unspoken words not to blow it. Her eyes found his. She looked away quickly. Time for telling Steven passed. Her future was now sealed with a lie.

Kari felt faint. She cringed inwardly as Steve slid his hand around her waist. He was just as bigoted and narrow-minded as her father and all the other people in her hometown. She accepted his almost chaste kiss on her lips even as she realized he had talked of marriage not to her, but to her father. This time the shivers turned into full- fledged shudders, causing Steve to pull her closer to his side.

His love for her and apparent hatred of race mixing stopped her from telling him the truth. What would she say? Admit that she was one of the women he could never marry? That she had done the one thing he found deplorable: She had not only slept with a white man, but also had lived with him. She'd have to tell him that she had been used by the man to thumb his nose at his parents and the town.

That all along the woman he loved was white. What advantage would it serve?

She could feel the heat from her parents' eyes burning through her. They were silently demanding that she not ruin her chances with a man they more than approved of. He'd passed the test. What good would it do any of them? She would never see Jonathan Steele again.

Kari smiled her assurance first at her father, then turned to include her mother. What did it matter if they all lied to insure her future with this wonderful man? Steven Anderson was her dark knight. He was what her family wanted for her.

She closed her eyes. Steve loved her and damn it, she was going to take the chance she had been given. Jonathan Steele would remain dead to her, just as he had been for the past seven years.

CHAPTER FOUR

A honking horn startled Kari, interrupting her quiet morning. *Don't let it wake them up.* As soon as the thought came, she remembered. Her parents were not ensconced in one of her extra bedrooms. They had insisted on staying at a hotel. Their not-so-subtle hint that she might need her privacy had surprised her. She felt as if they were trying to force-feed her to Steve

The horn sounded again more insistently. Padding to the window, she pulled back the curtain and watched as the mail carrier honked away angrily. For Rose to be honking meant Kari had a package.

One good thing about the Chicago suburb where she lived, the rural carriers would not just return special mail to the post office. Not even when they were annoyed by the length of time they waited for the customer to answer. Judging by the honks, there must be something pretty special waiting for her.

Better not push it, Kari. She hurriedly threw on the robe that was dangling off the arm of her bedroom chair and ran down the drive, smiling her apologies at the carrier.

Reaching for the extended pen, she signed for the thick manila envelope, wondering who could be sending her a certified package.

A cursory glance made her heart sink. American Resorts. She knew what it was. She was being sued. Several years before, she had bought into the campground and changed her mind. She had paid a lawyer a hefty fee to rescind the contract and thought it was all behind her.

Kari smiled and waved at her neighbors, though her heart was in the pit of her stomach. She felt panicky and afraid, unsure what she should do. She covered the few steps to her door quickly, wanting to be inside the safety of her home.

The envelope mocked her, forcing her to deal with it. *Get it over with, the papers can't hurt you*, she chided herself.

After a quick scanning of the papers her heart sank even further. At the bottom of the long list of lawyers was the name *Jonathan Steele*.

It can't be, not in Kansas City, Missouri. What would he be doing there? With that thought, the papers fell from her hand and scattered around her.

Why the hell am I being sued in Missouri? I've never even been there. I bought into the campground all right, but in Illinois. Her thoughts were going in ten different directions at once. Kari kneeled to pick up the papers, remembering having heard that the company had a charter from Missouri and had filed for protection under the bankruptcy act. There had been talk that they were going to call thousands of people who'd bought into the campground into court, people who'd changed their mind for some reason or other about paying.

Damn, she thought again, damn her for listening to Jackie. She was the one who'd told her there was no possible way the company could drag Illinois residents into federal bankruptcy court in Missouri. Well, Miss Know-it-all Jackie, they not only could do it, they were doing it.

Kari's eyes were drawn to Jon's name. She mentally calculated time. Yes, there had been enough time for him to have finished law school. After all, she had managed to finish her education when she moved to Chicago. Jon could have done the same thing.

For a brief instant she was granted a respite, knowing she had not damaged his career. Then memory of the last time she'd seen him wiped out the momentary joy.

She remembered the look on his face, when she had seen him chained. He'd hated her for abandoning him. The hate had been there in his cold stare.

Kari had wanted to tell him a million times that she was sorry but she'd remained too angry and too hurt.

Look at you, she scolded herself. *Just the sight of his name on a piece of paper and you come apart*. She had to give herself a pep talk. If she didn't she would remember all the things she had forced herself to forget for the past seven years.

Why now? she thought. *Steve has definitely made his intentions clear. He wants us to be together*. She was going to be happy with Steve. That was a promise she'd made to herself. She was going to marry him and have lots of babies.

Kari sighed heavily. What a mess. It was like having your thoughts become reality. The night before, Jon's presence had been very much in the room, in thoughts that had passed silently between her and her parents. Now the person her parents feared most might be back full force in her life.

But maybe it was a different Jonathan Steele. Surely Jon wouldn't take a case in which he might have to see her again. Then again, maybe it was, in which case she'd have to deal with him. *No, no that's wrong. I have to find a way to deal with the lawsuit.*

She forced her brain to remember. This matter should've been taken care of. Somewhere she had a receipt that said she had paid good money to make the problem go away.

A few hours later Kari smiled. Her search had paid off. She clutched in her hand the answer to her prayers, her receipt for attorney Williams. Maybe she wouldn't have to do anything. Maybe she wouldn't have to face the man who had caused her so much pain.

Don't forget you were deliriously happy for three years. She wanted to quiet the voice but thoughts of Jon had been stirred up the night before.

Kari thought about Steve. Dark, chocolate brown Steve with whom she had been positive she wanted to spend the rest of her life. Until last night. She didn't want to spend her life with a bigot but she was afraid now, afraid of once again losing her parents' approval. Loving Jon had been a lonely time in her life. She didn't want to go through that again.

Her body trembled slightly as she picked up the remaining pages of the summons. She allowed the tips of her fingers to trace Jon's name, almost as a caress. An involuntary shudder passed through her and she closed her eyes for a moment, lost in the past.

Stop it. Even if it is him, what does it matter? Her thoughts refused to be shut off. Kari could feel the knot twisting her intestines. Pain coursed through her body, jabbing her with the intensity of a red hot poker.

If it is him, I'll deal with it. I need a lawyer. She knew instantly that she would not be using the services of attorney Williams. *Damn,* she thought as she headed for the phone and called his office. She would demand to know what had happened, why this matter had come back to bite her in the behind after all of this time.

Kari ended the call to the attorney not at all satisfied. The secretary remembered her and the case and was just as surprised as Kari that the resort was taking Illinois residents to Kansas City, Missouri, to sue them. That didn't bode well in Kari's mind. If the people that worked in the attorney's office didn't know it could be done, she doubted that they would be much help to her.

Still, the woman had told her to bring in the summons and the attorney would look it over. No charge. As if she'd give him another penny. Again the thought came. She needed an attorney, though. Maybe someone at work could recommend one.

Kari thought of the staid accounting firm she was with. They wouldn't like it one bit if she was involved in a scandal.

To think that a woman that handled other people's money could have done something as stupid as buying into a campground she hadn't thoroughly checked out…no, they wouldn't like it at all.

She could kick herself for having done it, but it was too late now. The damage was done. There was no way she would ask her co-workers to help her find a lawyer. She had to do everything in her power to conceal it from her firm. She would find her own lawyer. If need be, she'd handle the case herself.

Kari slumped into a kitchen chair and closed her eyes. For once, she didn't fight the memories. Behind her closed lids, Jon smiled at her in technicolor and his scent invaded her nostrils. She could feel the heat rise from her nether regions and spread throughout her torso. She ached physically for Jon.

She knew what she had to do. Kari went to her bedroom and pulled the locked case from the depths of her messy closet. She didn't have to search for the key. It was worn next to the crystal around her neck, which was supposed to ward off the evil represented by the key.

She inserted the key and pulled out the package with trembling fingers. Angrily, Kari forced herself to look at the pictures. Feeling the hot tears that managed to seep beneath her lids, she whispered the lie, softly. "I have Steve now. I'm over him."

Jonathan might not have been a rapist but he never loved you, Kari, remember that. She shut her eyes tight against the pain. The hot tears slid from beneath her lashes while her heart broke yet again. *But I loved him.*

CHAPTER FIVE

Jon felt the eyes of his secretary burrowing a hole in his back. He knew the woman was curious but he refused to indulge her curiosity. Let her keep guessing. Besides, he didn't particularly like the woman anyway.

His fingers virtually tore the mail out of the woman's hands each morning. Sure, it was strange for an attorney to search for responses to a routine summons the firm had issued. But so what?

It had all begun innocently enough. Nothing made the day stand out in his memory other than that the work had been extremely light. He was bored and had started going over a list of names, people they were suing on behalf of American Resorts in Joliet, Illinois.

He had been going over the papers with a mechanical interest at best when almost at the bottom of the list he'd spotted her name. He snatched the papers up and stared transfixed at her name. Anyone watching would have thought the black letters on the white paper were speaking to him.

He was bombarded with so many differing emotions before he calmed himself. Worry was at the top of his list, along with anger. Lurking in the background was something darker, more sinister. He didn't have a name for it.

He closed his eyes for a split second before shaking his head slightly at the thought of suing Kari. When he reopened his eyes they landed on Elizabeth Dobis, his secretary. Her lips were twisted in a sneer, giving the impressions she had tasted something rancid.

His eyes fell back on the papers in his hand before he went to the next sheet. He couldn't let the woman know that he now had a personal interest in the outcome of one of the cases. He knew the woman found him strange and unconventional. For that reason alone he couldn't ask her for the information he craved. That was why he had begun his ritual of checking the mail. He needed to know what Kari planned to do, how she planned on handling the case.

For months their firm had been suing thousands of Illinois residents. Jon would never admit it to his bosses, but he felt sorry for the defendants. He figured most of them had probably tried to grab a piece of the American pie and had been scammed by corporate America once again.

He tried to remember it wasn't his job to moralize, just get as much money for the client as the courts would allow. Suing the little guy for big business paid the bills.

But spotting Kari's name amongst the suckers who had signed on the dotted line for the campground hit close to home. Kari wasn't stupid. She was one of the smartest women he knew and she was an accountant. How could she have let herself become involved in something so obviously ill fated?

He looked around the office, feeling the ache of loneliness he had carried for seven years. He shook his head ever so slightly, willing the pain away as he always did. Now was not the time.

Jon returned his focus to the lawsuit. The company had fixed a lot of the problems with the contracts and had changed them several times, bullying lots of their clients into signing a second and sometimes third more binding contract, and had issued gifts as an inducement.

If only those being sued had checked with an attorney before signing. Jon shook his head. Then he had a moment of pity. He assumed the defendants were probably trying to save the attorney's fee by not checking. Bad idea.

For the last few months Jon had found most people reached a settlement or just didn't bother to show up in court. When that happened a judgment was issued on their client's behalf. Rarely did anyone show up and even more rarely did they win.

American Resorts had managed not to deliver what they had promised and had sought restructuring under the bankruptcy law. They were still entitled to go after the little guy who had welched on payments for whatever reason.

Jon looked over the mail with a disgusted sigh, then at his expensive clothes. He made a good living. He should be grateful for the business American Resorts gave his firm.

Another sigh. He was fully aware that his thoughts would not be traveling so far if Kari were not involved. He couldn't help wondering what had happened to Her. Why hadn't she paid? For that matter, what had possessed her to sign in the first place?

His eyes fell on the legal documents in his palm. The paper he held in his hand had slowly been twisted into a ball. Suddenly he shook his head, disgusted with himself. *Why are you worrying about her? She sure as hell didn't worry about you.*

"Mrs. Dobis, would you get me a cup of coffee, please?" He didn't really want it but he knew she hated attending to the minor inconveniences of the attorneys and he wanted to needle her a bit. He would use her absence to copy the information on Kari, to make sure this Kari Thomas was his.

The sound of Mrs. Dobis's returning hastened his copying and he swung away quickly. He wondered absently if some of the lingering bitterness for Kari had spilled over coloring his attitude toward Mrs. Dobis.

"Here's your coffee, Mr. Steele."

"Thank you." Jon's voice was curt. "Mrs. Dobis, I'll be in my office. Please don't disturb me until I call you." He walked toward his door, then turned suddenly. "Hold my calls."

The door firmly closed, he waited a moment for any indication his secretary was spying on him. Elizabeth Dobis had been at the firm for almost twenty years and thought she was in charge of all the new young attorneys. He sucked in his breath while reaching for his cellular phone. This was one call he didn't want his secretary to be privy to.

CB

Within a matter of days one of the private investigators they used on occasion reported back on the several names Jon had given him. The information confirmed that the Kari Thomas the firm was suing on behalf of their client was his Kari.

Jon wasn't surprised. Somehow he had known the moment he spotted her name that it was Kari. He wanted to see her, to confront her, maybe to tell her to go to hell as she had told him. Or maybe not.

He sat in his massive leather chair remembering a time when every stick of furniture in his home cost less than the chair he was now using. For several minutes he sat looking at her address and phone number. After everything that had happened, he still wanted to find a way to protect Kari from the lawsuit. He knew she now owned her own home. If she didn't pay or couldn't pay, he didn't want anyone attempting to seize her assets.

He reached for his wallet, his throat tight with emotion. The picture was wedged in tightly against cards he never used. Her picture. For some reason he'd never tossed it. He changed wallet after wallet without looking at the picture, just placing it between other useless items. Now he wanted to see her face again. He pulled the picture free. The ache was as raw as the moment she'd stood before him ordering him out of her life.

For seven months he'd waited for her to come to him. It didn't bother him that he had been thrown in jail. If that was what it was going to take to prove to Kari that he loved her, then he would gladly go. But he had never expected her to leave him there to rot.

Jon looked down into Kari's laughing brown eyes. Her lips curled into a gentle smile telling him she loved him and that the moment he put the camera down she wanted to make love. Every day for seven months he had pulled out her picture, remembering the day he'd taken it.

For seven months Jon had caressed Kari's picture the moment he awoke, thinking it would be the day she would come and tell him she was sorry. That she believed him. That she loved him still. But it hadn't happened. She had not come.

In the end it had been his parents who had pulled the strings and sprung him. Shortly after, Sharon had recanted her lie and the whole ugly mess was over. He remembered making a beeline for his rented house and the feeling of dread that had come over him as he'd slid his key into the door. Something was terribly wrong. He could feel the fear wash over him in waves.

Despite her absence, Jon had held on, his faith unshakable, believing that when he was released Kari would listen. The door had swung open and the silence had come crashing down on him. She was gone. No one had to tell him. Everything was as he had left it, down to the candles in the makeshift bottle holder. It was her essence that was missing.

Jon had sunk into one of their rickety chairs, giving in to the pain for several minutes, the sound of his parents' voices fading into the background, feeling as though he had been kicked in the gut by a mule. He'd felt his spirit separating from his body and floating away.

His mother's good riddance to bad rubbish had brought him back. He wondered if Kari's mother had said the same about him. For the first time he offered no argument and he didn't attempt to defend Kari. He was numb with grief and anger. If he hadn't been, he would have laughed at the irony of the situation. His mother had more in common with Kari's Mom than she knew. Both women were fond of calling people rubbish.

He had tried living in the house for several months alone but it had proven too much. Memories assaulted him constantly, making him destructive. He lost a year of his life, part spent behind bars, the other time spent wallowing in self pity and booze.

When he could no longer take sleeping in the creaky bed alone, he'd accepted his parents' offer of help to finish school. Going to law school meant getting out of Lonett. It always had. Only he and Kari had planned to do it together.

Enough remembering. He replaced the picture in his wallet, then walked to the door. Seeing Mrs. Dobis should be just the thing to chase away his sadness. The woman hated taking orders from him, that much was clear. He had the distinct impression that she was looking for something to use against him in the company. His thoughts returned to Kari. That would do it, if she ever knew.

Seven years later and his past had caught up with him. He had never asked where Kari had gone, never searched. He had tried to get as far away from Alabama as possible. Now she was back in his life.

How ironic, he thought, *Kari wanted us to escape to a larger, more progressive city and look where she landed, smack dab in the middle of the same old tune just being played on a larger stage.* He wondered if she'd ever thought of that. *She ran away from me and straight into the arms of the thing she feared most, hatred.* The color of a person's skin mattered just as much in Chicago as it did in Lonett.

A few years before, Chicago reporters had revealed shocking information: The police department from Highland Park used racial codes. NUT. The meaning, "niggers up town." It was a code for the white officers to harass any black that was in the shopping district.

That day Jon had turned off his TV with disgust after hearing that R. Benedict Mayers had attempted to get his racial views actually placed on a ballot. The man wanted a law requiring that black prisoners be sent to Africa. He also wanted to outlaw interracial marriages. Jon couldn't imagine anyone with that much hate.

He shuddered. He did know people with that much hate, the people who'd helped Sharon destroy his life. As much as he wanted to, Jon couldn't put all the blame on Sharon. He'd been the one who'd agreed to take the compromising photos.

He'd known Kari would disapprove. That was the reason he hadn't told her. At the time he'd thought he was doing it for them, to give Kari the things they didn't have. If only he'd never agreed to the last set of pictures. He found out later that he'd been slipped a mickey. But by then it was too late, the damage was done. He'd provided the perfect weapon. Simply because he'd wanted to make some fast money.

Jon again felt eyes on him. He had to get control of his wandering thoughts. He couldn't change the past. He glanced at his secretary and decided not to ask for the latest mail. He had done it three times already. There was nothing there from Kari. Besides, his strange behavior was already enough to give the woman ammunition.

Walk away, Jon, don't look annoyed. He took his own advice and headed for his office. He resolved to stop going through the mail over and over. What was going to happen would happen, whether he looked through the mail or not. Kari would have to send in her answers or be required to pay fifteen thousand dollars. He didn't believe she would just give that kind of money away, even if she had it.

He paused midway to his office. Jon smiled at the new intern, his eyes traveling down her shapely form. Tanya was sending him signals. Had been from the moment she walked in the door. But he had ignored them, concerned only with his career. Now his thoughts of Kari plagued him, made him hunger for the things he'd once thought he had.

He could feel himself grow hard as his eyes lingered on the woman's derrière. He sent a mental message to his bulging member. *Forget it. We don't play where we work.*

He mentally added that crime of pleasures he couldn't have against Kari. Until her name had resurfaced he had been satisfied with his occasional bouts of recreational sex. Now he wanted more. Jon wanted what he was sure he had found long ago when he was young and filled with dreams. He wanted what he'd had with Kari.

As he sat at his desk, Jon caught a glimpse of someone over the top of the aloe vera plant he had placed to block out prying eyes. A deep sigh, a quick glance at his watch and Jon counted slowly to ten.

Feminine knuckles rapped on his door. For one brief instant he wanted to say, "Stay the hell out." His foul temper, though, was not the fault of anyone at the firm. Not even Mrs. Dobis. He needed to get about the business of law.

"Come in." He attempted to make the invitation pleasant but failed.

"Mr. Steele, You've got about thirty minutes to get to court. I've sent the files ahead by your assistants." Mrs. Dobis peered at him, her gaze unreadable.

"Sure, you're right." He smiled at her. "I was just getting ready to leave. It's time to collect another million for the resort." A short derisive snort followed his sarcastic remark.

"It is your job." Mrs. Dobis stared hard at him.

Jon was aware of his secretary's opinion of him. She'd thought he was a loose cannon from the beginning, not someone the firm should have hired.

He had accidentally picked up the receiver in his office one day and heard the woman regaling the listener with her tales of her horrid young boss.

"No, he's much better suited to be a struggling public defender. He's always putting down the clients as well as his own financial success."

Jon had coughed to alert the woman that he was on the phone. Even then, she had not apologized. They'd maintained a wary distance from each other since that time.

"You're so right, Mrs. Dobis. We all have our jobs to do. Even if we're being a prick about it, we have our jobs." He smiled, slow and easy, his blue eyes showing the depth of his emotions. He looked at the woman standing in his doorway frowning at him for another ten seconds.

Elizabeth Dobis then turned on her heel, not knowing if she had just been called a prick by her young boss.

He watched the woman depart, her annoyance obvious. *If she were sure of my words I know she would sue my ass for abuse of power. You'd better thread lightly, Jon*, he scolded himself mentally. It was time for him to leave. If she had not interrupted, he might have continued lost in thought. His fingers drummed the desk, his eyes resting on his locked drawer where he had put the information from the private detective.

He felt his hand sliding into his pocket. It was then he knew a decision had been reached in which he evidently hadn't taken part. He slipped the folded papers from the drawer and dropped them into his brief case. He was supposed to have the only key but he didn't trust Elizabeth Dobis.

Jon walked toward the door where the other two lawyers that were handling the cases waited for him. He gave a slight wave of acknowledgment. To his secretary he gave a playful grin. "Goodbye, Mrs. Dobis. I do appreciate your competence."

He walked away before the woman could respond. The look on the faces of the other attorneys told him they knew the game he was playing.

"She is a shrew, isn't she?" Tim asked.

"Shrew, I could take," Jon laughed. "The woman's more like a vampire, out to suck the life out of everyone around." He cast a suspicious eye at his companions. "Why is a woman with that much seniority my secretary? Why isn't she working for one of the partners?"

"Because they are the partners! I think it was unofficially decided that since no one could stand the woman she would always be placed with the newest attorney." Tim smiled at Jon. "That, my friend, happens to be you. Don't worry," he laughed, "when a new attorney joins the firm you get rid of her."

All three attorneys laughed but then Jon had more sobering thoughts. For the first time in the year and a half he had worked at the firm he could see the reason behind the woman's bitterness.

Jon's glance took in first his female counterpart, then darted over to Tim. "Maybe Mrs. Dobis feels humiliated at being treated like a joke and never promoted, just always starting over with some new hotshot lawyer." Cassandra glanced at Jon. He saw the amusement in her eyes before she spoke.

"Don't kid yourself that if you're nice to her she'll be nice to you. It won't work. Believe me, I tried. I was going to make the woman like me or die trying."

"What happened?"

"Tim came and he inherited her."

Cassandra and Tim began laughing again, but this time Jon did not join in. He still didn't like the woman but now his dislike was a little less intense.

To be the butt of everyone's joke, he knew that feeling. Kari would have felt sorry for the woman and would have been angry with Jon for making fun of Mrs. Dobis behind her back.

The cold Missouri wind whipped across their faces. Jon pulled the collar of his coat a little tighter, glad for the cold. He was in the danger zone, too much remembering Kari and worrying about her opinion.

The federal courthouse loomed in front of them. As always, he felt a shiver of pride when he walked through the door. Now he felt the familiar tug of aloneness. *Damn her*, he thought, *my life was going along just fine without her.*

CHAPTER SIX

Jon rubbed both hands across his face, letting out a groan as he mentally calculated the money he and his two coworkers had made for American Resorts. Almost three million dollars. He turned for a brief instant to scan the faces in the small courtroom.

They all looked the same. Desperation and fear strained at the faces of the few remaining defendants in the room. It was evident they had not consulted a lawyer. He wanted to yell at them they were all about to lose thousands of dollars but had chosen to hold onto the few hundreds it would have taken to give them a fair shot.

Jon turned away. Even with the lawyers they would probably still lose. He and his team were good, very good. They knew what they were doing. *She doesn't stand a chance.* The thought popped unbidden into his head.

For once, the end of the day was welcomed. Usually he wanted to remain in the courtroom forever, knowing he was a part of it, loving it, wishing...

"Anybody want to get a drink?"

Jon watched Cassandra turn toward Tim. A look passed between them. Tim was married but it was evident he had the hots for Cassandra. It was also evident that Jon's company was not really wanted.

"You two go ahead. There are some papers I want to look over for tomorrow."

"Why?" quipped Tim. "The cases could practically be won without us even being in the room. They're not that difficult."

Jon's smile was slow. He kept his eyes shaded deliberately, not wanting to give away any secrets. "I don't think we should let the partners hear that. They might find us so unnecessary that we're out of a job."

He laughed lightly, lifting his eyes toward his companions. He had struck a nerve. They joined his laughter a bit nervously.

"Maybe we should return to the office and go over some of the cases ourselves." There was disappointment in Cassandra's voice.

"No need for all of us to suffer. I'll do it tonight, then next week one of you can stay. We are working together." Jon smiled. "If the bosses check, finding one member of the team will be more than enough to pacify them."

He watched as smiles of relief broke out on both Tim's and Cassandra's faces.

"We owe you big."

Tim gave him a series of pats on the shoulder. Cassandra smiled at him, then turned her gaze on Tim. There was hunger in her eyes. Jon saw and cast his eyes downward again. He didn't want to see, didn't want to know, to judge.

Tim's wife appeared happy, yet Tim cheated on her constantly. Jon had lost Kari to a lie. He had never once thought of cheating on her yet he had been accused and found guilty of doing just that. *Jon, you'll have to admit it sooner or later, you did betray her*. He groaned, cutting off the voice that mocked him.

Again the sadness washed over him and his eyes closed automatically to shield his pain. An unexpected moan escaped. Jon forced a bright smile. *Walk away*, he commanded his feet as they slowly turned in the opposite direction from the pair.

"Please, dear God, for once let Mrs. Dobis leave on time." The short walk to the office was covered in record time. Demons were chasing him, making him move quickly. *You did betray her, Jon*. He

struggled against the desire to protect the woman he once loved and the desire to extract revenge. She should have given him a chance to explain about the pictures. Hell yes, he knew what was on them. Still she should have let him explain.

He met Mrs. Dobis at the building door. With his hand on the handle of the door, his eyes strayed to the glass partition. Elizabeth Dobis's frosty sneer greeted him. As he moved aside to allow the woman to exit, he murmured goodnight.

As Jon made his way toward the elevator, a strong spicy, albeit expensive, odor hit him. He should have wished that the intern would be gone also. The smell of Tanya's perfume and the invitation in her eyes could tempt him.

A string of nameless faces flashed across his mind, women he'd bedded in an attempt to forget Kari. He wondered if she was thinking of him. Had his name on the long list of lawyers caused her to remember as well? *Does she still think I lied, that I betrayed her?* *"You did,"* the annoying little voice that belonged to his conscience answered.

He turned the handle to his office door. *Snap out of it. She's just a woman you used to know. She's a deadbeat, a defendant who didn't pay her debt, no more no less. It's your job to make her pay.*

Jon sat behind his massive teak desk, the wood smooth and polished with a gloss so bright it mirrored his face. He slumped in his chair and covered his eyes with his hands, allowing image after image of Kari to dance behind his closed lids.

He saw her brown skin glistening with a fine sheen of perspiration just after they made love. Her hair long and tangled from his hands, his lips. He saw her smile and hold out her arms to him wanting more, needing him, loving him.

It's time, Jon, the voice badgered him. *It's time you remembered things as they really were.* For the first time in years Jon thought of Sharon and the pictures he had posed for. Kari had never known about their swelling bank account. If Sharon had not started blackmailing him, he would have been able to tell her.

God, the entire thing now seemed like a long ago nightmare. Sharon, her offers of friendship, her telling him of a quick way to make lots of money. Hell, he'd needed money. Who didn't? He'd planned on using that money to buy Kari an engagement ring. She was pregnant, and more than anything he'd wanted to marry her, have their baby and protect their family. All of his dreams took money, and the pictures had offered that. Money.

For a time posing with Sharon had been fun. Subtly the pictures had begun changing until even he no longer knew if they'd crossed the line. Then the day came when he didn't have to wonder, he knew beyond the shadow of a doubt. Sharon had fixed him a drink and the next thing he knew he was naked in bed with her. He could still hear the voice that had screamed out at him to run, but he'd been too groggy.

Somehow things had gotten out of control. He squeezed his eyes tightly shut. He didn't want to remember his part in the fiasco, but now that he'd begun, he couldn't stop. They had been only supposed to simulate lovemaking, it wasn't to be for real. But it had been.

It wasn't until many hours later when his head was finally clear that he'd realized two things: He'd missed Valentine's Day with Kari, and he was spent. The evidence of what he'd done clung to his limp penis.

He vaguely remembered Sharon spitting his seed into a plastic container. He'd found that strange, her obsession with him even stranger. It wasn't until a week later when he'd refused to pose for any more pictures that she told him what she'd done with his semen.

He couldn't believe it. She'd used it, inserted it into her body and gone to the police to make a report of rape. She'd ordered him to leave Kari to be with her or she'd name him as the rapist. She'd backed up that threat with another one-a promise to show Kari the pictures. He vaguely remembered the photo shoot, but hadn't realized that they'd captured the sexual act on film.

He felt again the shock of looking at the images of himself with his penis in Sharon's mouth. He'd done everything in his power to dissuade her from showing the pictures to Kari. More frightening than Sharon's accusation of rape was the prospect of Kari seeing the pictures before he could explain what had happened, tell her that he'd never meant to let things go so far, that he'd not betrayed her, that he loved her.

You betrayed her, Jon. The voice was now shouting at him. "Never my heart," Jon whispered, "that always belonged to Kari."

Jon allowed the breath he was holding to leave his body slowly. His eyes remained closed. He had done it for the two of them, them and their baby. But that was another story. In the end Kari had not wanted the baby or him. He had only wanted to make their life better. An easy way to make money, he'd convinced himself. There was no harm in taking pictures. What a fantasy.

Stupid, stupid, stupid. He rubbed his head remembering all the strange places he had posed. Jon again rubbed at his head, harder this time. It was a nervous habit. He would be glad when American Resort suits were finished. To put it truthfully, he would be happy when Kari's dealing with American Resorts was over.

He would see her and nail her as he had all the others. Then he would continue to put her out of his life as he had done for the past seven years.

He twisted his head slowly, trying to work out the kinks brought about by stress. The stacked folders lined one entire side of his massive desk. At least another two million dollars for the resort.

Perhaps two percent of the defendants thus far had won against the resort. A drop in the bucket, considering.

Jon's gaze took in all the corrugated boxes lining the walls of his office. He should be pleased that he had been trusted with one of their most lucrative cases, even more so because he was the lead attorney when his two co-workers had been with the firm longer.

For some unknown reason the partners had liked him from the start. When they put him as lead attorney on the case, Jonathan had expected resentment from Tim and Cassandra. It never came.

He was aware he needed to settle his feelings about Kari before they more seriously hampered his work. If that happened he knew his rising star wouldn't shine as brightly. The luster would be just a bit dimmed.

Yes, he definitely had to pull himself together. His conflicting emotions were playing havoc with his nervous system. One second he wanted to protect the woman he had loved, the next he wanted to crucify her.

Despite the contradictions of his feelings, he knew in the end he would take no pleasure in going after Kari. He didn't even want to see her. He wasn't at all sure how he would react. There was still too much hurt there.

I have to find a way to keep her from coming. He smiled to himself. A dismissal without prejudice. It was a draw, no losers and yet no winners. If only she would send the damn answers in he could begin.

His wallet was in his hand and yet he didn't remember reaching for it. For the second time that day Jon pulled Kari's picture out of its hiding place.

"I really did love you, you know." He spoke softly. To her picture, to her.

The heat began in his belly and continued upward toward his

chest. He could feel his throat beginning to constrict with the pain of remembering. He heard the sounds of Tanya moving about outside his door. She was finding things to do until he emerged. He needed temporary comfort, but it would not be with Tanya. He took a last brief look at Kari's image while reaching for the phone.

❧

Ahhh. Kari needed to come up for air. Steve's hands were caressing her body, making her forget the problem she had shoved aside for weeks. His brown eyes so much like her own were filled with an undeniable passion. She squirmed, successfully loosening his embrace.

"What's wrong with you?"

She was lying prone on the sofa and Steve was positioned above her, balancing his weight with his powerful hands pressed down into the couch on each side of her. His annoyance clearly showed on his face, the scowl deepening.

"Steve I'm sorry. I've got so many things on my mind right now."

"That's exactly what I mean. It's been weeks since we've been together."

Kari was truly puzzled. "What are you talking about? We made love last night."

"No, we didn't make love. You lay there and allowed me to touch you. You weren't there and you haven't been."

He took her hand and lifted it upward toward his face. He fingered the ring he'd placed there only a few weeks before.

"Kari, I know something's wrong. From the moment I placed this on your finger you've been somewhere else. What's wrong? Don't you want to marry me?"

"I want to marry you, Steve."

He was watching her face, noticing the lack of enthusiasm. He wasn't blind. There was a problem brewing. He sat up. "Is there someone else?"

Kari sat up also. She could hear the hurt in Steve's voice. How could she tell him that the someone else was a memory, especially a memory he wouldn't approve of.

She touched him hesitantly, loving the feel of his chocolate brown skin beneath her fingers. "There is no one else."

"Then tell me what's going on. We've planned this day for weeks. It's getting off to a rocky start. Where are you?"

"How far is Missouri?"

"What?"

"That's where I am. Kansas City, Missouri. I'm being sued."

Kari fell back away from Steve into the pillows and waited. She had never meant to tell him. She'd wanted to handle everything on her own, but so far, her fears had paralyzed her, causing her to do nothing, take no action. Coupled with Steven's hurt and suspicions, the words had just come tumbling out.

She remembered how it felt to know that the person you loved was hiding something from you. You always imagined the worst and usually you were right. She watched Steven's face, seeing the confusion there.

"Who's suing you in Kansas?"

"Not Kansas. Kansas City, Missouri."

"I stand corrected. Who's suing you in Missouri?"

"American Resorts."

"Kari, do you think you could give me a little more information? Who the hell is American Resorts, and where are they located?"

"Joliet."

A shudder passed through her body. Signing that contract was the dumbest thing she had ever done. She forced herself to go to the kitchen and retrieve the papers she had shoved into the back of her junk drawer.

She glanced at the clock, it was too early for problems. Steve was right. Their day off was being ruined needlessly. It was after nine and the only thing they'd done was eat breakfast. She'd have to make it up to him.

Kari returned and handed the papers over to Steve. She sat and waited while he read them through, then repeated it a second time, relief flooding his face. She saw the relief and knew she had been right to tell him. Her humiliation versus his sense of betrayal. She'd do everything within her power to see that Steven never felt betrayed by her.

"Have you been to a lawyer?"

"Sort of."

"What do you mean, sort of? Either you have, or you haven't."

"It's complicated," Kari sighed. "I went to the attorney I paid to rescind the contract. His office told me to bring the summons in and he would take a look at it. When I went back to pick it up, I found the secretary making copies of my summons."

"Did you ask her why?"

"No. There was no need. I knew the attorney was trying to find a way to protect himself if I came after him for not handling the case in the first place. That wasn't why I went to him. I wasn't out to make him pay for my mistake. I should have never let Jackie talk me into signing up in the first place."

"I should have known Jackie would be involved." Steve rolled his eyes and gave a snort of disapproval. "Okay, let's forget Jackie for the moment. What did the lawyer have to say about your case?"

"Good luck."

You're kidding."

"I'm afraid not."

"Didn't you call any other lawyers? Surely someone could help you with this."

"No."

"Why not?"

"I was afraid to."

He sat beside her and took her in his arms. It felt so good. She welcomed the feel of his hand against her back.

Steve glanced once more at the papers in his hands. "Was it the money? I could—" His words were stopped by her lips kissing him softly, tenderly.

"No, it's not just the money. I was afraid my company would find out somehow. Think about it. I have a plum assignment. I get to work on site with the clients, almost never having to go in. If I didn't have this assignment at the hospital I would have never met you." She shrugged. "Besides, I would look stupid. An accountant. I'm supposed to have better sense."

"Was there ever any warning that you were about to be sued?"

"Well, yes, I suppose so. The company sent me letters. After the first ones I didn't bother to open the others. I thought they were bluffing. I talked it over with Jackie. She didn't think that they would bring me out of state to sue." He was looking at her, smiling, and for some reason it made her uncomfortable.

"You should have come to me instead of going to Jackie, but that's okay now. Don't worry. I'll take care of this," he said.

That was it. Steven had voiced her apprehension. He was looking at her as though she were a helpless female. A dolt. She was neither. She felt his hand sliding back under her sweater, pushing away the flimsy lace bra. *Just like a man*, she thought. *Whatever the problem, sex should fix it.*

She moaned. She didn't feel it, but it appeared that Steven couldn't tell the difference. She listened to his voice telling her not to worry. She wanted to heed the voice, to relax and enjoy what he was doing.

It was more than the lawsuit though. Jonathan Steele had invaded her life again and she wasn't ready to face him. *Can you fix that, Steve?* If only she dared ask him.

She turned her mouth toward his, loving the feel of his lips on her own. She wanted so much to send her memories of Jon scurrying back into the darkness where they belonged. She pressed her body into Steve's. She'd do anything to banish her memories.

She felt herself being lifted up into his arms. She wrapped her arms around his neck, burying her lips in his flesh, as he carried her into the bedroom. She knew what it would take to make him believe and for now she was more than willing to give it. Hell, it wouldn't be the first time she'd pretended.

As Steve took her nipple in his mouth, Kari let out a small cry.

"That's it, baby," he moaned in her ear. "Let yourself go, come fly with me."

Kari moaned in agreement. It was expected. The more effort she put into it, the sooner it would be over. She reached down between their bodies, her hand reaching for and finding the zipper of his trousers. She reached inside, splaying her fingers around his aroused flesh.

She lifted her legs, giving Steven easier access. She felt him pushing her skirt up around her hips with one hand while the other tore at her panties and tossed them to the floor.

Within seconds after she began grinding her pelvis into his, he was pushing his engorged penis into her, pumping hard and fast. Kari did everything she knew to rush him toward orgasm. It worked.

Their lovemaking over, Steve lay with his head on her belly, his hand nestled between her thighs. He was pleased with her performance.

"See baby, see how high we soar when you don't hold yourself back? You should have told me sooner what was wrong," he murmured before falling asleep.

Kari attempted to lie quiet, not wanting to disturb Steve. His soft snoring told her that he'd fallen asleep. They had managed to pass a major trust hurdle. She didn't want her disappearance from the bed to be taken as anything more than that her body was cramping, begging for a stretch.

She lay as long as she could, a half hour, forty minutes, she wasn't sure. She wasn't sleepy. She was tired and Steve's head pressing into her body felt like one of those heavy medicine balls. She wondered why when you were in the midst of all the action nothing felt wrong but the moment it was over a mere twinge could turn into a major muscle ache.

She managed to ease her body away without waking the man she was to marry. He had never asked her directly. After announcing the decision to her father he'd given her the ring, then started on the planning, pulling her along, assigning her tasks. Not once had she complained. Not even when she was annoyed and it burned a hole in her to remain silent. She applauded herself. She was turning out to be the kind of woman it seemed her parents had always wanted. One who obeyed the rules and never made waves.

It had been a long time since Kari had made waves. Still waters suited her just fine.

On bare feet she padded silently into the hall bathroom. That was another thing Steve hated, that they had to shower before and after. He claimed to love the smell of sex that lingered on their sweaty bodies. She didn't.

The water ran over her body. She closed her eyes as she soaped up, remembering a time when she didn't rush for the shower. It would have been useless. For three years she'd lived in a constant state of sexual bliss. Through everything they'd had that.

She couldn't stop the smile that came to her lips on remembering Jon. They would make love lying close together making plans, then make love all over again. It would continue until they both fell asleep exhausted. When they awakened they would start again, leaving just enough time to shower and run to class or one of their numerous jobs.

In those days sex was the only thing they had that was not in short supply. No money, just them and their burning passion.

Kari's hand moved with the soap to the triangle between her thighs. She lathered gently, remembering also that not once had she ever faked it with Jon. There had been no need. He merely had to look at her and she would become wet with desire.

It had been seven years since she had experienced the peaks of passion they had climbed together. Her lovemaking with Steve was good on most occasions, just not earth shattering. She'd never had the soul connection with anyone that she'd had with Jon.

Kari felt the involuntary squeezing of her thighs against her palms. Who needed breathtaking dizzying passionate sex? She had more, much more. She had her parents' love again and the approval of her entire family. She was marrying a wonderful man, a black man, a doctor.

Since the night she'd had a peek at Steve's racist side, she had begun mentally recounting his positive traits. It was now her mantra. She had no choice but to repeat it or she would go mad knowing she was marrying a man who would hate her for her past.

Oh God, what am I doing? She caught herself, she had to stop. Steve was wonderful, handsome and successful. He was a sensitive and attentive lover.

She no longer needed to feel the earth move. She'd felt it—and the betrayal that came along with it. Now she'd settle for good loving. That was all she needed. She felt the lower half of her body convulsing, calling her a liar.

To her horror, the soap fell from her hand and clanged to the bottom of the shower. Another smaller tremble went through her body, ripping at her inner thighs. She had never intended to do it, had never even known she needed it. There was too much shame for her to enjoy the release. Hurriedly, she finished her shower, cursing Jon and her memories of him.

CHAPTER SEVEN

It took an hour for Kari to calm down. Once she did, she formulated a plan to end her nightmare. With an uncanny sense of clarity she knew without a doubt that she could not allow Steve to take over yet another area of her life. This problem she had to handle alone.

She held the sheath of papers in her hands, scanning them with an accusing glare. This wasn't supposed to happen but it had and now she would deal with it. She read the questions, one after the other, then proceeded to draft her answers. She made them as noncommittal as possible, not wanting to trip herself up.

"You need a lawyer, Kari." It was Jon's voice she heard in her head, scolding her on attempting to represent herself.

"Maybe you're right," she answered the imaginary voice. "Chicago has more lawyers than any city need."

Before she knew it, she had retrieved the yellow pages from a dusty pile of books under her sofa. She sneezed once from the dust lifting into the air and almost put off her task in order to sweep. The snoring sounds emitting from her bedroom reinforced her decision to continue. It was nearly noon. When Steve awoke, she wanted a clear handle on things.

Kari dialed several lawyers, some telling her outright they couldn't help her. She fought against the worries that were nagging at her and continued dialing, finally setting up an appointment for the following week. That should have done something to assuage her apprehension but it didn't.

"Honey, where are you? Come back to bed."

It was Steve's voice calling out to her, making her wish she were alone, that their long awaited day together was over. *Damn, why don't you go home?* It was only a thought. Hearing the annoyance in Steve's voice and feeling the same annoyance crawling through her belly, she took a moment to answer.

Kari glanced at the two karat, pear-shaped diamond that sat on her finger. Every since Steven had given it to her, it seemed he wanted her at his beck and call.

"Steve, I'm busy."

She listened to the sounds of his footsteps coming toward her, then looked up and saw him. Even unaroused the man really was well endowed. She allowed herself the luxury of wantonly gazing on his naked frame, knowing that it gave him pleasure to have her looking at him.

Her eyes moved across his washboard abdomen, then up to his chest. She loved the downy soft curls nestled there. A thick carpet of black on brown. Her eyes slowly moved downward, taking in the fact that her stares were having an effect. His erection appeared to swell at astronomical speed.

He walked toward her, his condition now jutting out proudly. A lascivious grin lighted up his eyes.

Kari ducked and pushed a chair in front of him. "Sorry, Steve, I have to get a lawyer. I don't have time for this now."

He looked hurt. She glanced down. Her words hadn't damaged him physically; there was not a sign of deflation. In fact, her refusal appeared to have had the opposite effect. He continued walking toward her, leering playfully.

Before she had a chance to think, Steven had positioned his nude body in a kitchen chair. With one swift movement, he managed to pull aside her panties and pull her onto his lap, placing her directly over his swollen erection.

Her body slid down despite her wishes to work. She felt him filling her and a shudder of pleasure coursed through her. Her upper torso went limp as she sank against his chest. The lingering smells from their previous sex caused her to gag and turn her head aside.

Gentle hands brought her head back into its original position. A powerful thrust and she forgot everything. This was indeed one of her favorite positions. Finding a decent lawyer could wait a little while longer.

Finished, they remained where they were. Steve's mouth was clamped to her breast, nibbling softly, pulling on her lightly. She was lucky to have him, lucky that he desired her and that for the most part, he pleased her.

There was something bothering her. *Don't be silly,* she chided herself, *a lot of men aren't good at saying it.* Still, she wanted to hear him tell her that he loved her, especially now. So far he had said it only to her father.

She felt him pressing himself closer to her, his hand running up and down her spine. "Hmmm, you smell so good," he moaned against her belly.

Kari felt embarrassed, self-conscious. "I do not. I smell musty, like I spilled an entire vat of pheromones in here and so do you," she teased.

He held her even closer. "I like it."

"I know."

She felt him stirring inside her. "What are you doing, pre-scribing yourself medications?" She truly was amazed at his stamina, always had been.

"No, he answered her. "With you I don't need a pill."

"Steve, this is important." She gestured toward the papers. "I have to take care of this."

"Go ahead, don't let me stop you."

Kari attempted to rise but felt strong hands pulling her back down.

"We both took the day off from work to spend some time together. I believe my exact words were, "I want to make love to you all day and all night.""

"I know, and believe me just as soon as I take care of this I promise I'll play. You won't be neglected."

"Not later," Steve purred into her ear. "I took the day off to make love to you, that's what I intend to do. Besides I already told you to leave the summons to me, that I'll take care of it."

Despite her best efforts, Kari was getting angry. She kept hearing Jon's voice telling her to get a lawyer. "Steve, I'm taking care of this now. I have to find a lawyer."

"Fine, you'll have to work from here, that's my only demand." His brown eyes were laughing at her, challenging her to ignore him.

"Can we at least slide the chair over so I can reach the papers?"

She watched silently as he rose carefully, an inch, no more, one of his hands keeping her locked to him. Kari thought of a pair of dogs she had once seen locked together and laughed out loud. She hadn't thought Steve would be able to move the chair, but he had.

"What's so funny?"

"Us. Do you really expect me to get any work done like this?"

His hands were roaming her body. "You have a choice. Stop worrying and let me handle this, or you work while I enjoy myself." He took one of her nipples in his mouth and bit down, a look of smugness on his handsome face.

For ten seconds longer Kari allowed Steven to enjoy her body while she replayed his words in her head. "You have a choice." It was as though she had been doused with a bucket of ice water. She closed her eyes, took several deep cleansing breaths that effectively shut Steve out. He was inside her, yet she managed to block out him and all that he was doing.

Kari dialed a couple of lawyers. In the middle of her conversation with a promising attorney, Steve came, clutching her and almost growling. Kari coughed several times to disguise the noise. Feeling annoyed, she told the attorney she would call back later, knowing she was too embarrassed to ever call him again.

Before her finger could push the button to end the call Steven was hauling her unceremoniously off his lap and heading for the shower. That meant he was through with lovemaking for the day. She could tell from his long-legged stride that he was angry. He had expected her to put the phone away, forget everything except his making love to her. She'd agreed to that, an entire day of lovemaking.

Why didn't you, Kari? Why did you have to make such an issue of this? For God's sake, you're marrying the man. He loves you and you love him. This is how it's supposed to be, that you can't get enough of each other.

Apologize. Her parents' voices were in her head hammering away at her. *Don't louse this up.* Part of her wanted to go into the bathroom. She knew he was waiting; she could tell from the amount of banging that was going on.

She rocked her body, trying to get her feet to move but they wouldn't. She opened her mouth to call out to Steven, to tell him that she was sorry, but no sound issued forth from her throat.

Steve was in the big shower in her bedroom. She could have joined him, stroked his ego as it were, and perhaps done a little physical stroking as well. Kari stood at the door of the linen closest instead and listened to the sounds from the bathroom before she walked in the opposite direction to the same hallway shower she'd used earlier. *Let him pout*, she thought, *who the hell cares?*

Showered and dressed, they stood three feet apart, neither speaking. She watched as Steve's hand went down to the center of the kitchen table. He lifted the court papers and glared at her.

"I'll take care of this."

Kari swallowed, closing her eyes for a brief moment. Her hand reached out to reclaim her papers. "No." Her voice was edgy, the anger almost brimming through. She swallowed again, needing a moment to soften her tone.

"No. Thank you, Steve, but I'll take care of this myself."

"Fine." With that he walked out of the door, hurt and angry.

She stood in the middle of the room, her eyes drawn to the last page of the document. *Damn you, Jonathan Steele. You ruined my life once. Now you're back for a repeat performance. I'm not going to give you the chance.*

With that Kari finished the questions, stuffed the papers in an envelope, pasted on the proper amount of stamps, slapped on an address label. Then she filled out the little green certified mail cards she kept in her kitchen drawer, another perk of living on a suburban mail route. You didn't have to go to the post office to send certified mail.

She ignored Jonathan's voice now screaming at her that she was making a mistake, to keep the appointment with the lawyer. "No," she screamed out loud, "I'm sick of lawyers. I'll handle it myself. As far as mistakes go, Jon, don't worry. It's not the first mistake I've ever made."

She proceeded down her drive to place the letters in the box for Rose, her mail carrier. She would handle her own life from here on out.

ॐ

Every fiber in Kari's being was geared up for seeing Jon, for fighting, for taking charge of her life once again. She could feel the adrenaline rush. She'd spent way too many years of her life missing that part of herself, the person she'd been with Jon.

Meanwhile, she had thrown herself into the thick of handling her case. She found one paper she had held on to from the resort, declaring an acceleration of payment.

She bought several law books and began looking up terms. She ran across the term *laches* and it was as though a light went on. According to the law of laches, you sat on your rights if you made your intentions known and then didn't follow through.

She had her way out. The resort had demanded payment in full over three years before and threatened to sue her if she didn't comply.

Kari was jubilant. So much so, that she decided to give lawyers another try. She took the document and the passages on *laches* to the lawyer, only to be told that he didn't think it would work. Kari left the office more determined than ever. The lawyer had failed to convince her that *laches* would not work. Her well-honed instincts told her it would. She would spend no more money on attorney consultations. They were worthless. She had already filed her answers, now she would defend herself, win or lose.

Time and again she went over the papers from Jon's office. When she spotted a long list of other defendants that were included in the same lawsuit as hers, she couldn't believe it. There in front of her were the names, addresses, and amounts each of the defendants owed.

She wondered why the law firm had lumped so many suits together, and why they'd made that information available to all those being sued. She wouldn't worry about it, she would use it, she decided, as she flipped the page and called the first name.

Only one couple was willing to work with her to defeat the resort. Several of the others had already made settlements with the law firm. Three had filed for bankruptcy and two were sending their attorneys to represent them.

None of this dissuaded Kari. She was on a mission and she was determined. When the law books housed in her town's library proved insufficient, she became a constant visitor at the Joliet courthouse and familiarized herself with the material that pertained to her case. She spent hours making photo copies of needed passages, lawsuits, anything that cited a case similar to her own.

She used the courthouse computers to get a printout of all the cases from American Resorts. She was able to learn the most personal details of all the people the resort had sued in Illinois. She was told by a court clerk that she could get that same information from the federal court in Missouri simply by calling and giving them the case number. She was surprised that her own legwork produced so much personal information on the people involved.

Kari then called the federal bankruptcy court in Kansas City, Missouri, and requested information on the resolutions of the cases tried there. She knew she was probably better prepared than any lawyer she could have hired. They wouldn't have cared enough to do all the research.

Armed with the information from the federal bankruptcy court, Kari now knew the disposition of the cases already tried. So far, not many defendants had won. She was undaunted. She would win. She had something they didn't have, that little declaration of accelerated payment from the resort. That was her ace in the hole. She wasn't worried that she was fighting against high paid attorneys, nor was she worried that she would be going up against Jon. She truly believed she could and would win.

She kicked her campaign into high gear and took her contract to a printer for examination. She had them write an official report for the court on the illegal size of the print used. She paid for the steady progression of sizes until the legal requirement was reached. She would go to court prepared. The judge would not have to guess what size was used and what size was legal.

She was beginning to enjoy her search through the law, comparing notes with the other couple on her list. It reminded her of another time and place when she had done the exact same thing.

Now it was for real. This was not a practice case. This was her case. She was being sued. And she was giving it all of her attention.

CB

"Let's go out for dinner." Steve's silky voice crooned enticingly to her a few days later.

"I can't, sorry, Steve. I have to work on my case."

"That's all you ever do lately. At least let me help you"

Kari ignored Steve's attempt to get her to allow him to help her in her search. She disregarded his pouting and hurt feelings.

"Kari, I'm beginning to feel a little like a beggar," Steve complained.

"A beggar? I don't understand." Kari was stunned. Where had that come from? What did Steven think he was begging for?

"Of course you don't understand." He walked over to her stash of law books and looked down at them. "You're consumed by this case. I'm going to be your husband; I have to insist that you allow me to help."

Kari glanced at Steve, knowing full well where this was coming from. Again she wondered what had made her get involved with a small town Southern man. She was very aware of the answer. He was a man her parents approved of.

"Don't force me to put my foot down, Kari."

This couldn't be happening. Her fiancé was giving her an ultimatum.

"Are you listening to me, Kari? I won't stay here and be ignored."

She smiled in his direction before walking toward him. When she stood directly in front of him she said, "Good night, Steve," reached for one of the law books and settled herself into the cushions of her sofa.

She ignored the daggers she was positive were aimed in her direction. She wouldn't be bullied by Steve. And she damn sure wasn't going to face Jonathan unprepared and look like a fool. She continued reading.

Kari heard the slam of her door and ignored that also. Whether or not it was meant for her to have a future with Steve, she must first prepare to meet Jonathan Steele.

Less than an hour later the phone rang. Kari debated answering, not wanting to continue the fight with Steve.

"Kari, what's going on?"

Damn. It was her father. If she'd had a choice she would have taken Steven, but just barely.

"Dad, what are you talking about?"

"He's talking about Steve," her Mother's voice. "Steve said something's wrong. He said you won't let him help you, that you barely have time for him."

Oh God, Kari thought as she listened to her mother's high-pitched, meddling voice. *Do they both have to be on the line?*

"Listen, Kari."

It was her father again. The idea of being scolded like a kid was as annoying as hell. "I'm listening, Dad."

"Are you being sarcastic?"

"Not yet."

"Don't talk to your father that way," her mother's voice chimed in.

"Well, I was just being honest," Kari defended herself.

"What's wrong with you, girl? For heaven's sakes, you're marrying the man. You should be happy a man like him wants to marry you."

That did it. It was the last straw. She was not damaged goods.

"That's just the point, Dad. I'm marrying Steve, but that doesn't give him ownership papers over me."

She waited as her father's voice rose with anger before becoming muffled. She knew what was happening. Her mother was calming her father down.

"Alright, Kari, if you won't let Steve help, then your mother and I will help you."

She dismissed her father's concern with a firm, "No thanks, Dad, I don't need any help."

She was annoyed that Steven had gone to them with her problem. When her father became insistent, she felt the anger she'd been holding inside for too many years bubbling to the surface.

"It's my business, Dad. I'm an adult. I would also appreciate it from now on if you don't talk to Steve about me. You want to know something, come to me. If I don't tell you, it's none of your business."

She hung up the phone, knowing she'd left her father puzzled and angry. And it concerned her not one iota.

She was aware it was time she informed her parents to back out of her life. Even though his involvement was indirect, it seemed to her anytime Jonathan Steele was involved, her life became crazy, choppy, filled with problems. This time she intended to keep the damage to a minimum. Her heart would not become involved.

CHAPTER EIGHT

Jon held the thick envelope in his hands at last. His breathing raspy, he tried to cover up the fact that he now held in his hand what he had diligently searched for, for weeks.

It took her long enough, he thought. He could tell he was about to work up a good head of steam before he even opened the envelope. He read her answers, getting angry at her for behaving like the other defendants he'd encountered. Her bold script revealed she'd filled out the papers herself. No attorney.

Why Kari? Why didn't you get any help with this? Jon felt his throat tightening up with the same lump he had experienced through the years. Some small corner of his heart refused to stop caring about her. He was truly worried about her, about her losing the case to his firm. To him.

His eyes came up. He saw Mrs. Dobis staring intently in his direction, a frown on her face. His response was immediate. He glared at the woman before proceeding to open the next envelope in his hand.

A tiny pulling began at the corners of his mouth. He wanted to smile but bit his lips against it. Kari had drafted a request for a dismissal. She was going to fight. He had to admit that was one of the things he'd loved about her, her fighting spirit.

Then with a sinking feeling, he realized what Kari's letter meant. She planned to come to Missouri. She was going to fight.

Anger, joy, curiosity and relief fought for the leading lineup. He would be seeing her again. Anger won out. Anger at himself for wanting to see her, for caring about her still. He couldn't allow those feelings to resurface. He had loved her, put his future in her hands and she'd bailed on him. He felt the tension invading his body. He had to find a way to make his thoughts of her fade. He lifted the phone from its cradle and waited for Elizabeth Dobis's dour voice.

"Mrs. Dobis, could you find Tanya and send her in, please?"

"What is it that you want her to do, Mr. Steele?"

Jon held the phone away from his ear, gripping it so hard that the blood drained from his knuckles, turning them white. Cassandra was right. He had been trying for weeks to be nicer to the woman but she was trying his patience. Even a saint could only endure so much. And a saint he wasn't.

"Just send her in, Mrs. Dobis."

He banged the receiver down on the base, cursing himself for the act he knew he was about to commit. He was aware it was stupid. How could he possibly erase almost four years of loving and living with Kari from his life by screwing the intern.

Seven months, Jon. You spent seven months in jail for a crime you didn't commit. She did nothing to help you.

He found himself rocking back and forth slowly, wanting to boil all his emotions into one: anger. Raw and simple. He didn't want to care for Kari, to worry about her and even feel pride that she was taking on the federal bankruptcy court. He wanted to remember that she had not loved him enough to let him explain.

Jon was so lost in thought when Tanya entered the room that he didn't hear her until she called his name. He turned and stared, getting the distinct impression that it was not the first time she had called him.

He wondered why he had called her into his office. He had avoided her purposefully. Until now. Now she stood before him radiant, purring his name, a look of hunger in her green eyes. She reminded him of a cat, a big predatory cat, and he felt much like a mouse caught under her paw.

"Did you want me, Mr. Steel?"

Jon watched as Tanya thrust her breasts out even more. A seductive sway of her hips toward him and the double entendre told him he was about to play with fire. For a moment he welcomed the inevitable burn.

Remember, Jon, don't play where you work. His eyes fell to his desk. Kari's handwriting stared up at him. It was the push into hell that he needed. With a sigh he allowed his eyes to explore the intern's body despite the fact that the term "sexual harassment" flashed before him.

"Tanya, would you like to go to dinner with me tonight?" He waited, his mouth dry. It was too late to take back his words. He watched as she ran one manicured nail slowly from the base of her neck, to her cheeks, stopping dramatically at her full lips, pretending to be contemplating the decision.

"I don't know, Mr. Steele. I need to think for a minute."

For crying out loud, he thought. *You've been after me forever and now you're playing coy?* "If you can't make it, maybe some other time." He shifted the papers on his desk. He wasn't about to beg for something that was constantly being shoved in his face.

"I didn't say that."

She walked toward him, coming around his desk, rolling her shoulders seductively, causing her breasts to jut out even farther. She stopped only inches from Jon's face and looked down at him, her eyes giving him permission to touch.

His mouth was extremely dry. Mentally, he called himself a fool. He felt the beginnings of an arousal, then sucked on his tongue. This wasn't going to happen. Not tonight.

"Cassandra, Tim and I need to go over some briefs for tomorrow. We need someone to take notes. I thought you could go to dinner with us. Of course we'll pay you for the overtime."

As Jon rustled the papers, he observed the cloud of confusion in her eyes. The blush of embarrassment that crept into her face made him feel guilty. She had correctly assumed that he was asking her out on a date.

He didn't know what had happened, just that at the last moment he'd frozen. He was still hard. Perhaps that's what scared him the most. It had taken tremendous effort on his part not to reach up and caress her ample breasts, to pull her into his lap, to feel her hands on him, touching, molding.

Stop it. His own voice screamed at him. He had worked too damn hard to blow his career on a piece of forbidden office ass. He would continue to seek his pleasures elsewhere.

"Well, Tanya, if you're not busy, can you work tonight? Of course dinner will be our treat. Whatever you want." He smiled at her, hoping to take some of the sting out of his abrupt turnaround.

Jon turned his attention to the papers before him, making notes, pretending he didn't notice Tanya's hands fluttering in front of her like a wounded bird. He felt bad about that. He moved even closer to the desk, making sure his uncomfortable bulge was hidden.

"Mr. Steele, I'm sorry. I almost forgot. I promised a friend I would go to the movies with her tonight. I do hope you don't mind, but I can't work tonight."

From the corner of his eye he caught the woman inching toward the door. She had managed to pull it off, to salvage something from the awful mess he'd made of things and for that he was grateful. He never should have gone against his instincts.

Jon kept his eyes glued to the folder in front of him. "Don't worry about it, Tanya. I'm sure we can find someone else to take notes." He stopped talking, dismissing her with his silence.

When he was certain the woman had left his vicinity, he called his co-counsels and issued an invitation to a working dinner. Though his request was met with hesitation and resistance, he overcame both, telling them they should really go over the next day's approach.

It was a flimsy excuse but the pair owed him for all the work he'd done alone. They would go along with him. At least this once they would. Jon wouldn't push his luck again, but he wanted to cover his tracks. He didn't want Tanya finding out that there was no dinner meeting.

He sank back against the expensive leather back of his chair and closed his eyes. There was no denying his erratic behavior in the recent past and it was all because of Kari. He thought back to the first time he'd seen her. He'd fallen in love with her before he had even had a chance to speak to her.

Her eyes, big and brown, had been a magnet for him, almost overshadowing the rest of her. So drawn he was to the warmth he saw in the depth of her pupils that it took him a second glance to take in the rest of her.

Her brown skin was the color of warm honey. Five foot, three, barely a hundred pounds, she wore her hair long, in dread-locks, a style he'd never cared for until her. She always had a smile. He had almost scared her off with his eagerness. It had taken him months to get her alone. She'd refused to date him and only after much persistence on his part had she allowed him to join her study group.

One by one the other students dropped out, annoyed that Kari had integrated the group without asking. Their hostilities had been apparent from the beginning. No one had held their tongue on advising Kari "not to go messing around with no white boy. He's just a redneck cracker."

He would never forget how he'd felt when she had turned to

him and flashed a brilliant smile before answering them. "I like him."

Their group had dwindled until it was only the two of them remaining. Still, she refused to date him. She treated him as though he were slow, perhaps a bit retarded. He put up with it because he still got to remain in her presence, love her and be around her.

Eventually the need to touch overrode her objections. Reaching for a book, their fingers touched. Jon couldn't help himself. He reached for her, his lips searching out hers. He was only mildly stunned when she pushed him away, a curious look on her face.

"Are you prejudiced against me because of the color of my skin, Kari?"

She had smiled at him then. "If that were true this room would be filled with my friends. Instead you're the only other person here."

He thought about that for a moment. "I thought we were friends."

"Jon, we are friends." She paused. "We both grew up in this town. Why are you begging for trouble? People are barely speaking to either of us because we study together. I can't imagine what would happen if we..."

He watched her lips as her voice trailed off. "If we what? I'm in love with you, Kari. I think having you love me too is worth any amount of trouble."

He paused. "Even if it's a lie, please humor me. Tell me that you feel what I'm feeling. Tell me that you love me a little bit too." His heart was pounding in his chest. He was so afraid she would toss him out on his ear, refuse to study with him. And yet...

He couldn't stop himself. Even if he had tried, which of course he didn't. He pulled her into his arms. Not feeling any resistance, he lowered his lips to hers and kissed her softly at first, tasting her, something he had wanted to do for months.

He pressed his hands against her back until slowly her hands came upward and embraced him. His exploration began in earnest. The sweet honey taste of her mouth reminded him of her honeyed complexion.

He pulled away to look into her eyes. "Do you, Kari? Do you love me even a little?"

"Do you think you would be here if I didn't?"

Her voice was low. He breathed in the breath she had just expelled. "I thought you were making a political statement by allowing me in the group."

She laughed, deep and throaty. "No way. I loved the look of adoration in your eyes. You've been good for my ego."

"Are you feeding mine now? I did ask you to lie to me. Are you lying?"

Jon shivered in his chair as he remembered how Kari had run her tongue across his lips, asking him, "What do you think?" After that night things had progressed quickly.

Memories of the first time they made love filled him with untold remorse for what they had lost. He opened his eyes, wrenching himself from the past. The feeling of loss permeated his soul till it filled the room with his grief.

He glanced at Kari's replies. Taking out a new legal pad from his desk he began to draft an order for dismissal without prejudice. He would run it by his colleagues. He already had an explanation for them. He would show Kari's petition to have the case dismissed.

So far no one had made that request. Their job, as lawyers was merely to collect the most amount of money in the shortest span of time.

He would tell them that fighting one defendant would take away the momentum they had built. Besides, he could always argue that if the firm wanted to bring her in later they could. No one need ever know he had a personal stake in the outcome.

Jon was pretty sure neither the firm nor the resort would go after one lone defendant. Not with all the millions they had collected and would continue to collect. Now if he could just sell Kari on the idea, he wouldn't have to see her.

He would not be forced to continue remembering how sweet it had been for them and how very painful at the end. He could return to forgetting how much he had loved her. He rubbed his throbbing groin. Apparently how much he still cared.

Jon glared at his phone as though the instrument were the enemy. Snatching it from its cradle, his voice gravely, he managed to croak out his instructions to Elizabeth Dobis.

As he listened to the ringing of the phone, his heart pounded, calling him a coward for listening in, not making the call himself. He couldn't.

ର

Kari had just ended the call with airline, having made plans to pick up her e-ticket to Missouri the next day, when the phone rang just as she was returning it to the base.

"May I speak to Ms. Kari Thomas."

The voice on the other end was cold, clipped. "This is Kari Thomas. Who am I speaking to?"

"I'm Elizabeth Dobis, secretary to Mr. Steele of the Davis and Jackson law firm."

The nerve endings along Kari's spine began to tingle. She listened for a sound. She heard none, but knew as surely as she knew her own name that Jon was on an extension. Listening.

"Ms. Thomas," the woman continued, "I have been instructed to call and advise you that the firm has issued an order to dismiss your case without prejudice. There will be no need for you to come to Missouri."

Kari made her own voice as cold and clipped as the secretary's. She wanted Jon to know she knew he was on the line. "Why would Mr. Steele want to offer me a dismissal? "Mrs. Dobis," she began, "I'm not a lawyer, so let's make sure we both have the same understanding of this. *Without prejudice* means you can bring me back to court. Is that true?"

"Yes, that's true."

Kari heard the hesitation in the woman's voice before she continued.

"Mr. Steele has no plans of pursuing this matter further with you."

"Oh. Thank you." Kari hung up her end without saying goodbye or letting Jon know her intentions.

So he has no plans to pursue this. She almost laughed out loud. *Does he really think I'm fool enough to settle for a dismissal of that nature?*

୧୭

Jon held the extension, listening to the sound of her voice. He could tell from the slight change in nuance the moment she became aware of his presence on the line. His body vibrated with an energy he thought had died.

Jon heard the click of the phone and prepared himself to meet Kari. Her last words spoke volumes. She would accept nothing less than complete and total vindication. He knew her well. She had always wanted to prove she was right. He was sure this time would be no different. He couldn't help wondering what he would do when he saw her face to face.

CHAPTER NINE

"Jackie, I'm going."

"I can't believe it. Why would you want to see Jonathan again?"

Kari glared at her friend. "This has nothing to do with Jon. I'm being sued, something, by the way, you told me wouldn't happen. You were wrong. They're dragging my ass to Kansas City, Missouri. Can you believe it?"

"I'm sorry." Jackie glanced away. "This is all my fault. I'm the one who took you out to that resort, the one who talked you into signing the contract, and I'm the one who told you to ignore their letters. Kari, I'm truly sorry. I'll go with you, if you want. I'm sure one of the other nurses will cover my shift for a day or so."

Kari had what she wanted, for her friend to get off the subject of Jonathan, but in the process she'd heaped guilt on her that she'd never intended. Kari reached out and punched Jackie's shoulder playfully. "It's not your fault, I'm a big girl, and, hey, I wanted the steak knives they gave me."

"Kari…

"No, Jackie, really I don't blame you, that would be stupid and wrong. When have you ever been able to persuade me to do anything that I didn't want to do?"

Jackie smiled, the relief evident. "You're right about that. You didn't listen when I told you to give Jonathan another chance and you won't listen when I tell you that the good Dr. Anderson is not what he appears to be."

"Will you stop it? My love life is not your business. Period. Steve is a wonderful man; we're going to have lots of beautiful babies together."

"That's about the only thing you've said concerning him that's true. I'll give that to him, he's fine. But..."

"But what? Go ahead, Jackie, say it. What's on your mind?"

"You're not the same with him that you were with Jonathan. You're so guarded it's almost like you're acting a part. I don't think you're really happy, not like before. I remember how much fun you and Jonathan had. I loved being around the two of you."

Jackie started to laugh. "Remember when you invited me for dinner and I came over and found the two of you in your garden, covered in mud?"

Kari smiled, she did remember. They'd gone out to pick fresh vegetables for dinner and Jon had decided to water the garden as she did the picking. He'd turned the hose on her and she'd wrestled it away, drenching him in water. When Jackie arrived, she'd found them rolling about in the mud, laughing like crazy. "What are you complaining about," Kari chuckled, "you got dinner."

"But I had to cook it."

"Because we had to wash off the mud."

"For an hour? And what about that God-awful pecan pie Jonathan made for us?"

Kari's eyes closed as she swallowed to prevent the tears. The pecans had come from their trees. She'd loved those trees, even the horrible pies Jon made from the nuts. Most of all, she'd loved Jonathan. She didn't need Jackie to make her remember. She had a million memories locked away in her heart: the two of them cooking together, taking walks, sitting around holding each other and watching television. No, reminders she didn't need. What she'd needed for the last seven years was a way to forget.

"Jackie, why are you doing this? You know what happened. He cheated on me, he'd only been pretending. Jackie, he didn't love me."

"I don't know what made him cheat, Kari. But I do know you're wrong about him not loving you. I was there. I witnessed his love. And I witnessed yours. Your feelings for Steve, they're not the same as they were for Jonathan."

"Of course they aren't the same. I'm not a kid anymore. But I'm happy. Why wouldn't I be? I have a damn good job. I get to go to different offices fixing their problems. It's never dull. I'm marrying a gorgeous man who's well off, generous and good in bed. And if that's not enough, my parents love him."

For a long moment the two friends were silent, eyeing each other, deciding who would be the first to speak. Kari shook her head and smiled. "You can't hold it in, can you? You're about to burst.

"You're going to get angry if I say it."

"That's never stopped you before."

"Well, in that case, I couldn't help but notice that you mentioned your job first in the things that make you happy. Shouldn't you have mentioned the man first?"

"Steve is first. You're just looking for problems where none exist."

"Dr. Anderson just doesn't seem your type, he's so, so…down home."

"Down home is just my type. Why can't you believe me? And while we're on the subject of Steve, why do you insist on calling him Dr. Anderson?"

Jackie hunched her shoulders. "Could be that he's a doctor, I'm a nurse, we work at the same hospital, that's how it's done." She stopped and sighed. "If it wasn't for me you would have never met him. You wouldn't have wanted the hospital account so badly if it hadn't meant we could see more of each other."

"God, Jackie, lighten up. Do you really think you have that much control over my life? Evidently it was my destiny to meet and marry Steve." This time it was Kari who sighed. "Listen, I think for now it would be safer for us to change the conversation."

"Okay," Jackie acquiesced with a naughty twinkle in her eyes. "How do you think you'll react to seeing Jonathan?"

Kari rolled her eyes. "Enough already. I have to go into the office today and see if I can get some time off. I'll call you later in the week. Maybe we can do something." She ignored Jackie's, "Yeah right," shouted to her back. To answer her would have started a whole new debate.

With surprising accommodation Kari's firm had given her no problem about requesting a spur of the moment vacation. She was a dedicated worker and had double-checked on each of the clients assigned to her, making sure none were experiencing any problems. She would only be gone a couple of days but just in case, she'd given them her pager number for emergencies.

She slept fitfully the night before she was to leave. Steve's strong arms around her did little to wash away her fears. He had given her a handful of mild sedatives the week before. Tonight she felt as if she needed one. She knew it wasn't the lawsuit. Even if she lost she could easily afford to pay. It was something else.

From the moment Elizabeth Dobis had called her with an offer of dismissal, something had happened to Kari. She should have been grateful that Jon didn't want to see her. The fact that he was throwing her a crumb, giving her a chance to back away, should have been enough.

She maneuvered her body even closer to Steve, her hand automatically sliding down the curve of her hip to reach behind and caress him. She drew imaginary circles around the tip of his flaccid penis, waiting patiently for her ministrations to take effect.

In a matter of seconds she felt the hardening followed by the rapid swelling. Her hand was no longer able to encompass him.

"Uhmm, nice." Steve's sleepy voice held a tinge of surprise.

He was awake, his hand rubbing her back, gliding over her buttocks, his breath warm and sweet against her ear.

"Want me to take a shower?"

"No. Not tonight," she replied, kissing away his surprise. She murmured the words into his mouth, not knowing if he heard. "I just need to feel you moving within me. It will be like taking some of your strength along tomorrow."

He heard her. "Why don't you let me go with you, Kari? Let me support you in this, I want to."

"I know you do," she replied, wishing she had kept her words to herself as well as her hands, but she truly did need a reminder to help her get through the thought of facing her past. She needed to have a clear picture of what was waiting for her at home.

"We're going to be married. I should be there for you. I should be the one taking care of your problems."

Kari felt her desire draining away and didn't want it to. She refused to allow Steven's words to annoy her. She didn't need taking care of. Correction. Her problems with the lawsuit she could handle. As for her body, she did need Steven for that.

She picked up the pace of her caresses, wanting to block everything from Steven's mind but the feel of her fingers against his throbbing loins. She needed him to make her forget. She felt an old ache deep within her soul. She wanted it gone.

Her hand found his special spot. She gave a squeeze, applying just the right amount of pressure. She felt the shudder go through him and into her, propelling her along. He was ready.

"Make love to me, Steve. No more talking. I want you inside me now." She was almost sobbing. Her reactions were scaring her.

As Steven rose on one elbow she spread her legs, waiting for him.

Her body clutched at him, her muscles tightening around him. All the while scalding tears cascaded down her cheeks. They came together and with their physical release a fresh torrent of tears burst forth. For Kari it felt as if she were saying goodbye.

"Kari, what's wrong?"

She couldn't answer him. She felt the slight ripples of his abdomen and was aware that her tears were causing him to panic. She wondered if he felt it too. The overwhelming sensation that they were about to lose something.

He gathered her in his arms, stroking her, comforting her. She clung to him, not wanting to ever leave his embrace. For the first time since it had begun she admitted to herself that she was afraid. Not of going to court but of seeing Jon.

How could she possibly share that with her fiancé? Kari had the strongest feeling that Steve was feeling something also. He was holding her with a tenderness that only made her cry more.

☙

Steven held Kari in his arms more sure than ever that something was bothering her. He didn't for a minute believe that nonsense about being sued. Fifteen thousand dollars wasn't enough money for the change he sensed in her.

He pulled her closer. He'd done his best to persuade her to allow him to come with her. Hell, for that matter, she could have just let him handle the entire thing.

When she'd refused, stating that she could take care of herself, it had taken him by surprise. There was little he could actually do, they weren't married yet. All that would change the moment she became his wife. He'd see to that. No more doing whatever the hell she wanted. He was the man. He would make the decisions.

cg

"Are you sure you don't want me to come with you?"

It was morning. Her crying jag was over. Steven had held her through the night, trying to ward off whatever it was that was causing her grief. He was smart. She knew he had to know it was something more than money that was causing a small tidal wave.

She gazed into his eyes and saw the hurt he was trying unsuccessfully to conceal. "I want you to come with me more than I've ever wanted anything," she answered him, meaning every word.

She went to him and began stroking his face. "But, Steve, I made this mess. Please let me clean it up. I can't always have you riding to the rescue to save me. I know you want to help me. I know my parents want to help, but you all have to trust me to handle this alone."

She brought her arms up around his neck, cradling the back of his head in her hands, her fingers raking through his short curly hair. She looked deep into his eyes and saw the hurt still lingering.

"I do trust you to handle it." He paused. "It just seems that you don't need me. I need you to need me, to allow me to take care of you. If that makes me outdated, what can I say?"

"Say that you love me, Steve."

His lips came down on hers a moment before he murmured, "You know I do."

Kari pulled away. "I know, but I need to hear the words. If you want to give me something, give me that. That's something I need, Steve, to hear you say it." It was so simple, three little words, no more, no less.

"Why is it so important to you for me to say the words? You know how I feel. You're wearing my ring, we're getting married. That should say it all."

"Women like to hear the words, Steve. We live to hear the man we love say that he loves us."

"Is there something going on that you haven't told me about?" He eyed her suspiciously. "Are you going to Missouri to meet someone?"

Kari laughed, moving out of the protective circle of his arms. "Steven, you've seen the papers. You know all the work I've been doing getting ready for this case. Why would you think there's someone else?"

"Because for weeks you've been shutting me out, not wanting my help. You were happy before with my taking charge, taking care of you. Now it annoys you. I'm not blind. I've noticed the change in you. So have your parents."

She bit down on her lip, realizing she still had not received what she had asked him for. She wanted, no needed, to hear him tell her that he loved her. She wondered briefly why he would go to such lengths not to tell her that he loved her. He'd had no such problems saying it to her father. But she didn't want to fight with him, not now. She needed to know she had Steve to return home to.

She attempted a smile. "You've spoiled me. So have my parents. I don't want you to marry a child, Steve. I want you to marry a woman, a strong woman whom you can lean on if need be. I want to be there for you as you've always been for me. I want to do some of the giving. Let me. Please."

She cast her eyes downward and pretended to be tearing up. God, how she hated using feminine wiles but sometimes you had to. She was determined to give him what he wanted without giving away her soul.

Moments later Steven was holding her, apologizing and agreeing with her that maybe she was right, perhaps she should make the trip without him.

"Thank you, Steve, for being so understanding," she said to him, though inwardly she was thinking, *Who the hell do you think you are? I don't need your permission, buster*. But she didn't say it.

Instead she kissed the man she was going to marry, the man who could make her dream of having a circle of beautiful brown babies come true.

Although she didn't need his permission, she needed to know that she had a life waiting for her in Illinois. She needed to know that within a few short months she would be married. She would be safe.

Safe, she thought and held Steve even closer. Now where had that come from? Her tongue explored Steven's mouth while her mind explored the origin of her thoughts. *Jon can't hurt you, Kari, not any more, you don't need Steven Anderson's protection*. Still, she clung to him, suddenly not wanting to leave.

ॐ

Kari met June and Hamid Ahmed at Chicago's Midway airport. Together the three of them prepared to fly to Missouri and slay the dragon.

They had chosen to go a day early to get their bearings and to avoid any possible delays in getting to the courthouse. No way were they taking a chance on not being there and having a judgment given in their absence.

After arrival the threesome fought their anxiety by enjoying the town. None of them had ever been in Missouri. They walked to the courthouse. Kari's idea. She had made sure to ask for a hotel as close as possible to eight-eleven Grand where the courthouse was located.

The Holiday Inn Crown Plaza was just down the street and around the corner at forty-four-forty-five Main street. She would not leave her fate in the hands of a taxi driver. Then a peek at the night life, some dinner, then bed with a request for a wake up call.

In the morning the trio found themselves too anxious to do more than have a cup of coffee. Kari had taken one of the sedatives Steven had given her. When she saw June's agitated state, she almost offered her one until she remembered Steven's dire warnings to her not to overdo the pills. She changed her mind about dispensing medication without a license. She was in enough hot water already.

They entered the courthouse and asked for directions to the correct room. Her steps resounded in her ears like the sounds she'd heard in movies when a person took the walk to their death. That's how scared she felt. A chill went through her as she turned to stare at the Ahmeds.

She had to remain strong. They were depending on her. They'd received a document in the mail before they left saying their case was dismissed without prejudice. A brief note had been included that said the law firm had no plans at the present time to bring them back to court. The Ahmeds wanted to believe it was over, but they were afraid. They wanted to end it.

Kari talked long and fast convincing the couple they could be dragged back to court later. She didn't trust that if they accepted the firm's offer, the resort wouldn't later try again.

She wasn't sure until she saw them at Midway Airport that they would actually come. Now they were all marching into a courtroom without a lawyer and she had promised them they would win.

"Please, Lord, let me be right," she prayed.

CHAPTER TEN

The moment he had been dreading, yet wanting, had finally arrived. He stood just outside the courtroom looking in, scanning the occupants for Kari.

He sensed her before spotting her. He observed the smartly tailored business suit she wore. Her hair was in a bun and she was sporting glasses. He smiled. He knew the effect she was going for.

"Jonathan, is something wrong?"

He turned and stared at Cassandra, trying to figure whether he'd done or said anything strange. Grateful that she repeated her question, he answered, "No, nothing's wrong," then proceeded to walk into the room wheeling the cart.

Jon refused to look in Kari's direction. It was hard enough for him to remember how to walk, let alone do the job he was being paid handsomely for when his entire being was screaming out her name. *Cool it, boy*.

He reached for a piece of paper. He needed something concrete, some plan to follow. He glanced at his nails and cringed, not wanting to admit that he'd gotten the first and last manicure of his life to impress Kari. *Geesh! I'm turning into such a wuss.*

It was all that he could do not to turn and stare at her. Since she'd resurfaced in his life, she was all that he thought about, admittedly alternating between wanting to strangle her and wanting to just see her smile once more, maybe give him a friendly hug. An immediate tightening in the front of his tailored slacks called him a liar.

Damn, this can't keep happening whenever I think of her. It has to end. We will behave as adults. When this is over, I'll speak to her, pretend she hasn't been on my mind.

The sound of wheeled carts drew Kari's attention to the open door of the courtroom. Her heart caught in her throat. There he was. Oh God, she wanted to turn and run but she smiled at the Ahmeds, a tiny weak smile, the best she could muster.

Jon wheeled in a contraption that resembled a luggage rack. It was loaded with at least four large corrugated boxes. Behind him came two others. They too were loaded down.

Kari tried to pretend that Jon's presence was not having any effect on her. Her stomach was in knots, and ribbons of pain cut through her intestines, causing her to gasp out loud, her hand clutching her belly.

"I hit my hand," she lied in answer to the Ahmeds' look of concern. *Steady, Kari, remain calm.* She took breath after breath, carefully inhaling and exhaling, her own personal calming technique.

It worked. She squared her shoulders and looked straight ahead at Jon's back. He'd gained weight, she noted. At least ten pounds. It looked good on him. His hair was also quite a bit longer and darker.

Her eyes moved from the top of his head down over the expensive material of his suit. He lifted one hand and she almost laughed out loud. She could tell even from where she sat that he'd had a professional manicure.

This successful man who'd put her life on a different course was standing twenty maybe thirty feet in front of her. Once again he was at the helm of her life. A surge of pride shot through her at his success. Unexpected. Jonathan Steele had fulfilled all of his dreams and she was happy for him.

She felt a tapping in her chest that she ignored. Sure, he'd reached his dreams without her. But she had done all that she'd set out to do. Once this case was settled all would be right in her world.

She watched as case after case was called and judgments entered in favor of the resort. She glanced around the almost empty courtroom and wondered where all the other defendants were. She listened as John and his partners received judgments for over five hundred thousand dollars.

Her name was called and she shouted out an answer. Two pairs of eyes turned toward her. She noticed with some irritation that Jon kept his eyes forward on the judge.

Kari gave June and Hamid a quick smile, followed by a thumbs up, before rushing toward the defendant's table.

"Your Honor, we filed for a dismissal on this case."

The judge turned his attention in Kari's direction but his question was to the female attorney. "When did you file these papers?"

It was all that Kari could do not to stare at Jon. She remained still, keeping her eye contact with the judge as she listened to the answer.

"We filed on Friday, the fourteenth of March, Your Honor."

Kari noted the stern look given to the attorney before the judge spoke again.

"That didn't give her much time."

Kari couldn't help noticing that the judge appeared annoyed with the attorney.

"Well, Your Honor, Ms. Thomas was also called and advised of this."

"Is that true, Ms. Thomas?"

The judge now had his attention focused on Kari. "Were you called?"

"Yes, Your Honor, they offered me a dismissal without prejudice. Your Honor, that is nothing more than a continuance. I've put in a lot of hours getting ready for this case and a lot of expense. I've done everything that was required of me."

Kari pulled herself up straighter, feeling that the sympathy of the judge was leaning in her direction. She noticed a slight smile around the corners of his mouth and what she took to be a twinkle in his eyes.

She glanced at the opposing table and saw the three attorneys had their heads bowed in conference. She smiled when the same attorney asked the judge for a continuance.

"Your Honor, I object to that." Kari's voice was clear, without a sign of nervousness.

She reached into her folder and presented the formal written objection to a continuance. One for the enemy. One for the judge. Kari's adrenaline was pumping. She could sense victory within her grasp.

She watched while the judge scowled at the three attorneys as he began flipping page after page from a folder he held.

"The defendant is correct," the judge declared. "She sent her answers back in a timely manner. This lawsuit has created an expense for her. You will proceed with the case today or it will be dismissed with prejudice."

Kari saw the woman attorney fidget before turning to her two male counterparts.

"Your Honor, we're not ready to proceed with this matter today. That's why we offered the defendant a...

The judge cut off her words. "She doesn't want what you offered and it is her right to be heard. Case dismissed with prejudice in the defendant's favor." He did smile at Kari then before adding, "Well done, young lady."

Kari smiled back and murmured, "Thank you."

She gathered her papers, thrilled. She resisted the strong pull to run to Jon and tell him that she remembered. All the nights they'd studied together, she remembered. And thanks to the man who was suing her, she had won in part because of him.

Kari turned. She was hurt that Jon did not even glance in her direction. She gazed out over the few remaining defendants and gave a quick victory sign to June and Hamid.

Her mouth opened wide in surprise. Steven was sitting there waiting for her, beaming, from ear to ear.

She walked toward him, pasting a smile on her face. She was happy to see him, wasn't she? She had not expected to talk to Jon, didn't want him back in her life. Why then was she finding it so very hard to resist the urge to look over her shoulder?

Steve held his hand out to her with what she thought was a quizzical look on his handsome face. *Why is he here?* The thought sat like lead inside of her.

She knew the reason. He had felt in her tears, in her lovemaking, that something was ending and he was there to prevent it. She should be happy. Deep down she knew this, but she wasn't.

Kari took her fiancé's hand and gave it a gentle squeeze. They remained like that, locked together in her victory, and waited for the Ahmeds to be called. When their case also ended in their favor, she was not surprised. She could barely contain her joy… and her sadness.

Now she would once again have to walk out of Jonathan's life without him ever knowing how sorry she was for the past. At least for the seven months he'd spent locked away.

That, she was sorry for. She owed him that much. But with Steven glued to her side, she didn't even dare glance toward Jonathan. Her instincts told her Steve was there for more than support. He was behaving strangely, a suspicious look in his eyes that he tried to conceal. Kari saw and understood. He felt the currents of emotions flowing from her, she was sure of it. The air practically vibrated with the electricity.

Maybe it was best that Steve had shown up. Now her past could be buried as it had been. Steve need never know about Jonathan. She'd done her best to behave as if he didn't exist. It was evident to her from his behavior that she no longer existed for him.

❧

Jonathan finally turned to look at the gallery. He wanted to look into the eyes of the woman he couldn't forget, to communicate to her to wait for him, that they needed to talk.

It had taken every ounce of strength he had in him not to congratulate her when she won. He'd held back, knowing his colleagues would think he had lost his mind. He'd watched her movements from the corner of his eye. The hurt flowed over him when she walked away as though she didn't know he was there.

Now spotting her in the gallery, Jon sucked in his breath. There was a tall, dark-skinned man holding on to Kari's hand as if he would never let it go. He was smiling down at her and she was looking back at him, a soft smile on her lips.

There was nothing to do but look away and absorb the pain. It was over. He never had to see Kari Thomas again. He heard the rustle of bodies leaving. *Good,* he thought *leave again.*

Before he knew what was happening, though, Jon found himself in the hall looking after Kari and the man. He watched the man lift her from the floor and twirl her around. He stood transfixed as the man's lips covered Kari's. Her arms wrapped around his neck and he heard her give a soft laugh filled with promise.

He couldn't move. He should never have left the courtroom. He was sure to receive a reaming out from the judge for that. Now he was forced to watch, unable to turn away.

This was one scenario he had never imagined. Sure, he had been with his share of women since Kari. He just had never thought of Kari being with anyone else. Had never imagined that he would witness her passion for another man. He felt sick.

"May I help you?"

It was the man. Kari's man. Jonathan locked gazes with him, ordering his tongue from the roof of his mouth. He wanted Kari to turn and at least acknowledge him, give him that much at least. She didn't.

"No. I'm sorry. I thought you were someone I knew."

Jon swallowed, wanting the floor to open wide and devour him, knowing he should turn away. She wasn't going to acknowledge him. She was treating him as if he'd never existed, as though he had not been a part of her life.

This was her second betrayal. The sword Kari had plunged into his heart more than seven years before was now twisting his insides with excruciating pain. All of his emotions coalesced into one clear one. Anger. He was angry with the man for putting his hands on Kari's body as though he had the right to do it. He was angry at Kari for giving him that right.

And he was angry at himself for expending so much energy over the past several months worrying about his reaction to her, her reaction to him. He wanted revenge.

You're not going to dismiss me that easily. You're going to talk to me face to face and you're going to answer my questions. He had a plan.

 ❧

Kari and her merry band went to the hotel dining room to begin their celebration. She was self-conscious as Steve's eyes never left her face. They were accusing. Of that she was sure.

Yet his voice remained calm and pleasant as they chatted with the other couple. He laughed in the right spots, congratulated them with a sound of true admiration in his voice. But there was something else there.

Kari could tell in the way he looked at her, in the precise way he buttered his toast, his attention never leaving the bread as though it were a patient's body. His every movement was rigid with annoyance.

Kari took several unladylike gulps of water. She could feel her pulse racing and her palms sweating. She would kill right now for another of those little tranquilizers Steven had given to her. Her heart was pounding, the urge to admit the truth so strong that she imagined the words pouring out and his reaction to them.

Steve stood to brush away a crumb. Kari's breath caught in her throat. For a long moment she thought she had spoken and that he was leaving her. He caught her looking at him. Panic filled her.

"Steve, I'm so glad you came."

He quirked one eyebrow in her direction, disbelief clouding his eyes. She waited in vain for an answer. *He knows*, she thought, *and he doesn't plan to make this easy for me*. At first she thought Jackie might have mentioned something, but the way her friend felt about Steve, she would have never volunteered information.

Kari cut into her ham and spinach omelet, the thick cheeses clinging to the tines of her fork. Though she attempted to eat, the food caught in her throat. Steven was watching her, watching every move she made.

She glanced at him. She didn't need to see his eyes to know that he was analyzing her behavior, her movements, even something so simple as taking a drink of water. Her hand trembled noticeably.

If he didn't know something was wrong, he does now. She gave up pretending to eat and sat instead like the village idiot, smiling until she thought her face would break.

Now that she had become completely unglued, Steven Anderson, her black knight, turned his attention to his food and began to eat.

"You know, if you're not going to eat that omelet, I'm starved."

Kari slid her plate over to Steve, wishing her fingers would remain steady. He took the plate from her. A small smile played around his lips as he gave a long hard look at her trembling fingers.

"So, I guess this means you're not hungry." He turned from her and toward the Ahmeds, directing his conversation to them.

∞

What the hell is going on? Steve wondered as he watched Kari's increasing tension. He observed the fine sheen of sweat that had gathered on her upper lip. Surely this tension in her was no longer about the case. She'd won. Sooner or later he would get to the bottom of it.

CHAPTER ELEVEN

Kari could feel the agitation she had tried to conceal mount at a frustrating rate. While Steven and the Ahmeds ate, drank and chatted amicably, Kari seethed internally, unable to ignore the intense looks Steven was giving her. When she decided to turn the table on Steven and stare at him, her actions only served to amuse him.

She would not make a scene, not in front of June and Hamid. She would not be the one to ruin their joyous mood.

"Were you as nervous as we were?"

Hamid was looking at her, waiting for an answer. Kari smiled at him before glancing at the man seated beside her.

"Yes, of course I was nervous," she managed. "Three lawyers." She blew out a long breath, hoping to release some of her tension with the action. It didn't work. "I have to admit it was a bit intimidating to see them wheel in all of those cases." She reached for her water glass and her hand trembled slightly.

"I'm glad we came. I can't believe so many people didn't bother to show up." She sipped from the glass, frowning in concentration as she watched her friends.

Hamid was answering her. She could see his lips moving. She saw the quick smile, then the look of affection light up his wife's eyes for whatever comment he had made.   Kari tilted her head a little to the right, her neck twisting ever so slightly, her eyes finding Steve's. For one long horrible instant she feared she was going deaf.

Kari savored the water as it went down her throat. She followed the sensation with her mind until she felt it reach her belly.

She could feel and hear the plop of each individual drop, yet she could not hear the conversation of the people seated at her table.

Steve was watching her intently. She could only pray that the fear she was feeling was not registering on her face.

His hand reached toward her and she followed the movement. He stroked the skin on the back of her hand and like magic the spell was broken. She could hear. But it was as though she had been in a fog. She wasn't sure what the conversation was about.

"Shouldn't we be leaving? Or at the very least we should think about packing and checking out." Kari glanced at her watch. "Our plane leaves soon."

"We've got over five hours, that's time enough. We don't have to rush."

As if to prove his point, Steve took another bite of his food, then leaned into the booth as if he had all the time in the world.

Her mouth was open slightly. She could feel her annoyance turning into anger. Her body sagged forward as the weight of the stress settled on her shoulders and made its journey internally through her body, coming to rest with a thud in her abdominal cavity. A thud that sent a sharp burst of pain racing through her spinal cord.

"Then you stay here and finish eating. I have to pack." She saw the shadow of confusion cross the faces of her friends and decided to amend her tone.

"I guess I was a little more nervous than I realized." She held her hands in front of her, the slight tremors enough to verify her words.

She smiled in turn at June and Hamid, not quite including Steven in the warmth. "I just can't get over the feeling that if we don't leave Missouri, the judge is going to send someone after us, to tell us it was all a mistake and to come back to the courtroom, that we didn't win after all."

She hated popping their bubble, stopping their celebration. They had a right to enjoy their victory. She watched as the expressions on June's and Hamid's faces changed from joyful, childish glee to uncertainty and fear.

Yep, she'd successfully ruined the mood. They shoved the plates away and stood. Now there were three of them staring down at Steve, who sat still eating slowly. Unfazed.

"Steve, maybe Kari's right. Maybe we should leave." June Ahmed spoke softly, almost apologetically.

Steve looked up at the slight sound of hesitation from the woman. He looked her over carefully. The contrast between her and Kari was evident.

Kari was filled with a quiet strength and determination. This woman was fearful, following Kari's lead, not even analyzing the statements Kari had made. It was ridiculous to think the judge would reverse his decision.

He took another bite, chewing slowing. He swallowed, then grinned up at June, letting her off the hook. "Perhaps you're right." He stood, at last reaching for his wallet, the light shining off his gold card. "My treat for your victory."

There was definitely something wrong; he could feel it. The same thing that had propelled him to go the airport and buy a ticket was pulling at him. Only now it was stronger. It was clear that Kari was annoyed with him, but there was something more.

He remembered the look she'd given him when he first saw her in the courtroom. There had been a quick flash of fear, like a child being caught stealing cookies from the cookie jar.

He positioned himself to be the last to leave from the restaurant. He analyzed Kari's stride, the pinched look on her face.

Steve shoved his hands in his pocket and made a decision. He lengthened his stride, easily overtaking Kari. His hand on her arm, he stopped her.

"What's wrong? There's something going on and I want to know what."

A part of him wanted her to say, "Nothing." Instead, she turned to him, the same guilty look clouding her eyes.

"Let's talk about this later," she answered.

Steve sucked in his breath. He was right. There was something wrong. His heart pounded in his chest. He couldn't wait for later.

"Did you come here to have an affair with someone?" There. It was out.

He felt himself tense in anticipation of her answer, watching as she turned toward him. Her face broke out in a huge smile as she laughed out loud. For the first time that morning his heart felt light.

"Steven Anderson, I do believe you're jealous."

Kari stood for a moment watching Steven's expression, relieved that his worry was just plain male jealousy. He didn't know. As she stood on tiptoe to kiss him, she whispered in his ear, "You're the only man in my bed and in my future."

His arms closed around her. She could feel the tension leaving his body. Tension that never should have been there. She had inadvertently shut him out. She would have to make it up to him.

Now that Jonathan Steele was safely out of her life for good, she would lavish all the care and attention on Steve that he deserved.

Kari felt Steven's fingers closing protectively around her own. He didn't deserve her inattention. He was a good man and until a few short months ago, she had been perfectly happy with him. She would be again.

Back in the room they made short work of packing the few items she'd brought. Kari and Steve waited in the lobby for the Ahmeds. For now they were at peace. Kari glanced at Steven, noting the look on his face, one of contentment. She wondered if she should tell him about Jonathan. *What does it matter*? she thought. *I'll never see Jon again*

She thought of the lonely years she had spent after Jon. Distrustful of men she'd built a wall around her emotions. Only on meeting Steven Anderson had she felt she had a chance to live again, love again, though it had never been what she had experienced in her youth.

Her comparison was unfair. Apples and oranges. Nothing could measure up to falling in love at eighteen. First loves were called that for a reason. They were meant to be just that, filled with emotions, passion and defiance. Yes, they'd had it all. *I should have known it wouldn't last.* Kari shivered from her thoughts and moved closer to Steve.

His look met her own. It told her that he had allowed himself to be pacified even though he realized there was a secret she was still keeping. She gave him a slow, lazy smile, part seductive and filled with promise, part apology for lying by omission. She knew he would center on the seductive part.

Steve slid his arms around Kari's shoulder easily, the way lovers do, allowing his thumb to discreetly caress her shoulder blades. Kari smiled up at him, pleased for now to put off any serious talks.

They had over two months before the wedding, more than enough time for her to tell him, if she decided to, enough time for him to decide if he wanted to spend the rest of his life with her.

"Kari, I can promise you we're going to be happy. We both want the same things, a big happy family."

"Yes, Steve, I know. I agree. We're going to be very happy." She glanced over his head, remembering those same words being spoken to her by another man she'd loved. He'd broken that promise.

She thought of Steven's position at the hospital. She thought of her parents and her family. They all approved of the man she was going to marry. With him there would never be whispers or stares.

There would be love, friendship, family get-togethers and wonderful babies growing up without the constraints and added burdens they would have had with a life with Jon. An image of four beautiful brown-skinned babies frolicking about flashed through Kari's mind.

In Steven's arms Kari remembered another time in her distant past when she'd thought about babies. She'd just found out that she was pregnant. She remembered the look of joy on Jon's face as he'd gathered her in his arms.

"I don't believe it. I'm going to be a father. We're going to have a baby. I'll take care of us, the three of us. I promise. Kari, I love you. I'll always love you."

Jonathan had crushed her to his chest, tears of joy streaming down his face as he once again proclaimed his love and renewed his promise to find a way to take care of them.

She had never told him that she had not shared in that joy, had felt only fear when she discovered she was pregnant, for her unborn child, for the two of them. What kind of life would their baby have in a world filled with prejudice and hate, despised by maternal and paternal grandparents?

Kari felt herself sinking into her fiancé's embrace, clinging tightly to him, trying desperately not to remember the look of pain in Jon's eyes when she'd informed him that she'd had a miscarriage. She had known he wanted to ask if she'd gotten rid of it. But he hadn't. He'd just held on to her, his pain evident.

Jon, Jon. I'm so sorry, her soul cried out within her. The guilt she felt about Jon, about the baby, threatened to consume her.

A tremble went through Kari's body, rocking her from the tips of her toes to the top of her head. Their last time together Jonathan had accused her of being the one who couldn't go the distance in their relationship, of her being prejudiced.

She had never believed him. Who would want to think they harbored such feelings? She had never thought herself a coward but more and more she could see a pattern emerging and she didn't like it.

"What's wrong?"

Steve's breath was warm and sweet against her face. This, she could have. She could and would be happy. *That in itself takes strength*, Kari thought, *to give up a childish dream and settle for a more mature love.*

"Honey, is something wrong?"

Kari realized it was the second time he'd spoken to her. *I'm not settling! Steve is who I want, the man who can give me the life I want and the babies*, she assured herself. *I'm not settling*. She repeated the words to herself silently while her lips stretched into a reassuring smile.

"There's nothing wrong. I just felt a chill. I'm anxious to get home, that's all, nothing to worry about."

As if on cue, the silver-patterned elevator doors opened with the musical ding accompanying it. Again Kari was granted a reprieve. The Ahmeds had appeared at last, their bags in hands. Now they could all return home. She could resume the life she'd made for herself. She was free now. Free to love Steve the way she always thought she had.

CB

Within a week Kari had almost managed to shove away her feelings from seeing Jon again. She was determined to close that chapter of her life. She had a life to live and she had all intentions of doing just that.

She was rushing about, determined to get the first ten wedding invitations in the mail when Rose honked, alerting her to the fact that the mail was there and she was not done with even that small batch.

Kari opened the door, waving casually at Rose as she did so. With her free hand she retrieved the finished envelopes and made her way down her drive for the mail. She exchanged pleasantries while accepting the outstretched mail.

Making her way up the drive, Kari had a smile on her face. She was going to be all right. She caught Rose backing the jeep backwards toward her and turned, thinking the woman had probably forgotten some junk mail.

"I'm sorry. I forgot, you have something else."

"Don't worry about it."

Kari reached out her hand for the envelope but sensed a slight hesitation from Rose

"It's certified mail. You'll have to sign for it."

Kari took the pen Rose offered, remembering the last time she had received certified mail. *Don't even think it*, she mentally scolded herself. *The case is finished, you won. Jonathan Steele is out of your life for good.*

No sooner had her words flitted across her mind when the explosion went off in her brain. *Damn. Another lawyer. What is this?*

Kari ripped the envelope open only moments before stepping into her door. She scanned the letter in disbelief. Jon was suing her for withholding useful information that would have kept him from being wrongfully imprisoned.

He had to be kidding. As she rechecked the name of the attorney, she saw that he was in Chicago. At least that was something. She wouldn't have to go to Missouri again. The phone was in her hand before she could change her mind.

"Hello, my name's Kari Thomas. I just received notice that your firm is suing me on behalf of Mr. Jonathan Steele."

"One moment please."

Kari waited while the secretary looked through her files. She was grateful that the woman had not played any of that horrible elevator music. The woman came back on the line, her voice much too cheerful for Kari's taste.

"Yes, I'm sorry to keep you waiting, Ms Thomas. I have a note here on that file. Mr. Steele has left a number for you to call should you want to discuss this."

There was a slight pause before the woman continued. "Would you like the number?"

Kari almost swooned, then shook her head. This couldn't be happening. Her life was turning into a nightmare.

"Yes, please, can I have it?"

She wrote the number down and thanked the secretary. She wasn't a lawyer but this sure seemed a strange way to handle a case. She held the phone in her hand, ignoring the annoying tone that told her that if she needed help to dial the operator.

Don't put it off, Kari, she prodded herself. *Get it over with. Find out what it is Jon really wants. He sure as hell can't be serious about suing me again.*

She dialed. The phone rang, the noise sharp. Each sound resonated throughout her body. His voice was a bit gruff as though he were irritated that his phone had disturbed him.

"Jon?"

Her voice stilted, she croaked out his name for the second time. "Jon?"

"Yes. Who's this?"

So that's the way he wants to play this, she thought. "Jon, it's Kari."

There was silence on the other end. She wanted to scream at him to stop the game, but she was having trouble keeping her teeth from chattering and her knees from knocking.

The sound of his voice was pulling her back into her past. An icy shiver traveled the length of her spine.

"Jonathan, this is Kari Thomas. The Kari Thomas that you're suing. Does my name ring a bell now?" She was trying for professional and cold. The slight crack prevented that.

"You called, you talk."

Kari could sense her entire skull filling with an unknown pressure. She wondered if that was how people felt before they had a stroke.

She sighed. "Okay. Why are you doing this? Are you angry that I won my case?" She heard his snort of disgust. He remained silent.

"Jon, for God's sakes, talk to me. You're the one who left the message with your lawyer for me to contact you. What do you want? The grounds that you're suing me on are bogus. You'll be laughed out of court. So it has to be something else."

Kari was running out of patience. The call had taken everything out of her. Now he was doing his best to prolong her agony. She let out a long sigh of annoyance, trying to force him to talk to her, knowing how much he hated the sound. It worked.

"We have unfinished business, Ms. Thomas. I spent seven months of my life behind bars for something that I didn't do. You'll have to excuse me if I'm not exactly sociable, but this lawsuit is no joke. I want to talk to you."

Jon was holding tightly to the phone, so much so that he was pressing it into the nerves running down the side of his face. He could feel the pain from the pressure but chose to use it to remain grounded.

He had thought many times through the years about the first conversation he would have with Kari. It had never gone like this.

She was supposed to be remorseful, telling him that she had searched years for him after realizing how wrong she'd been. No, this was not the scenario at all. She was annoyed, and not the least bit apologetic.

Jon bit his bottom lip before speaking. "We need to talk."

"Like you told me," Kari answered him. "Talk."

"Face to face, Kari. I deserve that much and I intend to have it."

"I'm not coming to Missouri."

"No one asked you to."

What were they doing? They had never spoken to each other in such cold tones. Even when they had fought it had not been with the distance they were displaying now. For some reason, that saddened Jon.

"Listen." Jon paused, trying to keep the pain from his voice. "Nothing will get settled this way. "Why don't we stop snapping at each other?" He waited a moment for her to acquiesce.

"Kari, are you still there?"

"Yes, Jon, I'm here."

"Do you think it's possible for us to meet and have a grown-up conversation? I'll fly to Chicago." Jon sensed Kari was struggling for a way to get out of a meeting.

"That's fine, Jon. I can meet you in your lawyer's office. Neutral grounds would work better."

There was silence again, then Kari spoke. "After the meeting, will you drop your case?"

"If the meeting is satisfactory."

"Jon, don't."

"Don't what? Don't ask for something that's long overdue?" he hissed. His hand gripped the phone while he concentrated on getting himself together. This really wasn't the direction he wanted to take. He'd been the one to ask for a truce.

His old feelings for Kari had surged to the surface, making him lose control. He was trying his best to push away the sadness that suddenly threatened to overtake him.

"Jon, I'm sorry it has to be like this."

Her voice was soft and he hoped that she was feeling a little bit of the pain that was tearing him apart. "Yeah, Kari, so am I."

ରଷ

He wasn't giving an inch other than to remove some of the frigid ice from his voice. He had no intention of meeting Kari at his lawyer's office. His lawyer had not even wanted to file the papers. He didn't want to be implicated for harassment.

Because they were friends, Jon had assured him the case would never reach court. He sure as hell couldn't ask the man for use of his office and make him a conspirator in a possible criminal charge.

Jon had other plans. His dossier on Kari had everything he needed. Their talk would definitely not take place on neutral grounds. He was going to her home.

"When are you coming?"

"I don't know," he lied. "I'll call my lawyer and let him know. He can call you with the details." He sensed a hesitation from Kari.

"Jon, I'll need some notice. I'll have to arrange things at work…and I have other considerations."

"Oh."

"I'm getting married."

"Congratulations. My lawyer will be in touch. Goodbye, Kari."

He didn't wait for her to answer. Instead he hung his phone up, keeping his hand on it for a moment longer, wanting to snatch it back up and scream at her that he wasn't someone that she'd had a casual affair with.

A lump stuck in his throat. Never had his imagined conversations with her ended with him wanting to sob like a baby. Kari was getting married to someone other than him. Apparently she'd had no trouble moving on with her life. A life without him. That knowledge hurt like hell.

Jon closed his eyes and felt the burning in his midsection. He removed his hand from the phone and murmured into the silent room, "God, how I loved you, Kari!"

CHAPTER TWELVE

Kari looked around the room. *Other considerations*. Had she really referred to the man she was going to marry as just that? *Other considerations*. As her gaze fell on the box of still unfinished wedding invitations, an eerie feeling came over her. She walked toward the boxes as if they would protect her from herself. Two fat tears escaped down her cheeks, followed by others. She lifted one of the cards in her hands, her vision blurred.

Why are you crying, Kari? Did you think Jon was going to be glad to hear from you? Remember, he's suing you.

She scolded herself to halt the flow of tears for she didn't for a moment believe that Jon would follow through with his threats. There was not a vindictive bone in his body. If she refused to meet him, the case would simply fade away. So why had she agreed to the meeting?

Probably for the same reason he's suing. We both need closure. She wiped at the tears that continued to fall. Somewhere hidden behind the anger in his words was the boy Kari had fallen in love with.

She willed herself to stop crying. She needed to concentrate on her wedding invitations. Steven had accused her of stalling. Once more he was beginning to look at her with a question in his eyes, judging every word, every caress, trying to detect the tiniest change.

Kari stared at the smiling black couple on the embossed invitations. They portrayed the very essence of happiness. In just a couple of months that picture could well be she and Steve. The invitations were the one thing the two of them had agreed on, and had gone to a specialty shop to get them.

Her gaze drifted over to the engagement photo of her and Steve on her mantle. Once again she thought of their future, of brown babies with thick curly hair. She wanted a little girl, someone whose hair she could braid. She could barely stop herself from picking up baby clothes whenever she went shopping. She drooled over the tiny barrettes and hair ornaments the way some women did over diamonds. This baby she could have. It would make up for...

Kari brought herself up short. She didn't want to think about that or about a pair of startling blue eyes. She didn't want to remember the owner of those eyes, using his eyes to make love to her. And she sure as hell didn't want to remember how very much she'd loved him.

She smiled to herself. A sad reminiscent smile as she remembered that Jon's words alone once brought her to orgasm without him so much as touching her. Kari licked her lips.

"That was a long time ago. All my feelings for him are dead." She chanted the words over and over but inside her head she heard the echo of another voice.

If that's true, why is your heart beating a mile a minute? Why didn't you call his bluff and tell him to go to hell?

The phone rang, breaking off Kari's need for reflection. She answered, knowing it would be Jackie.

"Kari, hi. What's up? I haven't really had a chance to talk to you since you got back. You barely mentioned Jon. What happened?"

"He's suing me, Jackie."

"What are you talking about? He's already done that."

"No, I'm not talking about the resort now. I'm talking about Jon. He's suing me personally. He's coming to Chicago."

"What are you going to do?"

Although Kari chuckled, neither she nor Jackie found humor in it. "What can I do? I'll see him."

"You okay with that? I mean, what about Steve?"

This time, Kari laughed out loud and she was amused. "I don't believe it. Now you call him Steve. Well, I know one thing for sure, I have no plans on telling Steve that Jon's coming."

A few minutes more conversation and Kari ended the call. She was exhausted. She'd barely hung up when it rang again.

"What are you doing?"

It was Steve. His voice was breathless, as though he had been running. She wondered what was up.

"I was working on the invitations."

"Good. How far have you gotten?"

He was pleased. She could tell it in his voice. Kari took another quick glance at the still full box and decided to lie.

"About halfway done."

"Need any help? Better yet, do you need a break?"

He was whistling, something he never did. "Steve, what's going on? You're up to something. I can't believe you would want me to leave the house once I started on the invitations."

His voice sheepish, he replied, "Not generally, but tonight I have a surprise for you. Think you can be ready in a couple of hours?"

"Sure," Kari answered. "What should I wear?" She waited, grinning, knowing he was attempting to find an answer that wouldn't give away his surprise.

"Well, something nice but nothing too sexy."

Kari's eyes rolled in her head. She hoped he didn't think an evening with the minister was a big surprise for her. Both Steve and the pastor had been after her for weeks to set a date for premarital counseling.

"Steven," her voice was stern, "I'm not up for a surprise attack, not tonight, especially if it's with the good reverend."

She heard his laugh. It must be something big. He wasn't nagging her about dragging her feet on the counseling. The minister had told them both repeatedly he wouldn't marry them without it. There was only so long she could put it off. But tonight she couldn't handle a conversation dealing with lifetime commitments.

"Don't worry, sweetie, this is one surprise you're going to love." She heard the sound of his lips coming together as he gave her an air kiss.

True to his word Steve was at her door approximately two hours later. Kari looked him up and down, thanking God that she had not been stupid enough to spoil things between them. Despite his seeming aversion to telling her that he loved her, he was all that she could hope for and more.

He smiled down at her, his face alight with his secret. He was almost dancing like a little boy in his need to rush her to where he was taking her.

Kari wasn't ready to leave. She wanted to taste Steven first, to have the feel of his hands on her body, reminding her to get busy with that box of still undone wedding invitations. She needed him more in that moment than ever before in the almost two years they had been together.

"What's your rush?" she practically purred. "Don't we have a few minutes?"

He stopped, looking at her with lust filling his eyes. She could tell he was fighting an inner battle, one she hoped she would win.

"We can't, not right now. But I promise later nothing will stop me." He ran one hand gently down her face, cupping her chin in his hand. "I can't wait until we're married. I'm going to take such good care of you."

There it was again. "We're going to take care of each other, Steve."

He growled at her. "You'll take care of me, our home and our kids." His lips moved against hers. "I'll take care of you and the finances."

For a second Kari froze. They'd never talked about her job before. She loved what she did and she was good at it. Her eyes glanced upward at Steven. Maybe she'd heard wrong. Maybe he wasn't suggesting she quit her job.

"Steven Anderson, if you're suggesting I stay at home and be the little woman you come home to, you're crazy."

For an answer he kissed her, his tongue thrusting deeper into the moistness of her mouth. Kari could feel the warmth spreading through both of them, Steve's hardness pushing at her. Her arms wound around his neck.

God, how she wanted this to work. She wanted nothing more than to be married, have babies and work at the job she loved.

Her eyes deliberately sought out the invitations. As soon as she was married, the past would be truly over. She could lay to rest any doubts. Her arms tightened a bit around Steven's broad shoulders, wanting him to say, " Let's stay in." Instead, she felt him pull away.

She looked questioningly at the bulge at his crotch. "Are you sure?" she asked him, her lips open slightly, her most seductive look. She knew, she had practiced it in the mirror.

"I'm afraid so. Your surprise can't wait."

She saw the hunger replaced by amusement. *It better be one hell of a surprise*, she thought.

Kari said little on the drive. They stopped in front of a restaurant they'd eaten in many times. What could be special about Terry's Bistro?

Steve ushered her in, his head swinging back and forth. She

looked for clues, anything that would tell her why Steven was so excited. She followed behind to the table, trying to linger for a peep at the door.

He turned, smiled at her, then gently positioned her in front of him. He was not giving anything away. She noticed he almost pushed the hostess out of the way to position Kari with her back to the door.

"Don't look behind you."

Contrary to his instructions, Kari's head turned automatically. It was her parents. For a moment she was confused.

She turned from her mother's and father's smiling faces back to face Steve, a feeling of dismay overtaking her. She attempted to open her mouth to speak but was robbed of the ability. Her fiancé's smile was as wide as that of her parents.

Does he really think this is a nice surprise for me? My God, he doesn't know me at all, she thought.

Kari rose automatically to greet her parents, shocked that the man she was going to spend the rest of her life with thought this would make her happy. *Damn, damn, damn. What had she gotten herself into?*

She ran her tongue over her lips, hoping her disappointment was hidden. "Mom, why are you guys here? I didn't know you were coming."

"Well, Steven called. He happened to mention that you were under some stress and hadn't had time to finish the wedding invitations. So we offered to come and help," her mother answered.

"Yes, we're glad Steve called. We've been worrying about how you've been behaving lately. Don't worry, baby. Marriage's a big step, but I guarantee you're marrying the right man. Now we're here to help you through this." Her father beamed at her. "Since you won't take our help with the wedding expenses, at least let us help you with some of the physical work."

Kari kissed both of her parents, then turned to Steve, barely concealing the glare. "I'm done," she lied. "I'm sorry you two made the trip for nothing."

"It's not for nothing, besides Steve paid for the entire trip. He has a beautiful room for us at the Sheraton."

She watched as her father pulled out a chair for her mother, knowing Steve was about to do the same for her. At the moment she felt the safest place for her fiancé was on the opposite side of the restaurant.

She shivered as his fingers brushed lightly down her bare arms. She wanted to slap him. He not only didn't know how to surprise her, but for all intents and purposes he had practically told her parents she was incompetent and needed them to bail her out.

He was nuzzling the back of her neck when she felt him tense. Kari glanced over her shoulder and saw what had caused his sudden change of ardor. A mixed couple was walking out of the restaurant. Steve's disapproving stare followed them.

"Steve, what's wrong? Do you know them?"

He turned his gaze back on her and walked to his own chair, not answering until he was seated. "I hate seeing our women with them."

Kari's mouth felt suddenly dry. "It's none of our business, Steve, you don't know either of them." Kari was trying desperately to calm the fury that was raging inside of her. "Would you feel better if the woman was white and he was black?" For an answer he stared at her in disbelief.

"Why don't we forget about this and order."

Kari stared at her father, surprised that he'd jumped in and answered, knowing he felt exactly the same as Steve. For once he wasn't stoking the fires.

Her eyes met her mother's. Kari waited. Five, four, three, two...

"Are you two having a fight?"

Good old Mom. "Just a difference of opinion," Kari quipped, "about whether or not we should stick our noses in the private affairs of others. It's nothing, we're done." Kari turned her smile to Steve, praying he would let it go.

He might have but the moment he took her hand across the table and returned her smile with one of his own, she again sensed a tenseness in him. His eyes were no longer on her face but looking over her head.

Kari turned. Steve was glaring openly at a black woman and white man that were being seated behind them. It was obvious the couple's presence angered him. *What else can go wrong tonight?* she thought.

"Don't start, Steve. I don't want to hear it." Kari's voice was sharp and filled with an intense anger she couldn't conceal, causing her parents to join Steve in glaring at her.

"What's wrong?"

Her father's voice, stern and parental, thrust her backwards into childhood. She didn't like the feeling. Kari took a sip of water, her finger tracing the beveled crystal. She needed desperately to regain control of her emotions.

For once she refused to back down. She was going to do something she should have done years ago. Maybe then she wouldn't have done everything in her power to distrust the man she loved.

Her voice was laced with ice as she addressed her father, her eyes scanning the table, taking in her mother and Steve's stony countenance.

"I'm tired of the three of you making judgments about other people's lives. If they love each other, that's their business, not yours."

"Don't you dare take that tone with your mother and me, young lady."

"Or what? You're going to take the car from me, not pay my tuition? What, Dad? What can you possibly do to me? I'm twenty-eight years old. I'm not a teenager. I make my own living, so what can you do? Disown me?"

Her voice held a threat. She was well aware that they didn't want Steven to know of her so-called horrid past. Kari was beyond caring. She wanted him to know. She had spent much too much energy hiding a very important part of herself and her life from the man she was going to marry. What kind of way was that to start a marriage?

"I'm sorry." Steve's apology was to her parents and that more than anything pushed her past enduring his blatant prejudices.

"Steve, while you're so busy kissing my father's ass, maybe you'd better sleep with him tonight."

She stood and smiled at her three dinner companions, almost enjoying the look of shock of their faces. Her father was sputtering, barely able to believe that she'd used profanity in front of them.

Kari's mind was made up. She'd exited the restaurant, determined not to speak to say anything else to any of the people she was with, when strong hands stopped her in midstride. She smelled the light spray of expensive cologne, the scent telling her it was Steve.

"What's wrong with you? Why are you acting like this? You've embarrassed me and insulted your parents. I think you owe them an apology."

Kari stood her ground. "I'm not apologizing, Steve, to any of you." She glared at him. "You have white friends. Why are you behaving like this?"

He looked at her. "There is a difference, you know it as well as I do."

"I may know it, Steve, but I sure as hell don't plan to spend the rest of my life with a bigot."

"Are you telling me that race mixing doesn't bother you? That you'd consider being with a white man, sleeping with him?"

Steve's voice was becoming angry as he glared at Kari. What the hell was wrong with her? How could she not feel the same way that he did? He held her arm a little tighter, his gaze on Kari unflinching, refusing to allow her to turn away.

"Would you ever think of marrying a white man, Kari, of having babies that wouldn't belong anywhere?"

Kari looked at him, quick tears springing to her eyes. "You get over this need to voice your hatred at people loving whoever the hell they want to or call this wedding off."

"Kari, you feel the same way about this as I do, as your parents feel. Admit the truth, Kari, to me and to yourself. Would you want a half-white baby?

His words were killing her. Each felt like a dagger in her heart. She wasn't like Steve and she sure as hell wasn't like her parents.

"Would you, Kari?" Steve insisted. "Would you want to be mother to a half-white baby?"

Kari stared hard at Steve, trying desperately to block out his words. She conjured up her circle of brown-skinned babies, hating herself for needing it. Hating herself even more for wanting it. She wasn't like Steve. She pulled away from him and proceeded out the door.

"Steve, I have to go home. I'm going to be sick."

"I can't just leave your parents sitting alone in there."

"Who asked you to? I don't want to be around you right now. I don't like you very much at this moment."

She turned and glared at him, the anger in her voice replaced by hurt. "Steve," she murmured softly, "don't bother coming by later."

CHAPTER THIRTEEN

Kari had been home for over an hour and still she was angry. It was time to tell Steve. She could not, would not, live the rest of her life with him, praying that he wouldn't find out.

She had never known what her mother meant when she would tell her that chickens always come home to roost. Now she thought she did. Her translation: Your past always catches up with you.

Kari paced back and forth worrying about her upcoming meeting with her past. Jonathan had refused to give her a date when he was coming to Chicago. She could do nothing but wait until his lawyer called.

The shrill ringing of her bell reminded her of why she was angry. She glanced once at the wall clock. Hrrump, I guess they're finished with dinner. She stood still for a moment, taking in a deep breath, fortifying herself to do battle. There was no doubt in her mind that it was her angry parents, or her angry fiancé.

Kari twisted the doorknob, pulling on it with all of her might. She would not cower down. And she would not apologize. The door opened and her anger turned to confusion. Then recognition.

"Jonathan." Kari leaned against the frame of the door and she sighed loudly.

Why not? she thought. *Everything else has gone wrong. Why not top it by a visit from Jonathan? Thanks, God, you are a big help. Not.*

"What are you doing here?"

Shocked, she was trying her best to still her heart from the thumping. He was the last person she'd expected at her door in the middle of the night. She stood blocking his path, taking in his frown, his eyes still the blue she remembered, but filled with an arctic coldness. Kari wavered a little from the stab of pain that pierced her heart.

Jonathan stared at Kari, his eyes still purposefully cold. "Are you going to let me in?"

He was stepping around her before she could answer, seizing advantage of her surprise. His eyes searched the room for some memento, maybe a picture of the two of them, anything from their past which would tell him he had meant something to her. Maybe they could both move on with their lives, but first they had to settle seven years worth of hurt.

"Don't you think you'd better close the door?" He pointed toward the door, observing Kari's look of confusion. He watched as she moved in slow motion to close it. That done, she glanced at the clock, then at Jonathan. His eyes followed her movements.

"Why are you here? I thought we were meeting in your attorney's office, that you were going to let me know before you came."

"I changed my mind." He looked her over, then turned away. He had a sudden urge to hold her in his arms, an urge so strong that if he had not turned from her, he surely would have bridged the distance of space and time to do just that. Instead, Jonathan moved around the room, picking up odds and ends of bric-a-brac, not making any comment.

His gaze slid down to the box containing what looked to him to be formal invitations of some sort. Jon stopped and looked again. Wedding invitations. The need to do what he'd come for was more evident.

Suddenly he felt dry. "Kari, do you think I could have a drink of water?" He watched her reactions. She was flustered and confused but moved toward the kitchen. Without thinking, Jon moved swiftly, picking up one of the sealed invitations and jamming it into his trousers pocket. The imprint of the bulky card was noticeable, the upper top corner poking out. He didn't care.

Kari returned with the water. She stood a little away from Jonathan. He noticed that she wasn't looking at him and for some perverse reason it gave him pleasure. He walked toward her, taking the glass from her hand.

He touched the tips of Kari's fingers with his own and felt the slight tremors from her shaking hand. An electric shock passed through him, reminding him of their very first kiss.

His eyes fell on the water. He needed it now. He brought it to his lips and took a drink before he dared another look at Kari. She was watching him intently, her mouth slightly ajar. The moment her tongue flicked out swiping at her lips, his heart filled with a yearning he had denied for almost eight years. He loved her still.

"Jonathan, can't this meeting wait? I'm expecting someone." She hesitated. "My parents are coming." She was twisting her hands together nervously.

He saw and understood. She didn't want him there. He looked at her, his eyes closing of their own volition, the remembered sadness competing for his remembrances of love.

He turned from her, fighting the threatening erection. Only she had ever had the power to make him hard with a thought, or a mere glance. She opened her mouth to speak and spoiled the moment.

"My parents are on their way over, Jon."

He noticed this time her voice didn't waver. "I don't care. I'm not leaving until we talk. I think it's time."

"Great, you think it's time. What about me? Don't I get a say in this?"

"No."

"No?"

He saw the frown immediately crease her face. "You heard me. No. You weren't the one who spent seven months in jail waiting to be forgiven."

"That wasn't why you were in jail, Jon. Sharon said you raped her, the police had a sample of your DNA. You want to blame someone, blame yourself."

"I didn't rape her. That's a lie and we both know it. Hell, I was with you the night she said it happened. At any time you could have cleared it up, but you didn't. Why? Because you were angry with me?" He was shouting now.

"Jonathan, keep your voice down, please. I told you I'm expecting company."

Jonathan stopped speaking and glared at her. "You want me to talk softly, Kari, because your lover might come and hear what I'm saying." His hurt and anger walked hand in hand.

"I'm not going to be accommodating, not any more. I waited for you every day to come to me. I never gave up hope. Not once... His voice broke. "Not once, Kari, did you bother to come and see me, not once. I couldn't believe it then and I'm here now because I want to know why. I deserve to know." With that he slammed the glass on the coffee table with such force it broke.

"You were supposed to love me, Kari. How could you turn your back on me? How could you leave me there to rot? Was it all a lie, all the promises we made to each other?"

"Have you forgotten Sharon?" Kari could feel the beginning of angry tears springing to her eyes. She glanced again at the clock. She didn't want to have this conversation here, not in her home when she knew darned well they could be interrupted at any moment. But she couldn't take Jonathan's pious behavior a moment longer.

"If there was someone living a lie it was you." The last she screamed at him, no longer caring who would hear them. "I loved you, Jonathan. You're the one who destroyed that."

"If I did, I sure as hell had some help from you. I was never truly involved with Sharon but you never gave me a chance to explain the pictures. Why do you think I went willingly to jail? I trusted you, believed you would come. Yes, you were angry and you had a right to be. But I expected you to come once you'd had a chance to cool off and allow me to tell you what happened."

"I know what happened, Jon. I saw the pictures. I saw you in bed with her, her mouth on you. I saw the look on your face. You weren't faking that." She turned from him, not wanting him to see that the pictures hurt her still. "It was for real so don't lie to me any-more and try and make me believe that the pictures were staged."

Kari glared at him, the tears brimming over. "You had an orgasm, Jon. The proof was there in the pictures." She walked away, hating herself for crying, despising herself for feeling the hurt as intensely as she had the first time she'd seen the photo of the man she loved being made love to by another woman.

Jon closed his eyes, rubbing his face, trying to think of a way to explain what had happened. "Kari, I didn't make love to her, not that night. Not ever. She gave me a blow-job, pure and simple, that's all that happened." He saw her shoulders convulsing with her sobs and walked toward her. Her back was to him. He intended to make her turn around to face him to witness the truth in his eyes.

Instead his fingers took on a life of their own and he lightly massaged her shoulders, then encircled her with his arms.

"Look at me, Kari, there's no need for me to lie. Not after all this time," he pleaded. "Sharon never meant anything to me. I'm telling you the truth when I say we were taking pictures, and it got out of hand. I'd had something to drink and…" His voice trailed off.

"Sharon…" His throat closed. "Sharon doing that to me, it wasn't making love."

For a moment she wanted to succumb to the feel of him, to the memory of their love. Wrenching herself free, she took a step away and swung with her open hand. The sharp sound of the slap reverberated throughout the room.

"Don't touch me, Jon, I'm not your whore. You don't have the right to ever touch me again. That line didn't work for Clinton, and it's not going to work for you." Kari walked toward the door. "I think you should go now."

"No." Jon rubbed at his reddened cheek. "I haven't gotten what I came for. I want an explanation. Why didn't you come to the jail?"

"Why did you make love to Sharon?"

His hands flew up into the air and his breath left his body in an overly-loud exaggerated whoosh. "I didn't make love to Sharon. She gave me a blow-job. Period."

"You enjoyed it!"

"I was drugged, Kari. There was something in my drink."

"You still enjoyed it!"

His hands covered his eyes and he shook his head as if to clear it. "Damn it, Kari. It was a job. I did it for you, for us."

"You made love to another woman for us? Well, at least that's original."

Her eyes searched the room for something to throw at him. He saw what she was planning and in one easy motion had her arms pinned to her side.

They stood like that, the hurt between them alive and raw. He rubbed his chin against her forehead, the stubble of the hairs tickling her. She was trembling so hard that he held her tighter to calm her.

"I saw the pictures, Jon." She swiped her eyes across the soft material of Jon's shirt, not trying to free her arms. "Tell me the truth. You enjoyed it, didn't you?"

She was staring into his eyes, her pained expression begging him to say no. Whether or not she believed him, he had never lied to her and would not now. What happened between him and Sharon he'd never once thought of as making love.

"Yes, I did," he answered at last as he released her.

He watched as she closed her eyes tightly and clutched her hands around her abdomen. A moment later she pushed him farther away, as he had known she would do.

"That was the first time the photographer had us in bed for the shots." Damn, even after all this time it was hard for him to tell her, but he had to. Neither of them should go a day longer not knowing the reason they weren't together.

"I was nervous. I didn't want to do the shots. Sharon gave me something to drink. I don't know what she put in it, but she told me it had a mild sedative effect. That it would relax me."

His tongue flicked across his lips. He was feeling dry again. "We weren't supposed to take off all our clothes, just give the illusion that we were nude. Several more people gave me something to drink. Just to ease my fears, they said."

He exhaled. "I don't know why I kept drinking, but it made me feel different. It was like I was flying. I don't remember taking my clothes off but there I was, naked and parading around in front of the camera smiling. I remember that."

Jonathan wavered, looking over at Kari to see if she was listening, if he would at last get to tell her what had happened.

She was watching him, disbelief clouding her face, but at least she was still in the room. Jonathan continued, thinking maybe she was finally as ready as he was to know the reason they weren't together.

"When Sharon first started kissing me, wrapping her lips around my… He looked down at his crotch. "I did try to push her away once. I remember that, but it felt so good… I know it sounds crazy but somehow I thought it was you."

He attempted to walk toward her. "You may not believe me, but I'm telling you the truth. One minute I was in bed with Sharon, posing for pictures, the next I thought I was home in bed, with you."

Kari was crying openly now. "Is all of this supposed to make me feel better, Jonathan? It doesn't matter, you slept with *her*. How else did the police get a sample of your DNA?" A crushed feeling overcame her and for a moment the tears ceased.

"This happened on Valentine's Day, didn't it?" She looked at his face and had her answer. "I remember, you missed the dinner I made for us to celebrate." Her tone was sarcastic. "Of course, we were only going to have spaghetti. I guess that can't compare with what you had to eat, does it?"

"Kari, I didn't. Don't make me say it, please." She was glaring at him. He had no choice but to continue. "Sharon saved my semen. I saw her spitting it out into a plastic container. I didn't think anything about it at the time. When it was over, and I realized what I had allowed to happen, that sobered me up pretty fast.

"But it was too late. She called a few days later and told me if I didn't break up with you, she'd come to you, show you proof. At the time I didn't even know they had pictures of…of her, of us. I didn't know they'd taken pictures of the entire act.

"Then she told me she'd gone to the police and reported that she had been raped. She told me she'd saved my semen, had put it in the freezer and later she'd inserted it. She threatened to give them my name. I told her I would never leave you and, well, you know the rest of it. She was nuts. She was determined to break us up, that much I know. Is that so hard to believe?"

"It doesn't matter, not anymore."

"Kari, I swear I didn't have intercourse with her and I didn't have oral sex with her either. She only did me. I didn't return the favor."

"Even if you didn't, Jon, you let her touch you and when you came home you pulled away from me and went straight to the shower. I should have known. And maybe in my heart I did, but didn't want to believe it. You didn't sleep in our bed that night. I remember. It was a week before you touched me again."

"I couldn't." His voice was soft, filled with his own pain. "I was too ashamed of what I allowed to happen to be able to touch you."

Kari was staring at him. Jon knew her so well. He was aware of what she was thinking.

"No, I didn't take any more pictures like that. You know the one I mean."

"Why didn't you ever tell me any of this before Sharon came to the house?"

"I was scared. Hell, I didn't want you to see the pictures and once I realized how far Sharon was willing to go, I didn't know what to do. She even told me she'd gotten a friend to slap her around and have rough sex with her, using a condom, before inserting my semen. When she went to the police, they believed she'd been raped and was too traumatized to give her attacker's name right then. All she had to do was give them a name. My name. I…I…knew I was in serious trouble. I was planning to tell you the same day Sharon came over."

He watched the expression on her face change. She was struggling with something.

Don't imagine things, Jon. She's probably wondering how to get you the hell out of here. Too much has happened. There's no room for you any longer in her life. He licked his top lip with his tongue and waited.

"Jon, I did come to the jail to see you. Twice."

He looked at her in disbelief before looking away, her lie stinging him to the core of his being. "Someone would have told me. Everyone knew I was waiting for you. They would have told me, if only to harass me with the fact that they didn't allow you in."

God, how he wanted to believe her. But he'd spent too many hours straining his ears, trying to hear through the thick metal doors. He had eavesdropped on every conversation in the cells, hoping that someone would mention seeing Kari. No one had. "I don't believe you," he whispered.

Kari saw the doubt on his face, heard it expressed clearly in his voice. *Too much pain,* her heart whispered to her.

"So, Jon. I should believe you, that you allowed her to take you in her mouth, that you had an orgasm, but that wasn't making love? But it's okay that you don't believe me? Would you like some details, Jon? Your mother was there the first time. She told me you didn't want to see me. She even had a guard go back and check. He came out and shook his head that you didn't want to see me."

"You believed my mother? That's a first."

His remark stung but she chose to ignore it. "No, not really, but I left anyway. I was still angry with you, but I didn't want to see you locked up. I started thinking about you saying that you had a ring on layaway, so I went through your things. I didn't find a receipt."

She looked at Jonathan, her mind no longer on the length of time Jonathan was there. She no longer cared if Steven or her parents arrived. Jon was here now and he was accusing her of not caring. If only he knew how much she'd cared.

"I went back a couple of days later. I wanted to give you a chance to explain, to tell me where the receipt was.

Your mother must have taken a room there because there she was again. Only this time she wasn't alone. Sharon was with her. She showed me the engagement ring you had given her. You had a ring and a receipt all right, but you gave them to another woman."

Kari bit her lip, then stopped, reminding herself that those days were long gone.

"Sharon told me that she was pregnant and the two of you were going to be married in jail."

"How could you believe that?"

"Reverend Bob came in. The guard took him back. Sharon went with him. I remember, Jon. Your mother sneered at me, then went back also."

Jonathan held his finger to his lip. "Shhhh. Not now, Kari. I'm the one who's owed an explanation. And all you're giving me is a pack of lies. My mother doesn't know Sharon, and Sharon never came to see me while I was in jail. Reverend Bob came, but never Sharon. The last time I saw her was the day I threw her out, so please, no more lies."

His head was beginning to pound. *Why did I really come?* he wondered. *We're just standing here, two people with their past spread out before them, each wanting to believe the other, pain keeping us from it. Now we've got lies on top of the pain.* That he couldn't handle.

"You were looking for reasons to end it, Kari. You want me to be honest, why don't you try it? Why don't you admit that you hated being in love with me. Don't blame your prejudices on some stupid pictures. You knew I loved you."

He glared at her. "You also know in your heart that I would never cheat on you. Not intentionally, Kari."

"Jon, what you did, what you allowed Sharon to do to you, is cheating, regardless of what some people might call it. It's cheating, Jon."

"It wasn't. How can I make you understand that it wasn't?"

"You can't."

"My God, Kari, drugging me was the only way that could have ever happened. You wanted an excuse to bail out on us. Now you want me to believe my own mother conspired with Sharon to have me thrown in jail. I can't believe that. It was my mother who bailed me out."

Jonathan walked away from Kari. His resolve was too weak when he was in close proximity to her. That hadn't changed, not since the first day he had spotted her on campus. She was still able to make his heart race. He started grinding his teeth to keep from kissing her.

"My mother's not on trial here, Kari."

"And I am?"

Jon looked at her, holding her stare. "Why didn't you try harder? You pushed me out of your life and forgot about me, just like you did with..."

"With what, Jon?" She knew what he was thinking, it was time to bring it out into the open. "Were you going to say with the baby?"

His face flushed red. He had promised himself that he would never accuse her of— "You didn't want it! You didn't even cry after." He stopped again, wetting his lips, not wanting to go on.

"After I had the abortion? That *is* what you were going to say, isn't it?" Kari waited, anger leaping into her veins like wildfire. She saw Jonathan's rigid self-control leaving him and the same anger she was feeling stretching his features, making his azure blue eyes turn smoky with anger.

"Did you?" he managed to grind out between clenched teeth.

"Isn't that what you decided years ago that I did? You never bothered asking me."

"I'm asking now. Did you?"

"What does it matter now?" She walked away as he approached her, menace in his eyes.

For *God's sake, tell him, tell him the truth. that you never had an abortion, that it really was a miscarriage.*

Her eyes closed and the sting of tears wet her cheeks. She wondered if he would hate her even more than he did at that moment if he knew the whole truth. If he knew what she'd prayed for, what would he do?

She opened her eyes and looked at him. As angry as she was with him, her guilt kept her quiet.

"What does it matter? For God's sake, Kari, what's wrong with you? That was our child. I wanted it even if you didn't."

"Why Jonathan? We wouldn't have been able to take care of a child. We worked ourselves silly, still we had no money for us, let alone a baby. Why should I want a baby I couldn't take care of? Jonathan, the two of us had a hard enough time. A half-black, half-white baby was just asking for trouble."

Jonathan whirled away from Kari, furiously breaking the glass that he'd missed before. "You talk about you, Kari. It wasn't just yours. And it wasn't your decision to make alone. I would have taken care of our child and you. No matter what."

"How Jon? What was next, making porno movies?"

Jon turned again to face her, feeling as though she had slapped him for the second time that evening. "You didn't trust me to take care of you and the baby." It was a statement, not a question.

His eyes widened with pain. She had doubted his ability to take care of them. Why shouldn't she? The thought flashed across his mind that she was right. "I didn't do a very good job of taking care of us, did I?"

"What were you going to do, Jon, quit school? You were doing the best you could. We both were."

Her tone had softened. She had seen the look on his face and regretted having made him feel inadequate. He had done his best, so had she.

Before she had a chance to think to not do it, she crossed the few steps to Jonathan Steele. Her hand reached out to caress his face.

"You did the best you could, Jon." She felt his body shudder as he pulled her into his arms and held her to his heart.

"I loved you, Kari."

She didn't answer. She couldn't. She was drowning in sadness.

He raised her head and his lips closed over hers. She couldn't have prevented the kiss if she'd tried. At the first taste of him, her soul cried out in remembrance, welcoming him home.

She clung to him out of desperation. The room was spinning, she was spinning, lost in his arms, in his embrace. "Jonathan, she moaned, "I loved you too." She heard the chime of the clock, the sound waking her, bringing her back to reality. She took a step back from Jon, attempting to pretend the kiss hadn't happened. She needed to pretend that she no longer felt anything for Jon. She couldn't allow her heart to welcome him back.

Kari's eyes swung again to the clock. "What about the lawsuit, Jon?"

He glared at her. "Is that all that you're interested in?"

For a brief second he thought he saw something in her eyes, heard a sound in her voice that said she was sorry for the way things had turned out, that she cared, if only a little. He was wrong. She only wanted him out of her life. The kiss had meant nothing. It was her pity she'd given him. He'd mistaken it for more.

"You know, Kari, you were the only one who saw color in our relationship. I never did. I didn't think of our baby as half-black."

He glared at her. "Tell me you didn't have those thoughts. That you never thought of our baby as being half white. Is that why you didn't want the baby?"

He waited, unable to stop the tears that ran down his face. She was crying also. He didn't care. He had loved her with everything that was in him. He loved her still.

It was she who'd bailed. She was the one who hadn't loved him enough. Knowing that hurt him as much as it had seven years before.

"Is that all the baby meant to you, Kari? Just another problem? One more reason to prove why we shouldn't be together? I loved that baby, Kari, and I loved you." He pierced her with a look.

"You know, I'm glad that our lives took the paths they did," Jonathan said through his tears. "I'm glad it was my mother who got me out of jail. Otherwise I would have to feel I owe you something. And I don't want to owe you ever!"

He looked at Kari, disgust filling him. "You don't have to worry about the lawsuit or seeing me again. I don't know what I expected from you.

"I guess I was fool enough to believe that we meant something to each other. That the color of our skin didn't matter. That what our parents and our town thought didn't matter. Even the world, Kari.

"I never cared about color, but it was never that way with you, was it? Lies, that's all it ever was."

Kari held herself erect. "Is that what you think, Jon, that I was playing some kind of game with you? I suppose you're right about the lies, but maybe you should ask your mother about that. Maybe you should ask her why it took her seven months to get you out of jail."

"If you've got something to say, spit it out."

"All right, here it is. I called your parents over and over, pleading with them to help you. Even after I thought you had married

Sharon, I still begged them to help you. Your mother said she would not lift a finger until I was out of not only your life but out of town."

She could see the shock on his face, his eyes telling her he didn't know if he should believe her. It no longer mattered, he thought the worst of her anyway. She had never wanted him to hate her but it seemed inevitable.

"Jon, the day I left town I called your mother. I told her I was leaving, that she could now help you. That was the last call I made."

"I don't believe you."

"I don't care."

She walked toward the door, wishing he no longer held the power to hurt her, knowing wishing wouldn't make it so.

"Why would my mother leave me in jail?"

"Why would she tell me you were getting married to Sharon?"

For a moment he appeared to be digesting what she said. "Even if that's so, my mother's not the one who killed my child without asking me."

Tell him, tell him, a little voice screamed out in her head. *Don't let him keep believing that.* Before she could decide, the moment passed. He was glaring at her, his pain and her guilt like a knife in her heart.

He turned on his heels and slammed out of the door, but not before he saw the tears spilling down Kari's face once again.

He had to get out. He wanted to take her in his arms again in spite of the anger and the hurt. He wanted to kiss some sense into her, kiss her until she said she was sorry, that the color of his skin didn't matter. That she loved him still, always had, always would.

He felt the bulge in the pocket of his slacks, ran his hand over the ridge of the wedding invitation. It was too late. Kari was getting married.

CHAPTER FOURTEEN

His eyes moist with unshed tears, Jonathan almost walked into the man coming up the drive. Both men stopped and gave each other the once-over. Then Jon walked to his car but turned back toward Kari's house in time to watch Steven Anderson, Kari's tall, dark, good-looking black fiancé use his key and go inside.

Jon stood for almost ten minutes watching Kari's house, thinking over the things she'd said to him. She was right. It no longer mattered. She was getting married to someone else. His hand went to the stolen card tucked inside his trouser pocket.

He leaned against the hood of his car. They had never spoken about the baby, not since that night. He had never asked her before if she'd had an abortion, just assumed she had. He knew why he hadn't asked her. If she had said yes, it would have killed him. *How could everything have gone so wrong for us*? he wondered. He sucked in his breath, the pain intensifying with every passing moment. He waited.

Two seconds before he was going to drive off, he noticed another car pulling up to Kari's house. He glanced at the watch on his arm. *It was awfully late for so many visitors.*

As the couple emerged from their car, all of Jon's feelings of rage, pain and betrayal culminated into anger at her parents. Before he could stop himself, he was heading toward them. This was also something he should have done a long time ago.

He was no longer thinking, just reacting to his pain. The couple in front of him symbolized the hurt he lived with. Yes, it was more than time that he confronted them. He no longer was in danger of losing the woman he loved. He had lost her a long time ago.

"Mr. and Mrs. Thomas," he said, a sardonic grin pulling at the corners of his mouth. "It's been a long time." He watched as the couple stared at him, their looks of bewilderment becoming filled with panic.

"Kari's getting married. Why are you here?"

Jon turned to Kari's father and glared at the man. "I just wanted to thank you two."

"What are you talking about?" the older man practically barked at him. "We've done nothing for you to thank us."

"I'm sure I have the two of you to thank for playing a part in Kari's abortion. My parents surely would have been just as happy about that decision as you were." He watched their expressions as Mr. Thomas turned and looked questioningly at his wife.

"What are you talking about?" Kari's mother inquired. Kari was never pregnant or at least she never told us."

"Besides," her husband growled at Jon, "that was a long time ago. She's getting married now. The past doesn't matter. She's getting a chance to start a new life."

Jon looked toward the house. "You approve of him, don't you?"

"Yes, why shouldn't we?" The couple spoke in unison.

"Look, he doesn't know about you," Mr. Thomas continued. "Why the hell did you reappear after all this time? Why don't you go away and leave her alone? If it's even true that she was ever pregnant, she didn't have your baby and it was for the best."

Jon glared at first one, then the other of Kari's parents. "I loved your daughter and I loved our child, so I want you to know that even though I was the only person to love that baby, it was not for the best."

At last he walked away from them, but not before making one final crack.

"I'll give you something that should help you sleep better tonight. I still love your daughter. And in spite of your hand-picked choice of a black husband for her, she still loves me. Ask her, if you're not afraid of the answer."

With that he got into his car and drove away, knowing he had spoken the truth. Kari's tears had told him she still cared.

The flow of water running down his cheeks unchecked would have dubbed him a liar if he had attempted to deny his feelings for her. As angry as he was with her, he loved her still.

The bitterness was all a cover for the pain of losing her, of losing all they had been to each other, of all they had promised. He drove off into the night, leaving behind the woman who for more than a decade had controlled his heart and was now about to marry another man. He licked at the salty tears dropping on his lips but did nothing to wipe them away.

ം

Steve entered the house slowly, cautiously, something about the man in the driveway niggling at his brain. He had seen the man before. Of that he was sure. Where? He would have to remember.

He spotted Kari huddled in the cushions of the sofa, tears streaming down her face. She looked up at him as he entered the room, making no effort to stop her flow of tears, guilt filling her watery gaze.

There was something else, some hint of something he'd sensed before. But it was the guilt that did it for him. It was the same expression she'd worn in Missouri at the courthouse.

Then it hit him. The man walking down her drive was the lawyer who had run out of the courtroom. Steve stood in the room looking down at Kari, her temper tantrum earlier making sense.

"Are we getting married?" he asked, his voice devoid of emotion.

For an answer Kari wiped at her eyes. "We need to talk."

"Are you sleeping with him? For God's sake, Kari, he's white."

"I know he's white. And the answer is no, I'm not sleeping with him. Not now."

"Then we don't need to talk."

"Steve," she paused, "I'm sorry."

She looked at him. His eyes were veiled to her, making it impossible for her to read him. She didn't know what else to say to him. She had lied. She knew from the beginning what he wanted. She had been planning to marry him under false pretenses.

"You need to go wash your face. Your parents are not far behind." He glanced at the floor at the broken glass. "I'll take care of this." He walked toward the kitchen for the broom. "Did he hurt you?"

"Not physically. We hurt each other," she answered him, then walked away to wash her face.

When she returned, Steven was holding the still undone invitations in his hands. "Is he the reason it's taken you so long to get these finished? They should have gone out a month ago." His voice held a touch of reprimand he didn't try to hide.

"If you're asking me if I've cheated on you with him, the answer is no. He's part of my past." She saw him look away as though the sight of her repulsed him. "It's time I told you."

He turned back toward her. "He's your past. Keep him there."

She watched him, knowing she needed to tell him. So she tried again. "Steve, I never expected to see him again. It's been over seven years."

He ignored her. Instead, he held out the box holding the beginning of their future.

"We're going to get these done tonight if we have to stay up all night to do it. Then tomorrow we're going to go see the pastor." His manner left no room for debate.

"That's fine, I would have finished them tonight anyway. You're the one who told me to take a break, that you had a surprise for me. Remember?" She gave him a weak smile, not feeling the gratitude that he undoubtedly thought she should. The door bell chimed and she turned away. "Steve," she stopped. "I won't marry you if you're judging me."

"Get the door, Kari."

The bell rang again. This time Steven walked past Kari and answered the door himself. He stood in the threshold blocking the way of her parents. Three pairs of eyes stared at her before anyone spoke.

"Is everything all right?"

Collin Thomas was asking Steve, not his daughter. Everyone was aware of the unasked question. Would he marry her now?

"Everything's fine," Steve answered.

He glanced over his shoulder at Kari, then gave a convincing smile to her parents. "But we need to be alone, there's a lot we have to do tonight. We're seeing the minister in the morning for premarital counseling."

Collin Thomas beamed. "You are? That's great."

He still had yet to acknowledge his daughter. Instead, he pulled his wife by the hand and led her away.

Kari watched them, thinking her father looked like a man who'd made a trade and had stuck someone with damaged goods and was now trying to slink off into obscurity before he was found out. She grimaced. That's what she felt like, damaged goods.

For four hours, she and Steven worked together until the last envelope was stamped and ready to be mailed. They worked in a polite silence. Several times Kari attempted to tell Steven about Jonathan, but each time he stopped her.

"Don't! I'm too angry with you right now to talk about this rationally. A cracker, Kari! A redneck cracker!

"Don't, Steve, don't go there. You know how I feel about this." He was glaring at her, his eyes cold and angry and for a moment she had the urge to run.

"And you know how I feel about our women dating them." He looked at her then, long and hard. "Well, this is one time that it won't work. He won't have you. I'll see to that."

"Steve, Jonathan's not like that, I swear he's not. Please listen to me. I need to tell you about him and you need to know."

"You're wrong, I don't need to know. Let's forget about him. He's your past; I'm your future. The right future." Steve stood, the heavy box balanced in his hand. "I'll pick you up at ten."

"It's late." Kari glanced at the clock. "It's almost morning. Aren't you staying?" She noticed that his eyes didn't meet hers when he answered.

"Not tonight."

He glanced over her head and out the window at the faint pinkish rays indicating daylight would soon be approaching. He corrected himself. "Not this morning. I think I'll drive these to the main post office. We don't have much time."

Kari didn't answer. His actions, loud and clear, told her he didn't trust her to turn over the invitations to Rose in a matter of a few hours. He was going to do it himself.

When he walked out of the door after giving her an obligatory peck on the cheek, she cringed inwardly.

Damn you, Jonathan Steele. Why now, why not years ago? She'd promised herself she'd stop crying, but the tears came despite her determination.

Why, after all this time, after all that happened does he still hold the ability to hurt me? Why did I go after him, trying to hurt him, wanting him to hate me? Why didn't I just tell him the truth, that I didn't have an abortion, that it really was a miscarriage?

You know why, she answered her own question. *Because you looked in his eyes and you saw that he loved you still. You lost yourself to him once and didn't want to do it again.*

Kari remembered how just a few short hours ago she'd stood in the middle of her living room screaming at Jonathan, saying horrible things to him and remembering how much she had loved him.

Still loved him. She held on to the back of a chair for support as she admitted to herself what she could no longer deny. She loved Jonathan Steele. Always had. Always would.

But what about Steve? Kari paced the room. *Seven years*! She wasn't marrying Steve on the rebound. She did love him. If she had never bought into that damnable campground, she would never have come in contact with Jonathan Steele again. She would be happily going about the business of her upcoming marriage.

Kari leaned against the refrigerator, feeling the cool metal against her skin. She brought her right hand up before her and stared at it, as if it were a foreign object. She had never struck Jonathan before, not even when she had found him with Sharon. Why, after all this, time had she?

Because when he put his hands on my shoulders I wanted to hold him so badly that I ached. I wanted to forgive him, tell him that I believed him. I wanted to tell him that I loved him.

The feel of his arms around her lingered with her still. The taste of him was fresh in her mouth. She'd been left with no choice but to spew words of anger and to finally hit him. If not, she would be in his arms now and nothing would have changed for the better. She would be unable to have the future she'd worked so hard for.

The tears rolled down her face furiously and she allowed her body to sag until it connected with the cold ceramic floor.

"Oh God, help me," she pleaded. "I can't, not now. My life is perfect. Please give me the strength not to mess it up. "

Kari remained on the floor until she thought she could talk without crying. Then she reached for the phone and dialed the number of the one person who would understand, the one person who'd been there through it all. Her eyes fell on the clock. It was only then that she noticed the time. Five-thirty on a Saturday morning. She could only pray that Jackie wasn't working today.

When, Jackie's voice answered, Kari's resolve not to cry melted and she sobbed, "Jackie, Jon was here."

"Kari, are you alright? Tell me what happened."

"He kissed me."

"What did you do?

"I kissed him back."

CHAPTER FIFTEEN

Since returning from Chicago Jonathan had regularly paced the rooms of his home, alternating between wanting to prove Kari a liar and knowing in his heart she spoke the truth. He dialed his childhood home, almost praying his mother wouldn't be home, that she wouldn't answer.

As he waited, he ordered himself to act natural. If he was going to get the truth from his mother, it would have to be a sneak attack. She couldn't suspect what he was after.

Even if his mother had maneuvered his arrest, it wouldn't change anything between him and Kari. What good would it do him to know? It wouldn't change anything. Kari had still... He stopped. He couldn't allow himself to think about the baby now. It hurt too much.

"Hello."

He heard his mother's crisp, cool southern drawl. He didn't want it to be true but if it was he couldn't continue living a lie.

"Mother?"

"Jonathan, is that you?"

"Yes." He forced cheerfulness into his voice. He didn't want her to suspect.

"Another minute and you would have missed me. I was about to go over to the church. Reverend Bob wants my help on the bake sale."

Jonathan made himself laugh. "I can just taste your cakes now, Mom. Why don't you make an extra one to send me?"

"Why don't you come home and get it yourself?"

Jon listened to the wistful tone of his mother's voice and for the briefest of seconds thought about not going through with his plan.

"I just might do that, Mom. I've been feeling kinda homesick." He changed his voice from the clipped tones he had adopted to his own drawl.

"Then why don't you come home? Your friends would love to see you."

That was the perfect opening. "Yeah," he drawled even deeper. "Have you seen my friend Sharon by any chance?" He waited, his heart in his throat, praying.

"No, I've haven't seen her since you were in jail." She stopped. "Jonathan, why are you asking me about Sharon?"

"Because I never introduced you to her or told you about her, Mom." He sucked on his teeth. "How do you know her, Mom?"

"Jonathan, why does it matter? That was all so long ago. I don't know, maybe she was one of your friends that came to the house looking for you."

"Do you think it might have been the jail, Mom?"

"I don't know, Jon. Why, what's wrong?"

"Mom, did you hire Sharon to try to break up my relationship with Kari?"

"No."

"Mom, don't lie, not now. It's too important. Sharon was the reason I was in jail. Remember?"

"What does it matter how I know Sharon?"

"I lost Kari because of Sharon."

"Jon, it's over and done with, isn't it? I hear tell that gal's getting married to some fancy black doctor."

"How would you know that?"

"Talk gets around."

"Mom, answer my question. Did you hire Sharon? Are you the reason she lied and said I raped her? Are you the reason I went to jail?"

"What if I did?" his mother yelled at him. "I would do anything to keep you from making a mess of your life."

Jonathan sank against the chair. "One more question, about Kari. Did you tell her you wouldn't help me until she left town?" He heard the sharp intake of breath.

"How do you know? Who told you?"

"You just did, Mom. No one else could have ever made me believe you had anything to do with this. No one but you."

"You talked as if you knew already. Someone had to have told you that. Who, Jonathan? Only one person knew about this."

"Don't worry about it, Mom. What I had before was only veiled innuendoes I wasn't sure about anyway, but you've filled in the blanks."

"What are you going to do, Jonathan? I did it all for your own good. You wouldn't know, not unless you're a mother. You nearly killed your father when you took up with that girl."

"So you did this for Dad?"

"No, Jonathan, I did it because you were making us into a laughing stock. We worked hard to build our good name and you were willing to throw it away on that, girl, that—"she hesitated, "on that, nig-"

"Don't Mom, or I'll never speak to you again. I loved her. You had no right to do what you did."

"I had every right. I love you. I'm still here. Where is she, Jon? She sure as hell didn't stick around to help you. I did."

Jonathan laughed, not believing what he was hearing. "You helped? Mom, you destroyed my life. What you did didn't make me stop loving her."

"What are you talking about? You're not seeing her again, are you?"

He heard the panic in her voice and stopped, the pain filling him. He had wished many times that his life had not been what it was but it had been. There was nothing he could do to change his town, his parents, or people's view. He closed his eyes briefly. Even the woman he loved was tainted by bigotry.

"Mom, I still love Kari. I always will."

"No, Jonathan, leave it be. She's getting married to one of her own. That's the way it should be." Her voice changed to one of cajoling. "I can help you find a suitable girl, Jon, give me a chance."

"No thanks, Mom." With that, he disconnected the phone. He thought about Kari and their life together, of all they'd gone through only to have both of their families undermining them every step of the way. They'd never stood a chance. Not in Lonett, Alabama. Maybe not anywhere.

We might have lost it, he thought, *but what we had was real.*

He rubbed his cheek. The imprint of Kari's hand was no longer there but he wanted to feel for it just the same. The look in her eyes had told him what he wanted to know. Her body clinging to his had said what she refused to say. Her words were a lie. She loved him still. Just as he loved her.

What am I doing? It's too late. He sat for over an hour thinking about the past and about the way his life and Kari's had turned out, thankful that his law career had not been washed down the toilet with the rest of his life.

At long last Jon stood and stretched. There was one more piece of unfinished business. He could not let go until he proved to Kari that his love for her had been true. He was aware that it would take hours to search through the dusty trunks stored in his garage. It didn't matter, he would find it.

Then what, Jon? What are you going to do once you have it in your hands?

He didn't allow himself time to answer the question. He rolled up the sleeves of his silk shirt and headed for the garage.

છ

Jonathan was right. It did take hours. When he held the mauve-colored velvet jeweler's box in his hand, he let out a deep groan before opening it.

The top opened smoothly. Jon lifted the ring and read the inscription. *Kari, my soulmate, my love, my life.* He held the ring in the palm of his hand licking his lips slowly as he did so, wondering if he'd had it with him three weeks before, when he'd gone to Kari's home, if it would have made a difference.

He looked again at the inscribed words. He had meant them. His pounding heart said he meant it still. *So what's next?* He peered at the ring as if it held the secrets of the universe. *It's too late*, he thought as he replaced the ring in the case and shoved it into the pocket of his now ruined silk shirt.

Jon looked at his filthy shirt, knowing it would never come clean. *What the hell, finding Kari's engagement ring was worth the price of a shirt.*

Jonathan threw the shirt over the back of a chair in his bedroom. He would decide later what to do. For now he would resist his instinct to fly back to Chicago and shove the ring in Kari's face. It was his proof that he had loved her.

Damn, why should I need proof? Didn't I show her every day that I loved her? He was getting angry again. *Women,* he thought. *Who the hell needs them? I do,* he answered silently.

He felt the pain stabbing him in the chest. "I do," he whispered aloud. "I need her."

He shucked off his ruined pants. Don't be a fool, she's getting married, to a black man. *Something I can never be for her. That was the real reason she left.* As the thought crossed his mind he felt another stab of pain and fell against the chair for support.

"If I could be that for you, Kari, I would!"

He needed to focus on the one thing he did have. His job. He had clients still that needed attending to. None of them were interested in his history or his pain. He was being paid to do a job.

If he didn't keep his mind on business there would be another young lawyer breathing down his neck, eager to replace him. Then where would he be? He wouldn't have Kari or a job.

He sighed as he made his way to the shower. Making Kari believe him would have to take a backseat for now. Besides, he was still angry with her.

Maybe he should let her keep thinking that he had only used her. It would serve her right for what she had done. She had admitted she had— He had to stop thinking about the baby.

But he couldn't stop thinking of what might have been. What if everything he had believed for the past years had all been lies, including Kari allowing him to believe the worst? It was then he realized Kari had never actually admitted to having an abortion. What she'd said was, "What difference does it make now?" There had been hurt in Kari's eyes when he'd finally accused her of having an abortion. *If she had actually had an abortion, guilt would have been in her eyes. She wouldn't have been hurt*ing.

This kind of thinking was getting him nowhere. It would change nothing. She was still going to marry her doctor.

Yet his heart felt the familiar tug of love. It wasn't just wishful thinking. No matter what Kari had said or what she had done, he knew in his heart she'd loved him once, and more than likely still did. His thoughts flew back to the baby. *She didn't do it,* he thought as he toweled dry.

Jon dressed quickly before he drove himself crazy with his imagination. He would work. That was the only thing he could think to do for now.

ℝ

Once he dug his heels in at work, he stayed until midnight every day for over a week. He knew he was trying to avoid the inevitable, another meeting with Kari.

He went through his file double-checking the address for where she worked. He called and was told she was on assignment at Chicago's University Hospital. The overly helpful receptionist gave him everything he needed, including the address of the hospital and Kari's schedule.

Jon had always known he would see her again, especially after finding her ring. This time there would be no fighting, no hurting. No pain. He would show her the ring, show her the yellowed receipt. He didn't know for sure where Sharon's ring had come from, but he had a pretty good idea.

This time when he left Chicago it would be a closed chapter. He would give her his proof, give her the ring.

Are you going to tell her that you love her? He heard the voice whispering in his ear and turned quickly, half expecting someone to be in the room with him.

I must be going crazy. Now I'm hearing voices. The echo of the question lingered in his mind as he checked his appointment book before dialing the airlines for a ticket.

He could swing a meeting if he waited until Thursday. All he needed to do was shuffle around a couple of meetings. Those he would take care of himself. The less Mrs. Dobis knew about what he was doing the better.

He got an open return ticket, not admitting that he was hoping he wouldn't need to turn around and come straight back to Missouri.

At the airport gift shop he had an idea. He went in and searched for wrapping paper. *I'll tell her it's a wedding gift, nothing more. If I'm wrong, I won't look like such a fool.*

Less than two hours later he was pushing the button of the elevator, heading for the office where Kari was working. His walk, sure and quick, belied his lack of confidence. As he was walking in the direction he'd been pointed, he heard someone call his name and turned.

"Jackie, Jackqueline Jackson, is that you?" He smiled in remembrance. She was the only friend of Kari's from the old days who had eventually accepted their relationship.

"Jon, what are you doing here?" Jackie crossed the few steps to him and hugged him warmly.

"I'm here to see Kari, I have to show her something."

"You do know Steve works here, don't you?"

"I don't care." He noticed that Jackie was grinning at him. He understood. She didn't like Steve.

"Good luck, Jon," Jackie said. "I would love to see the look on Kari's face when you walk in her door, but I'm on duty."

For the first time, Jon noticed the patient in the wheelchair a few feet from where they stood talking. "Thanks, Jackie. I'll probably need it." He gave her another quick hug and continued toward the offices where he expected to find Kari.

☏

"I'm here to see Kari Thomas." He smiled at the pretty receptionist, half flirting to insure she would not lie and tell him Kari was out. He had come too far. He didn't know if he would be able to repeat this again.

He listened to the woman say his name into the phone. He waited, expecting burly guards to rush up and throw him out of the building. Instead, the receptionist turned to him, smiled and pointed toward a door.

"You can go right in."

Jon looked at her for a moment, glanced at her nameplate and said, "Thanks, Amy." It had all appeared too easy. He had expected resistance not admittance. He noticed the receptionist's smile dropping as he hesitated. *Probably wondering if you're as dumb as a block of wood.*

He turned and headed in the direction she pointed after giving her a smile. He didn't want the woman to think he was a total moron. He knocked twice lightly on the door, then entered.

Kari was seated behind a desk, a pencil in her mouth. She barely looked up from her work. Her face was scrunched up in a frown over a mammoth adding machine.

He wondered why she just didn't use a computer for her figures. Then he remembered. She always double checked the computer. Jon smiled slightly, waiting for some sign from her.

She absentmindedly pointed toward a chair, her concentration on her work. "Give me a few minutes." She didn't wait for an answer, but continued with her task.

Jon took the seat she pointed to and watched her. He noticed the slight trembling of her hand. Anyone entering the room would have thought he was merely a client. He knew better.

She was trying to give herself an edge by pretending to be hard at work, ignoring him as if he were simply the delivery boy, but he had seen her Achilles heel. She couldn't help it. Whenever she was nervous her hands would tremble.

He sat and watched her and as he did he felt a leap of fire soar through his loins. His own Achilles heel around Kari. In an instant

161

he had a massive, rock hard erection that would be impossible to hide. He draped the package he was carrying across his lap but it did little to camouflage his condition.

Think, Jon, think. He didn't want her to see him like this. The balance of power was slowly shifting in her direction. He knew all she had to do was smile at him and he would be unable to prevent himself from taking her in his arms, slap or no slap.

He forced an image of everything disagreeable into his mind but nothing seemed to work. Then he thought of Elizabeth Dobis, his secretary.

That did the trick. He could feel his monumental hard- on losing power. It wasn't gone, but at least he could stand and turn around until he was able to send it back into submission.

❧

Kari had been expecting this moment. She had lived with the man for three years. When he left her home, hurt and angry, she had known she would see him again. She had been waiting for him to pop in at any moment. His coming to her office was no surprise. It was like him to try and throw her off balance.

Well, what he didn't know was she was ready for him. She had felt her hands tremble when he walked in and prayed he hadn't noticed. Now that he was here, however, she wasn't as confident as she had been in her dreams. She was sitting across from him wanting to look at him, to tell him that she was sorry.

Why don't you admit it, Kari, you want to be twenty-one again, before Sharon came into your lives, and try it all again.

Her hands trembled a little more noticeably. She knew Jonathan had seen it. She dared a glance at him beneath her lashes and saw him staring at her. She saw something else, something she was sure he had not meant for her to see. He was not as unaffected by her as he wanted her to believe.

Okay, Kari, you're both still sexually attracted to each other. It doesn't mean a thing. It's not as though you want to forget about Steve and run away with Jonathan.

A sudden flush flooded her body, causing her to bite into the pencil in her mouth. Where had that thought come from?

She punched in figures furiously, then scribbled the useless numbers on a piece of paper. Her work was all in vain. She had no idea of what she was adding or writing, but she would do it for a few minutes more before addressing Jonathan.

She felt more than saw him squirming around in the seat. She was aware that he didn't want her to know what was happening. That knowledge gave her reason to almost smile. Had he forgotten the many times they had practiced enticing each other without using words?

The sexual tension was so thick in her small office that even a person devoid of the five senses would know it. The two of them in a room together had always spelled untamed, lustful passion.

Her thoughts flew back to Steve. There was never this kind of energy with them, not even when they were in the throes of love-making.

Stop it, Kari, she scolded herself. *Stop it. Sex isn't everything, remember that.*

Her eyes followed Jonathan as he stood and turned away from her. She allowed herself the hunger for the few seconds it took for him to turn around. It was the look in his eyes that caused her the problem.

In seven years no one had looked at her in that manner. Her body felt hot. She was tingling all over. She could feel the tiny beads of moisture gathering in the vee of her thighs. In seconds she would be climaxing if she didn't put a stop to it.

"Jonathan." Kari coughed, still caught under his spell, fighting desperately to save herself from drowning in his eyes.

He didn't love you, Kari. Remember that. None of it was real.

She waited while the ebb of electricity receded enough to allow her normal use of her voice. She felt the sticky wetness in her panties. Since Jonathan, she'd had no need to wear panty liners.

She decided to try again. "Jonathan, I wasn't expecting you."

The words rolled off her tongue. Her head lifted and her eyes met his. They laughed together at her obvious lie.

"So are there a few more insults you want to shout at me, something you might have forgotten a week ago?" There was no sting in her words, amusement only. Their laughter had managed to dispel some of the tension.

"No, I'm here with a peace offering."

Jon was still standing. He placed his hand on the back of the chair to anchor himself. She was smiling at him. And he wanted her so badly he could feel his salivary glands releasing their juices, his memories of the taste of her filling his mouth, making him want her even more. He gave his head a shake. Kari was speaking to him and yet he hadn't heard.

"I'm sorry." He smiled again at her. "I didn't hear you. I saw your parents, they seemed happy to see me. We had a very long and pleasant discussion."

He cocked his head at her, thinking how beautiful she was. He watched her face as her lips stretched into a smile. The sound of her laughter shattered the last of the reserve around his heart.

Yes. He loved her still.

"My parents happy to see you, Jon? That will be the day." She wiped at the tears of laughter brimming from her eyes. "Seriously, why did you come back?"

"I said I brought you a peace offering."

"Why?"

He looked away before answering. "I don't know. I talked to my mother," he continued. "I know the truth."

The atmosphere of the room changed. They could both feel it. For a moment it had looked as if there might be the slightest chance that one day they could attempt to be friends. Now this ominous cloud hung between them.

Kari let out a sigh before glancing out her window to look at the Chicago skyline, changing her mind about giving him the peace he sought. She wouldn't clear up his misunderstanding about the abortion. It wasn't his belief in her that brought him back, it was his mother.

"You didn't believe me until your mother verified it?"

"That's not fair. We both had some problems with trust. I wasn't the only one."

"No, but you were the only one to have the doubts blown up in Technicolor."

Kari was becoming angry. This wasn't how she wanted it. Since she'd last seen him, she'd wanted to do nothing more than to go to him and tell him she was sorry for hurting him. That she had not done what he accused her of.

It hurt that he thought she had. It also hurt that he thought she left because of the color of his skin. He should know her better than that.

She wanted to tell him those things now, but she didn't. She couldn't help it, but whenever she thought about the pictures she still wanted to cry. She wanted to hit something, someone. It wasn't fair that she should be the only one hurting.

The very idea that Jonathan's mother's word was what it had taken for him to believe her hurt even more. She wanted to make sure Jonathan hurt as much as she was constantly hurting.

In an attempt to calm herself, she closed her eyes and brought both elbows onto the surface of her desk. She cupped her hands together and placed them over her nose and mouth, massaging the creases by her eyes with her fingers.

"I never cheated on you, Kari, never in my heart, never in my love for you. You should know that."

"It doesn't matter, Jon, that was a lifetime ago."

Something he had never thought of flashed into his mind. "If I was going to cheat on you intentionally, why would I photograph it? Just think about that, Kari. I was working, the pictures were staged."

Before she could answer, the door opened and Steve walked into the room. Kari was about to ask him what he was doing there but stopped herself in the nick of time. She could feel the unwanted guilt clouding her eyes and wished for the billionth time she wasn't such an open book. All of her emotions were easily read.

She saw the angry expression on Steve's face and without thinking the lie came from her mouth. "Steve, this is Jonathan Steele, a college classmate of mine. He just happened to be in town and decided to look me up."

Both men turned toward her, both wearing surprised looks, their eyes flashing a warning for her not to continue. She ignored them both. "Jonathan, this is my fiancé, Dr. Steven Anderson."

"Oh."

Steve advanced his hand tentatively, his dislike masked by two rows of gleaming teeth. "You're the lawyer from Missouri, aren't you? I hope you didn't get in any trouble when you were beaten by amateurs."

"Well, Kari isn't exactly an amateur. She used to help me study for pre-law."

Kari's gaze took in first Steve, then Jonathan. She lingered on Jon, watching him. His eyelids were at half-mast, and the left corner of his lip quivered just the tiniest bit, negligible to most observers, not for her. She knew that look well. He was angry.

Jon accepted Steve's hand, his smile lazy. Kari could feel her heart pounding against her ribs. She cast her eyes downward to observe her own body. Surely her heart was about to come unhinged from its nest in her body. She concentrated on the two men, listening to the hostility in their voices.

"Nice to meet you, Jonathan. As you can see, Kari's doing things the right way now. She's not into experimenting anymore."

Jon's glance slid over to Kari, cold and angry, yet she sensed the hurt. One minute they had actually been laughing, the tension gone. She had finally been going to tell him the truth. Then the next moment, he had mentioned his mother and she'd wanted nothing more than to hurt him. Again. Now Steve was here, and she was hurting Jonathan even more.

Steve looked at Kari, wondering why she'd bothered to introduce Jonathan as an old classmate. He decided to continue the pretense. "So you and Kari were classmates? It's nice that you could stop by while you're in town."

Again Jon smiled at the man. "I would like to think Kari and I were more than classmates. We used to be friends. But of course that was a long time ago."

He turned up the power of his smile. "If you want to know more than that, you'll have to ask Kari."

His statement was filled with innuendo. As he swung around to face Kari, his eyes issued a challenge.

Kari's gaze flew to Steve's face. She watched him, noting the vein popping out on the left side of his neck.

She saw him clench his fingers into fists, his head twitching as though he had a tic. There was no mistaking the anger.

She glanced back at Jon. She had fired the first shot. Of course he would send an answering volley. She refused to allow his comment or his presence to upset her.

She smiled coolly at Jon. "More to know? In Lonett, Alabama? I don't think so." She laughed, then answered Jon's challenge. "We were never that close. I wonder what your family would have thought of that idea? Besides, I never knew you thought of me as a friend. If anyone had asked me to name your friends," she paused, "I would have probably said Sharon. You know, Jon, the blonde who was always plastered on you."

Kari didn't know why but she seemed to have no control over what was coming out of her mouth. She knew she wasn't fooling anyone. They all knew exactly what she had been to Jonathan Steele.

Again Jon's lips twitched. Kari saw and smiled. "Anyway, that was a long time ago," she muttered as she came from around her desk. "I can barely remember my childhood or the boys I talked to."

She gave Jonathan a wicked grin before winking in Steven's direction. "As you can see, I've also outgrown boys. I prefer men now." Steve might not have been aware of it, but she was doing this for him.

She watched as the two men turned toward each other, squaring off, both angry. She was not going to be their prize. She had made her choice.

She stepped indifferently between them and leaned her head against Steven's massive chest. All the while her eyes never left Jon's face.

Kari slid her hand along Steven's wrist, circling his hand. She slowly ran her fingers up the entire length of his arm until she reached his shoulder.

She held her left hand toward Jon. "I don't think you've seen my ring yet, have you?" There was an undertone of sarcasm in her voice. "Go ahead, take a look, it won't disappear."

Jon looked first at the ring, then at Kari. He took two steps and was holding her left hand in his, his eyes drawing her. What the hell was she doing? He barely glanced at the ring, knowing that Kari was telling him she still didn't believe he'd bought her a ring.

If he were smart, he'd get the hell out of there and just forget he ever knew her, forget he'd ever loved her. But how could he? He loved her still. The last thing he would wish on her was the racist bastard she was about to marry.

That knowledge made his entire body pulsate with anger. With trembling fingers he took her hand as if to examine the ring, and felt the surge of desire spring once again into his loins. He felt the trembling of Kari's own fingers.

Then slowly, ever so slowly, he traced her fingers with his thumb, through the tiny crevices up and down, through each opening, going over the back of her hand.

Jon continued right in front of Kari's fiancé to make love to her with his hand holding hers. He reclaimed her then and there. If not her love, then her body. He saw the small gasp of pleasure escape her. Her eyes were about to close, signaling her release, when abruptly his hand was knocked away.

"What the hell do you think you're doing?" Steve was livid, glaring first at Jonathan, then Kari.

Jonathan turned his attention to Steve. He saw the man was furious and didn't give a damn. "I was admiring the ring." He gave a short and derisive laugh. "Congratulations. You have a lovely bride. I'm sure it'll be a lovely wedding."

He looked again at Kari, not bothering to conceal the wanton lust in his eyes, knowing his look would elicit the same from her. He saw briefly that it had before she looked away.

Steve pulled Kari away from Jon, then stepped in front of her before answering him. "Yes, it will be. Sorry you're not invited but all of our invitations have been mailed out." He stretched, flexing his chest.

Steve advanced even closer to Jonathan. "I've decided to hire several guards to keep out unwanted, uninvited guests." He smirked at Jonathan. "You do understand, don't you?"

"I think I do. But what if your bride changes her mind and decides it's not you she really wants to marry after all? What if she decides that she loves someone else? What are you going to do then, force her?" Jonathan attempted a smile that looked more like a sneer. "Are you going to hire guards to intimidate her?"

Things were getting out of hand. Kari blamed herself for the over-abundance of male hormones stinking up the office. She should never have attempted to bait Jonathan. What did it matter now that he'd never bought her a ring?

"Jonathan, Steve doesn't have to worry about the bride. He's the only man I've ever wanted to marry. The only man whose ring I've worn."

"Touché," Jonathan said.

Kari bit down on her lip, sighing, as her eyes closed automatically. She wanted to stop her meanness, stop hurting Jon, but she couldn't. She wanted him gone from her life. She couldn't have him.

"Listen, Jonathan, I'm sorry to cut this visit short but Steve and I were about to go out for lunch."

"Oh." Jon smiled in her direction, ignoring her obvious dig. He glanced at his watch, knowing full well what time it was.

"It's only a little after ten. That's funny. In Missouri we eat lunch about one, two o'clock. You folks sure are spoiled here."

Kari was annoyed that Jonathan wouldn't just leave. It was obvious they would never be able to be friends. They loved each other too damn much to just settle for friendship. So they settled for the only thing they had left between them that they could use, their ability to inflict pain on each other. She had one thing left in her depleted arsenal.

"I said we were going to lunch, Jon. I didn't say we were going to eat."

"No, you didn't say you were going to eat, did you? I guess I should be leaving anyway. I only came by to give you a gift, call it a wedding present if you want." He glanced at Steven. "Actually it's not for you."

He could care less that the man was steadily advancing on him, wanting probably to smash his face in. Well, just let him try. He wanted to do some smashing of his own.

He turned his eyes toward Kari, burning her with his searing gaze. He watched as her hands twittered nervously at her side.

"He handed her the package. "Don't be afraid. It's not a bomb. It's only a gift, Kari."

He walked toward the door, stopped, turned to look at the couple facing him. "Good luck. I hope you both get what you deserve."

Kari and Steve looked first at each other, then at Jonathan's retreating back. Neither answered. His comment, though cheerful, was dripping with sarcasm.

Jonathan smiled at the receptionist on his way out. He needed a diversion to keep him from returning to the room and smashing Steven Anderson's face in.

How could Kari have ever gotten involved with such a stuffed shirt, pompous ass. The man was an exact replica of her father, only younger. Well, if she wanted to ruin her life, let her.

He was determined that he would never set foot in the entire state of Illinois again in his life. He had tried to mend the fences between them. If she didn't care, then to hell away with her, he thought. She deserved what was going to be her life.

The moment the elevator doors closed Jon punched the metal

walls in frustration. Out of nowhere a thought flitted across his mind. *Why didn't you just tell her that you love her?*

"She never gave me the chance," he answered out loud. He sagged against the cold walls, his head hitting the metal with a bang.

He never thought he could feel more pain than he had when he returned home from jail and found Kari gone, but now he did. Now it was a thousand times worst. He could do no more. He would do more. The next move was up to her.

CHAPTER SIXTEEN

"Damn it, Kari, you didn't have to lie to him about why I was here. You shouldn't have told him we were going to lunch. If anything, you should have told him I was here for a quickie. I have a right to be here any damn time I choose."

Steve could not remember the last time he'd been so angry, not even when he'd spotted the bastard leaving Kari's home had he felt such intense anger. He shoved several items from Kari's desk to the floor and watched as they hit, clanging on the hard ceramic tiles with a deafening thud.

A few moments later there was an urgent rapping on the door. "Miss Thomas?" The door flew open and the receptionist stood there, her eyes wide. She looked first at the mess on the floor, then toward Kari. "Do you need any help, Miss Thomas? Are you okay?" She glared angrily at Steve before her eyes came back to rest on Kari.

"It's okay, Amy, don't worry, just minor glitches," Kari lied. "Listen, why don't you take a break for a few minutes. I'll cover the phones."

"Are you sure?" the receptionist asked, looking warily in Steve's direction.

"I'm sure, now go ahead don't worry. I'm fine." She waited while Amy switched the calls from her own desk to Kari's office.

Kari retreated back behind her desk, Jonathan's gift in her hand. She waited for Steve to turn from the door, glad for the few moments she had to compose herself.

How could he do that? she thought. *How could I allow him to do that right in front of Steve*? Her body still tingled with sexual desire and it wasn't for the man she was going to marry.

If Steve hadn't pushed Jon's hand away, she knew what would have happened. She was on the verge of an explosive orgasm and could feel the pull of it still. Only Jonathan had ever been able to have that effect on her. He'd done it deliberately, that much she knew.

And she was also aware of the reason he'd done it. She'd forced him by treating him as if he meant nothing to her. The truth of it was, it was the exact opposite. He meant everything to her.

At last Steve turned toward her, the fury in his face making his ebony skin gleam.

"You were looking at him as if you were hypnotized, as though I wasn't even in the room. What was that?" He waited for her answer, then roughly took her left hand. "That's my ring you're wearing. We're getting married in a few weeks and I don't appreciate being made to look like a fool."

"I'm sorry, Steve, I didn't mean..."

"Didn't mean what?" he interrupted her. "Didn't mean for me to catch you in here with him? Didn't mean to let him hold your hand, caressing you? I was here," he screamed. "He didn't care that I was in here and neither did you."

Kari stared at the man in front of her desk shouting at her. "Why are you here, Steve? And why didn't Amy announce you? Have you been stalking me, waiting to see if I were faithful?"

She watched as his eyes bulged out. The veins on both sides of his neck were throbbing with rage and for a moment she feared the internal rage within him.

"Don't you dare turn this around. I work here, damn it. Why was he here?" He snatched the gaily wrapped package from Kari's hand. "This gift. Is this the reason?" He ripped the paper into shreds, tearing into the box without her permission.

The sight of a jeweler's box stopped him and he glared angrily at Kari before lifting the top. His mouth opened in shocked surprise as he spied the engagement ring sitting there. He plopped it down in front of Kari.

"Explain!"

She reached for the box. The yellowed receipt fluttered out and she picked it up. She fell back into the chair from which she had arisen only moments before.

*He hadn't lie*d. That knowledge alone sent a thrill through her. *He actually had had a ring*. She pressed the box to her chest and looked at Steve. *Oh, God what have I done*?

"What the hell is this all about, Kari. Why is he giving you a ring, an engagement ring?"

"It's not what you think, Steve."

"Are you telling me that's not an engagement ring in your hand, that the man who just gave it to you wasn't the man you had an affair with?"

"I never had an affair with Jonathan. I had a relationship with him. I was in love with him."

Kari stared at Steve. "Jonathan and I were committed to each other, we were planning a future together. An affair is just about sex."

"I don't give a damn how you word it. Why the hell did he bring you an engagement ring now? Is he trying to get you back?"

"He didn't bring the ring here to try and break us up. He brought it as proof that he had loved me."

"Exactly what happened between the two of you? I never for a minute thought you'd ever consider marrying one of them." He closed his eyes, pacing around the room to control his fury. "What does he mean to you?"

"I've tried to tell you. You never wanted to know."

"I want to know now. I will not be in competition for your affections. That's a promise."

"You're not in competition, Steve, you're the man I'm planning on marrying. What I felt for Jonathan was a long time ago." A chill flew through her entire body, settling around her heart, encasing it in ice.

"My God, Kari, when I saw him at your house you led me to believe that he was only someone you'd dated. You never indicated that you'd loved him. I assumed the dating was it. You lied to me."

"Yes, I lied, by not telling you—even if you did tell me you didn't want to hear about my past, I should have told you anyway. It was a long time ago, Steve, more than seven years. I never thought I would see Jonathan again."

Kari turned away from Steve's gaze that was filled with a barely controlled fury. She brought the ring along with the yellowed receipt downward from her heart. She lifted the ring and read the inscription inside.

Kari, my soulmate, my love, my life. Her eyes filled with tears despite Steven's presence and his yelling.

What have I done? She wished she had not hurt Jon yet again. He really had brought a peace offering and she had literally thrown it back in his face. She moaned softly and replaced the ring in the box.

Oh God, give me strength. He was telling the truth, he loved me. What have I done? She wanted to run to Jon, tell him what she should have told him before Steve came in.

"Kari," Steve screamed at her. "Have you completely lost your mind? You're mooning over that dumb-ass redneck."

"Don't, Steve. I told you before, I won't stand for you calling Jonathan names."

"You go to hell. Who do you think you're talking to? I'm the man you're going to marry. I told you before how I felt. Are you a frigging idiot? Or are you just deaf?" He knocked several more items off her desk and advanced on her.

"Get your eyes off that door. If he comes back in here you'll both wish he hadn't."

Kari hadn't realized she was staring at the door. How could she be, with Steven in her face shouting obscenities at her. Jonathan she would have to take care of later. For now, she would have to deal with Steve.

"First, if you want me to listen to you, stop shouting at me. I don't appreciate your talking to me in this manner."

She glared back at him. "You never told me anything Steve, you told my father. You never even asked me to marry you, you discussed the matter with my father." She stood. "You've never even told me that you love me. Again, you told my father." She walked toward him, taking off the huge diamond as she did so. "Maybe it's my father you should be marrying."

Steve walked toward her, meeting her, disbelief in his eyes. "You're calling off the wedding? I come in here and find you with him, you let him touch you like that in front of me and I'm not supposed to be angry? You lied to me, Kari. What did you expect was going to happen when I found out?"

She held out the ring. "Like I said, I didn't know it was an issue, I never thought I would see Jon again. Here, take the ring back. I think it's for the best. You're right. I did lie to you, by omission."

A heavy sigh escaped her. "Steve, I didn't just happen to date Jonathan. I lived with him for three years. We were going to get married."

"You lived with him? I told you I would never marry a woman who had slept with a white man. For that matter, why the hell didn't you tell me that before? Why did your father quiz me about race mixing when he knew you had... Steve turned away in disgust.

"My parents disowned me. The only time my mother called in the entire three years was to berate Jon and to tell me she saw him with another woman."

"Still, I don't understand. Why did your father say anything at all about the subject?"

"Because he's a bigot, just like you." There was no malice in her voice. She was just stating a fact. "If you

were into white women, do you think they would approve of you?" She laughed, a harsh angry sound. "I'm their daughter. They consider that period of my life, the time when I went crazy. They think I was mentally unbalanced."

She laughed again. "They think Jon kept me doped up for three years. They would much rather believe that I was strung out than that I loved him."

Steve's eyebrows were pulled into a frown. He looked at Kari. "You still love him, don't you?"

"He was my first love. I suppose some part of me will always love him." She observed the horror-stricken look on Steve's face. "I don't want to marry him, though." She shivered, then crossed her hands over her body. "Once in an interracial relationship was enough."

"Then why was he here?"

Kari glanced toward her desk at the jewelry box. Steve's gaze followed hers. "This is a peace offering, nothing more."

"You know you have to give that back to him." He reached for the box but Kari took it in her hand.

She looked at him, a puzzled smile at the corners of her mouth. "Yeah, I know I have to give it back, but I also have to give back yours." She opened her right hand. There sat the ring he had chosen for her, that she had worn for the last few months.

"Are you saying that you don't love me?"

"No, I'm saying that I won't marry you. I see the disgust in your eyes. I'm sure if I told you how ashamed I am to have loved Jonathan and lived with him you would be able to forgive me. But I can't do that."

She opened the box and looked at Jonathan's ring again. "I'm not ashamed of having loved him."

Steve turned away from her, running his hand over his face. How the hell could this have happened? A lot of care had gone into picking Kari Thomas to be his wife, the mother of his children. He'd watched her, asked questions. She'd never dated anyone but black men, not like a lot of the other women he knew. That was the reason he'd first approached Kari. Now to find the whole time it had all been a lie…

He could barely stand to look at her A part of him wanted to snatch his ring away, to leave her to that dumb ass white lawyer.

Another part resisted, unwilling for the other man to win. He'd seen the way he'd looked at Kari, the way she'd looked at him. She still felt something for him. If he didn't marry Kari, she might very well return to Jonathan Steele. He wouldn't let that happen. Kari Thomas was one woman he was determined would stay in her own race. He'd see to it. He'd marry her, then heaven help her if she ever looked at a white man again. Heaven help her if she ever looked at any man.

He mentally attempted to calm himself. He had to talk rationally to convince her that he could get over it. What- ever it took to make her marry him, he would do. She would pay for her lies and deceit later.

When he could speak, at last having brought his emotions under some semblance of control, he stared directly at Kari. "Are you telling me that if I were hiding a secret, you wouldn't be upset with me? You would just say okay, let's forget it?"

"No, I would be upset if I found you were hiding a secret."

Good, he thought. He could tell he was getting to her. Just a little more and she would be slipping the ring back on her finger.

"Steve." She stood, slipping Jonathan's ring into her pocket and walked toward her fiancé, her hand outstretched holding his ring.

"You have every right to be upset with me. I should have told you about Jonathan the moment I knew we were getting serious."

"Why didn't you?" He was staring at her.

"Because it had been seven years. If I had never bought into that campground I would have never been sued, and Jonathan would have never reentered my life."

"Why did you two break up? You said something about your mother seeing him with another woman."

Kari smiled, this time a smile of sadness. She felt the dark cloud of grief seep into the marrow of her being. "You hate him, Steven, I saw it in your eyes and you hate me for having been with him. Why do you want me to tell you this now?"

His arms were around her before she had a chance to stop him. He was holding her tightly, so tightly she could feel the beating of his heart.

"I don't hate you, Kari. I won't lie, I hate the fact that you were with him, that you lied to me about it. But I don't hate you."

He kissed her forehead. "I want you to make me understand how you could have been with him after everything our people have been through. I want to know how you could make love to me knowing you had slept with him."

Inwardly, Steve was seething. Kari was right, he had no interest in hearing of her sleeping with anyone, but he was determined to make her follow through on her promise to marry him. Jonathan Steele would not win her.

Steve's breath was raspy. If possible, he was holding her tighter, making her want to move away. It wasn't love she was sensing from him or even desire. For some strange reason she felt he was holding onto her as he would one of his possessions he didn't want to lose.

His right hand slid up until it came to rest at the base of her throat. He applied slight pressure, not enough to cause her pain but enough to make her blink.

"I asked you a question. I suggest you answer."

She stared into his eyes before glancing down toward his hand at her throat. She glared at him, her look every bit as cold as his own. "Remove your hand."

She held his stare, refusing to speak until he took his hand away. He was still holding her close. Too close. She gazed into the depths of his eyes and saw something lingering that she'd tried on several occasions to ignore.

She exhaled long and loud, worrying her lips before continuing. "We broke up because the odds were against us. We were young. Jonathan's mother hired a woman to go after him, entice him. The woman talked him into posing for erotic pictures for magazines, then she brought the pictures to me, told me they were having an affair. When Jonathan refused to leave, she accused him of rape."

Kari leaned away from Steven, breaking the hold he had on her. For the first time since her breakup with Jonathan she was seeing things in a different light. For the first time she wasn't reliving something that had never happened. For the past seven years she had blamed Jonathan, thinking he'd lied to her. Nothing was as she had believed for all these years.

Steve interrupted Kari's remembrances. "How did she do that? You have to have proof."

"She had proof." Kari shuddered. "Oral sex. She kept the semen and used it when it became apparent he wasn't going to leave me."

"Didn't he have anyone who could alibi for him?"

"Yeah, me."

Steve looked at her. "If you loved him, why didn't you?"

"The pictures, they were awful." she paused. "I came home and found them together. Sharon was all over Jon. He threw her out, said she wanted to destroy us. I thought they were together, that he didn't love me, that he had only been using me to anger his parents."

"Is that what she told you?"

"Yes and so did everybody else, except Jon. He was the only one I didn't believe."

"How long was he in jail?"

"Seven months. I went to the jail twice to try and help him. His mother and Sharon, that's the woman's name, were there and things got ugly. No one was going to help Jon until I left town. Eventually I did. When he got out I was gone. I never heard from him or saw him again until the lawsuit in Missouri."

"Is that the reason you didn't want me to go? Did you think when you saw him you were going to want him back?"

"No. I thought I hated him. I knew he hated me. I thought the scene in Missouri would get pretty messy. I didn't want you to find out about this, at least not that way."

She walked closer to Steve. "I did try to tell you even before he came back. You never wanted to know about my past."

"There weren't any black guys in your college?"

"I didn't fall in love with Jonathan because of his color."

"Then why did you? What was it about him that made you forget who you were?"

Kari gave him a wan smile. "His love, Steve. He loved me. That was the reason I fell in love with Jonathan."

"I thought you said you didn't believe in his love."

"After three years of everyone whittling away at us, I guess I forgot the things I loved most about Jonathan."

"What?"

"His honesty, his loyalty, his gentleness. I allowed my own doubts and fears to eat away at me until I saw Jonathan as the man my parents saw."

"How could you put up with all the crap from the entire town?" He looked at her with some confusion. "How could you go against your family like that?"

"I think that was the hardest part. I missed my parents. Other than Jackie, Jonathan and I only had each other. By the time I thought he was pulling away from me, Jackie had moved. I had no one."

"I don't know if I could do that, Kari. To give up your entire family like that, be hated by both sides. I don't think the pain would be worth it."

"In the end that's what I thought too." Kari watched him, his face. She had been wrong in not telling him before. She didn't blame him for his anger. It was justified.

"You must have loved him a lot to go through all of that."

"I did. I went through it because I loved him, only in the end love didn't appear to be enough."

Steve studied Kari. Some of the anger had left his voice. The tenseness in his shoulder had eased just a bit, he could feel it. He had known for months that Kari was hiding something. He had to admit he had been afraid to find out what it was.

"Are there any more secrets?" he asked her, trepidation in his voice.

"No more." She licked again at her lips then returned the intense stare he was giving her, his eyes unwavering as though he could plum the depths of her soul. She held his gaze. "No more."

She would not tell him about the baby. That one secret remained hers and Jonathan's alone. How could she tell anyone about that until she had told Jonathan the truth? She held the ring out in her palm, pushing it toward Steve.

"Now you know."

He took the ring from her outstretched palm and placed it back on her third finger, left hand. "That's where it belongs. We'll work through this. I may not like it, but I'll try to understand it."

Like hell, he'd try and understand it. He never would understand how she could have done it. She spoke of loyalty, but where the hell was her loyalty to her race? Didn't she think she owed black men her allegiance?

He tilted her chin toward him so she was looking directly into his eyes. "Are you sure I'm the one you want, Kari?"

Kari closed her eyes and as always when she contemplated her future with Steven Anderson, she saw beautiful brown-skinned babies.

She wanted those babies desperately, the babies she couldn't have with Jon. She wanted those babies, enough to forgive Steven his look of horror. He was right. They would work it out.

"Yes, Steve, I'm sure."

Steve pulled away a little to peer into Kari's eyes. He smiled, then walked away from her. "If you want me, Kari, prove it."

He held his hand out, waiting, knowing if she took it she was taking him also. She did. He gave her hand a squeeze, steamrolling any objections, leaving her with no choice but to allow herself to be wrapped in his strong embrace.

"Give me the ring; I'll send it back for you."

"I don't have his address."

"You still have the address of the law firm, don't you?" He pulled back to look into her eyes, unsure whether he had her under control. "You're planning on seeing him again, aren't you?" he accused. He allowed his weight to be supported by the corner of Kari's desk. His hands were low on her hips, cupping her buttocks. "I don't want you to go."

"I know, but I have to do this." Kari reached up to touch her hand to his cheek. "Nothing's going to happen. I'll come back."

She saw the doubt in Steve's eyes and understood. Why wouldn't he worry after what he had witnessed? She moved her leg forward, brushing her thigh against his and felt the wetness in her panties from earlier, when Jon had...

That's why he's worried. There's reason to worry.

"Steve, Jonathan came to make amends for the hurts, the misunderstandings. He didn't come to win me back. He came with a peace offering. He only wanted to say goodbye, the way we should have before, not with me leaving without a word. I owe him the same. I need to tell him I'm sorry. If I don't, Steve, Jon will always be between us."

Kari's fingers moved in her pocket against the soft velvet. She decided to take a gamble as she lifted the box from her pocket. She held the ring toward Steve.

"You decide. You're going to be my husband so we need to start building trust now. I'll do whatever you say." She watched as he toyed with the box, his brows furrowing in deep concentration.

This was his chance. She was giving him the ball, acknowledging that he was the man, the one in control. He sucked on the inside of his jaw trying to gauge her response if he said, "Hell no." He thought of the things she loved about Jonathan. The bastard was probably sensitive as well. Okay, if she wanted sensitive, he'd give that to her. For now.

"Are you sure you're coming home?"

"I'm sure."

"Why?"

"I have someone to come home to. And Steve, one last thing. Don't follow me to Missouri."

"Is there any reason that I should?"

"No, Steve, none."

Her voice was soft, her eyes piercing his reservation. She moved closer, knowing what he wanted, what they both needed to hear.

"I love you, Steve."

"I'm going to make you forget about him. I promise."

He leaned down and kissed her, his tongue forcing her lips apart.

"Just tell me that you love me," she whispered into his mouth.

"I do," he whispered back into hers.

She gave herself over to his kiss, his touch, ignoring the screaming of her heart telling her it was not enough. She still had not heard him say the words she desperately needed to hear: "Kari, I love you."

CHAPTER SEVENTEEN

Jonathan stormed into his office angrier than he could ever remember being in his entire life. Enough mooning around like a lovesick teen. *I gave her the damn ring. I hope I never see her again.*

No sooner had the thought come, than he knew it for the lie it was. *I won't chase her, that much I can control. I've lived my life just fine without her.*

"Mr. Steele, I thought you were going to be out of the office for the entire day."

Jon turned and glared at his secretary. "Mrs. Dobis I'm not in the mood for sparing with you today. So I want to warn you. Don't start."

For the first time in a year and a half, Jon saw the woman back down slightly. She was glaring at him with as much intensity as always, but he almost thought he spotted concern in her eyes.

"Listen, I don't mean to bite your head off. I'm sorry." He watched as the woman cast a glance at the file cabinet, then back at him. That would be his only acknowledgment.

"Mrs. Dobis, if Kari Thomas calls me, tell her to go to hell."

A few hours later he found himself in bed with a woman he had slept with a dozen times in the past. With them there was no need for conversation, for a building up of passion.

They both used each other for release, no strings attached. It had been enough in the past. Tonight he repeated the act over and over and still found no release. Physical release yes, but it was no longer enough.

Jonathan punched the pillow, trying to make a hollow for his head. He thought of spending the night, but as he lay next to the woman whose body he had used for hours, he realized he had no reason to stay.

He didn't want to cuddle with her, to hold her in his arms and he sure as hell didn't want to spend the night. With that realization he pulled his clothes on hurriedly, not bothering to shower. She was sleeping, that was good. He wouldn't have to speak. He knew she didn't expect him to be there when she woke up. That made it easier.

ভ

For weeks Jonathan worked like a demon. Tim and Cassandra were beginning to avoid him. He was working too hard and wanting them to do the same. He understood their annoyance. He was working away his pain. They weren't.

He tried hard to push Kari from his mind, not believing she would come. He had spent a big chunk of his life waiting for her and twice she had managed to disappoint him. First, leaving him in jail, now—He sighed. What did he expect her to do? She was getting married, she didn't want him. She'd made that clear.

Jonathan shoved the file he was working on across his desk. He couldn't concentrate. Maybe he should buzz his secretary, needle her about something. He was almost glad when his silence was interrupted by his phone.

"Mr. Steele, Kari Thomas...

Jonathan glanced up at his ceiling, surprised that his thoughts had been turned into reality. After all the thinking he'd done about Kari, she was bound to call. His heart beat a little faster as he decided not to take her call.

"Mr. Steele," his secretary repeated. He didn't let her finish. "I told you if she calls, to tell her to go to hell."

There was a slight pause, then a muffled conversation. Jon wondered what the woman was doing. Then she spoke to him again.

"Mr. Steele, she didn't call. She's here, in the office waiting to see you. What do you want me to do?"

This was what he'd wanted, for her to come to him, but he didn't intend to make it easy for her. "Mrs. Dobis, have her wait twenty minutes, then send her in."

"But…but…," the woman stammered.

Again Jon stopped her. "Just do it. If she wants to leave, let her. Just don't let her in here for twenty minutes, not one second sooner." With that he hung up the phone. His palms were sweaty, so he rubbed them together.

What the hell are the two of us doing? We're playing games, acting like children.

Still he sat down to wait, his eyes glued to his watch as he sent mental commands to his feet not to move. Three times he had gone to her, the first time only to find her gone. The last two times they had fought. No, this time he would make her wait for him. He was through with trying to put an end to their pain.

For the first time since arriving at Jackson and Davis, Jonathan was not grateful for the thick oak office door. He wanted to hear what Elizabeth Dobis was saying to Kari. He wanted to hear if Kari was still there, but it was impossible to hear anything through the massive wood.

ᙟ

"Ms. Thomas, Mr. Steele asked me to have you wait. It might take awhile, he's busy." She looked toward her boss's door. "It might take as long as twenty minutes."

Kari knew the woman was curious. She smiled. "Don't worry, I didn't expect to go in immediately. I know how busy lawyers are."

She watched the secretary's reaction, her eyes telling her that Jonathan wasn't busy but had chosen to make her wait as she had done to him.

Kari smiled to herself. She thought she had let enough time pass so that he wouldn't still be angry. Evidently she hadn't waited long enough.

She spied the counter with the fixings for coffee and tea. "Would it be all right if I make myself a cup of tea while I wait?"

"Help yourself."

Kari took two cups and placed a tea bag in each before filling them with hot water. She carried one to the secretary. "I don't know what you take in it. I'll be glad to get whatever you need."

She saw the look of astonishment cross the woman's face and she looked around, wondering what was wrong.

"Is there a problem?" Kari asked.

"No. It's just... The secretary stopped and smiled a genuine smile at the beautiful black woman that her boss was keeping waiting. "I've worked here for twenty years and this is the first time anyone has ever given me a cup of anything. I do the fetching around here."

Kari was incredulous. "You're kidding. Not Jonathan, he's the kindest...She felt her face warming. "He's a real gentleman."

"Well, I've never seen that side of him."

The woman stopped and Kari knew she was wondering if Kari was going to repeat what she had said. She laughed to allay the woman's fears.

"Maybe Jonathan has changed, it's been a long time." She laughed harder. "After all, a real gentleman wouldn't make me wait out here while he pouts in there," Kari continued, laughing. This time Jon's secretary joined in.

Kari saw several people turn around to look at them. "What's wrong, you people don't laugh here?"

Elizabeth Dobis stopped laughing, but the smile remained on her face. "I don't laugh."

Kari stared at the woman, then at the women who were still glancing toward them. "If that's true, I'm glad that I was here to hear you. You have a wonderful sound."

This time the secretary looked away, her features twisted as though she was thinking of something.

"Kari Thomas. Your name sounds familiar. I think I've heard it before, but I don't recall meeting you."

"You haven't, your firm sued me several months ago." She saw the woman's puzzled look. "I'm sorry. I was part of the Resort suit. The ones sued in the federal bankruptcy court." For a moment Kari wondered why she was being so candid with a perfect stranger.

She saw the woman's eyes light up and knew she was more than likely the woman she had talked to months before, the one who'd offered her a dismissal without prejudice.

Her own smile dropped a little. The woman on the phone had seemed cold. This woman was warm, despite what her co- workers seemed to think.

"You became friends with Mr. Steele, after he sued you?"

Kari didn't blame the woman for being puzzled. "No, Jonathan and I...I've know him for almost eleven years."

"You were friends?"

"Yeah, we used to be friends, but it was a long time ago. I'm hoping we can get that back."

For a few moments neither spoke. Then the door to Jon's office opened and he stepped out.

"Ms. Thomas, you can come in now."

Kari turned toward Jon's secretary and smiled a secret smile between women.

"I'll be there soon," she said to Jon's retreating body. She watched him stop, knowing she had caught him off guard and intended to keep the advantage.

"Fine. Suit yourself." He slammed the door behind him but not before he heard Kari's laughter. *Damn that woman*, he thought.

Kari saw the amusement in the older woman's eyes. "What?"

"He's in love with you."

Kari turned away slightly. "How do you know that?"

"Because he's been working here for a year and a half and he's never looked at anyone that way. Besides," she chided gently, "I've been in love myself. I know what it looks like. What about you? Are you in love with him?"

Kari didn't understand why, but she felt a kindred spirit with Jon's secretary. She turned back to face her, her voice low and secretive. "I'll tell you, if you tell me something. You don't care for Jonathan. Why?"

Mrs. Dobis didn't hesitate. "It's not that I don't like him. Like I said, I've worked here a long time. New lawyers come and go all the time. To all of them, I'm only a fixture and they're only the people I work for, nothing more."

"Why?" Kari asked, startled. "Do you mean to tell me you've never had friends here at work?"

"I just prefer to keep my private life separate."

Kari was truly puzzled. "That can't be, you're a warm person." She looked at the woman and thought for a moment she was going to say more. When she didn't, Kari spoke. "Give Jonathan a chance. He really is one of the good guys."

"I'll keep that in mind. Now you were going to answer my question. "Are you in love with my boss?"

Kari held out her left hand displaying her diamond. "I'm engaged."

"That wasn't the question, Ms. Thomas."

"Okay, okay. I used to be in love with him."

Kari was saved from having to answer farther when Jonathan's head popped back out the door.

"It's been very nice talking with you, Mrs. Dobis." She smiled, then gathered up her belongings and headed for Jon's office.

CHAPTER NINETEEN

Kari closed the door, noticing Jonathan had positioned himself by the window with his long arms folded over his chest. She took a long look around the massive office, feeling pride at Jon's success.

He turned toward her, waiting for her to speak, though his eyes refused to meet hers. Kari smiled and walked toward him, a manila envelope in her hand.

"I would have come sooner but I know how you are when you're angry. I wanted to give you some time to cool off."

She waited until he looked at her. Then he was watching her so intently she felt the searing burn begin in her toes and work its way through every cell in her body. The room was crackling with their combined vibrations.

She sucked in her breath, knowing he was feeling the same things. Her free hand went to his ring in the pocket of her slacks.

"The ring's magnificent, Jon. I love it. I waited a long time to see this ring so I wanted to keep it for just a little longer before giving it back."

"You don't have to give it back. The ring was bought for you. I knew you would love it."

He smiled at her, a tiny little smile that pulled at the corners of her heart. She gave him an answering smile, grateful not to be lying to him or herself anymore.

She looked steadily at him, knowing without words he would understand what having the ring even for a little while had meant to her. He had loved her. As she had loved him.

"What's that?" he asked, catching sight of the envelope in her hand.

"It's the last barrier preventing us from getting past this," she waved her hand in front of her body and toward Jon, "this—hostility. Jonathan, you were right all along. We should have talked. This is my peace offering to you. I think it's time I let go of the pain and anger."

"Are those the pictures?"

For an answer she nodded.

"Why did you keep them?"

"Why did you keep the ring?" She pursed her lips, not wanting to start another argument. She decided instead to tell him the truth.

"The pictures were my insulation. Whenever I thought of you and was tempted to find you, I pulled out the photos and looked at them."

"So what do you want to do with them?" Just knowing that the pictures still existed made him feel ill.

Kari glanced at the envelope in her hand before looking again at Jon. "I think we should destroy them. It's symbolic, don't you think? After all, they helped to destroy us."

Was that sadness he heard in her voice? He wasn't going to push it.

"I have a shredder." He held his hand out and finally accepted the package. "Did you look at them again?"

"Yes."

"And?" he queried.

"And you were right. They were staged." She felt foolish. "I don't know why I didn't see that before."

"You believe me now? Even the picture where…"

"Where you," her voice dropped low, "let her make love to you? I took a good look at it after you left Chicago. I thought your eyes were glazed over with desire, but then I looked really close. I believe you when you say you were drugged."

Jonathan fed picture after picture into the shredder, not looking at them. There was a lump in his throat. When the last picture had been turned into confetti, he shredded the envelope.

"I don't think shredding them is enough," he finally said. "For all the pain these damn things caused, I think we have to do more."

"What?"

Kari waited. They had already destroyed the pictures. What more could they do? She watched as Jon picked up his phone and pressed the button, asking his secretary to bring matches.

She listened to him shout into the phone, "I don't care, find some."

She walked away from him. "I'm not the only one who's changed, Jon." She turned back to face him. "Why do you treat her like that?"

"She hates me."

"If you talk to her like that, I don't blame her." She ignored his glare. Pointing at the phone, she sighed. "That's not you."

The light knock on the door stopped her. She waited until the woman handed the matches to Jonathan and was about to walk out before she spoke again.

"That's a lovely blouse you have on, Mrs. Dobis. Do you mind if I ask where you got it?"

Kari could tell she had caught the woman by surprise and wondered if the camaraderie they had forged in the outer office would hold up in Jonathan's office.

Without turning from the door Elizabeth answered her. "I bought it at Peaches's, a little shop about three miles from here."

The woman had her hand on the knob of the door poised to leave when Kari asked, "Would you mind if I bought one like that for myself?"

She saw the blush of pleasure spread up the woman's neck before she answered, "No," and managed to scamper out of the room. Jonathan was watching her, not speaking.

She pulled the ring from her pocket. "It's lovely but I have to give it back."

She placed the box in his hand and stepped away. She had promised Steven nothing would happen. She intended to keep that promise and she would begin by keeping her distance.

Jonathan pocketed the ring and then struck the first match and threw it in the can. "I've never stopped loving you, Kari."

"I know," she answered him, marveling at how easy it was for him to tell her he loved her, even now, after all that had happened.

They stood side by side and watched the shreds catch and finally burn. Still Jonathan didn't stop throwing matches into the pile.

"What about you, Kari?"

"What difference does it make? No matter how it happened, our breakup was for the best. We both have our careers and new lives. Let's not complicate things."

She watched him as he turned toward her. He had the same look in his eyes that he'd had at eighteen and had kissed her for the first time.

She really couldn't tell who made the first move. It seemed to have happened in a flash. One moment she was remembering her promise to Steve, the next she was in Jonathan's arms, tears streaming down both of their faces.

"I love you, Kari. Please forgive me for hurting you."

His words made her cry harder. She wound her arms tightly around his neck. It might be too late, but she had to tell him.

"Jonathan, it should be me asking you for forgiveness. I

wasn't there for you when we lost the baby. You were grieving alone. I've always wanted to tell you I was sorry for that."

She held him tighter as she felt the vibrations of his body. She knew the memory of that night haunted him still as it did her.

"Jon, I didn't have an abortion," she sobbed into his neck. She felt him moving away.

"All of this time, why did you let me believe that?"

She could barely get the words out. "Because what I did was worse. I prayed Jonathan. I prayed to God to help me not have the baby."

She covered her eyes with her fingers as she felt his hands fall from around her. "Now you know why I couldn't share in your grief. It was my fault. You were right to blame me."

"Is that what you thought, that I blamed you? Why, Kari? Why didn't you tell me? I thought it was because you didn't trust me to take care of you, to take care of us. I would have. I would have done anything to keep us a family."

"That was part of it, Jon. I thought you were going to quit school. At first you were so happy, then about two weeks after I told you, you started disappearing. There were days when I didn't see you. Between school and work, there was no time for us.

"I thought you had changed your mind, that you didn't want a baby. When you stopped coming home, I thought—"

Kari's arms came up in a protective manner covering her body. She licked repeatedly at her lips, pulling on the top one with her teeth. She wanted not to cry. "I thought you'd changed your mind, that you didn't want me."

"My God, Kari, not want you? Everything I did, I did for us. I wanted the baby, Kari. I thought you knew that. I was working to make sure you could receive medical attention, that we'd be okay."

"Jonathan."

It finally hit her, the pictures. It was all so clear, everything she had been too blind to see. If only she had listened to him.

"That's why you took that job posing with Sharon, because I was pregnant?"

"We needed the money, we were going to have a baby. I was so happy, it took me a week to see that you were miserable. I thought that you were afraid, that you didn't trust me to look after us."

Jonathan crushed Kari to him, his own throat constricted with tears. "What have we done? Why didn't we talk?" He pulled away just enough to look into her eyes. "Are you ready to listen now?"

He saw her affirmative nod, then kissed away the tears that continued to flow down her cheeks. He was finally getting the chance to tell her what he should have told her years ago. *Maybe if I had told her before I did* it…,maybe *this would never have happened*.

He closed his eyes tightly, breathing in the essence of the woman he had always loved, wanting never to let her go. Now he had his chance and this time he would tell her.

"Sharon had tried to get me to pose for months," Jon began. "I always said no. When I found out we were going to have a baby I called her."

A violent shudder wrenched his body. He held on to Kari, never wanting to let her go. "I wonder if we had talked all of this through, if we would have been able to figure out my mother was behind it."

He couldn't stop the sadness that invaded his body and his words. For a long moment they looked into each other's souls, plumbing the depths.

"It seems we made our mistake because of our love, not because we didn't love enough. We were both so busy trying to protect the other that we forgot to talk."

Jon let Kari lie against him, feeling complete for the first time in years. He could feel the rapid pounding of her heart and knew she was still afraid of loving him, just as in the beginning. It wasn't going to be easy to get her to change, that he knew.

"Kari, you can't marry anyone else, not now. Not when we know the truth."

She pulled away. "Don't you see it doesn't make any difference? I didn't pray because I thought you couldn't take care of us. I prayed because I was worried that I wouldn't love our baby."

Her stomach was tightening in knots. "Your mother's face kept flashing before me and I thought, what if the baby looks like her? I know this sound awful but that's how I felt."

She brought her eyes to meet Jonathan's. "I knew it was wrong, but I couldn't help it, it was how I felt. Your mother hated me so much." She shuddered. "I didn't want the baby because I was afraid I wouldn't love it. If I didn't love the baby, then, I wondered, did I really love you?"

He had a puzzled frown, as if he couldn't follow what she was saying.

"Not love our baby? How could you have believed that? I know you, Kari. It would have been impossible for you not to love our child, you wouldn't have cared if the baby looked identical to my mother."

"How can you be so sure? I wasn't."

"Because I love you, I know. This time we'll correct all the mistakes of our past, we'll talk. You won't be afraid anymore, Kari."

"Jonathan, I'm going to marry Steve."

"I don't believe you. How can you possibly marry him now? We have a chance to make things right."

"We can't change the world. Besides, I love him."

He took her in his arms, felt her trembling, but she didn't move away. "That's a lie. I don't believe you." He tilted her chin upward. "Why are you trembling in my arms if you love another man as you say you do?" His eyes pierced her, demanding that she tell him the complete truth.

"Jon, I do love him. I love who he is. I can have the kind of life with him I could never have with you. With him my life is easy. I don't want to fight constantly, to put up with stares, with your parents hating me and mine hating you. I don't want people waiting and guessing what kind of babies we'll produce. I look at Steven and I see a good life. I see babies that look like me, babies I can love."

His hands loosened and she saw the pain in his eyes. This time she truly had not meant to hurt him. She had only wanted him to know the truth.

"Love isn't enough, Jonathan. It wasn't then, it's not now."

"I guess it's not." He looked at her, pity in his eyes and voice. "Not if we're not willing to fight for it."

"It's not worth it, Jonathan. We've been down that road before. Yes, I still love you, but as for spending the rest of my life fighting for that love…" She spread her hands out. "It's not worth it."

"I don't believe you, and I'm going to prove it to you," he said as he walked away from her. She watched as he locked his office door, picked up his phone and instructed his secretary to hold his calls.

"It's not going to happen, Jon," she said softly. "I'm not going to allow it."

"It's going to happen," he answered, as he came toward her, lust in his eyes. "It's going to happen and you knew that when you got on the plane and came here."

"Jonathan, I'm engaged."

"Walk away from Steve, Kari," he whispered in her ear as his fingers found the buttons to her blouse and began, one by one, to open them.

She was moaning softly, loving the feel of his hands on her body, needing him to touch her at that moment more than she needed air to breathe. Still she attempted to keep her word, her promise to her fiancé. "Jonathan, don't. It won't make any difference. I'm still going to marry Steve."

"Well, if you do, I'm going to make sure you know your body no longer belongs to him. And despite what you said, Kari, regardless of what you tell him, your heart never did. I'm the man you love, Kari, we both know it."

He slid the blouse down her shoulders, watching as it fluttered down her arms. Her hands moved up to stop him and he kissed them and continued. He buried his lips in Kari's honeyed skin, kissing the hollow between her breasts. He felt the tremors in her body, heard her whispering his name.

"It's going to happen, Kari," he repeated, and with one swift motion he'd discarded the blouse. His attention was on her, her body, the sight of her making him want nothing more than to enter her, take her, reclaim her as his own.   He closed his eyes for a moment. This wouldn't be fast, he'd take his time, he'd show her the difference between making love and having sex. He intended to make love to her, just as he'd done every night they'd been together. She was looking at him her eyes glazed over with passion. She was shivering.

"Are you cold?" he asked. "Let me warm you up." He kissed her bare shoulders and worked his hands around and down to the lacy bra she was wearing. He felt her nipples, hard and pebbled, through the flimsy material.

He was watching her watch him as his hand slid under the front clasp and he slowly undid the hooks. She was shivering even more. "I must not be doing a very good job of keeping you warm," he purred as he discarded the bra onto the floor with her blouse.

Jon couldn't resist. He took one of her warm nipples into his mouth. The first taste of her and something was unleashed that had been dead since she'd gone from his life. Tremendous shudders raced through him, forcing him to pull away. This would not be wham-bam-thank-you-ma'am. He was going to take his time.

For a long moment he stared at her, wanting to remember the sight of her. Her breasts, firm and luscious, again called to him. As he took her right nipple into his mouth, his hand fondled her left breast and he suckled her as if his life depended on it.

Kari felt the wetness running down her legs as Jonathan's mouth feasted on her. Her arms tightened around him. "Jonathan," she moaned, "Jonathan." His lips were burning her, scorching her skin. She felt her pants sliding down her hips, heard the soft swoosh, as they hit the floor.

She no longer wanted to stop him. Her very soul cried out for him, his touch, his love. She wanted Jon. She wanted what she'd craved for over seven years. Her hands grasped his buttocks. As he pushed her against the wall, her legs lifted, encircling his waist. He stumbled slightly, righted himself and moved closer.

His lips still on her breast, he made one quick move of his hand and ripped her panties away. Then his hand was between her legs rubbing her furiously, tenderly. As her tremors turned to shudders she loosened her legs from his waist and slid downward.

He inserted one finger into her moistness, then two. Her body tightened and she felt tremors gaining strength, building, as she tore at the belt to Jonathan's trousers.

"No," Jonathan whispered to her, "not like that." He fell to his knees. "I love you, Kari. He pushed her thighs open with his head and dove in, lapping at her juices, his hands caressing her buttocks, pulling her ever closer. She grabbed his head, shoving a fist into her mouth, to drown out the sounds of her pleasure.

"Oh, God," she moaned, "Jonathan, Jonathan." She gave up and surrendered to the ecstasy that was claming her. Her body, mind and spirit belonged to Jonathan and Jonathan alone.

It seemed to her that she was climaxing forever. Her body seemed to float. Then at last she returned to awareness, Jonathan's mouth was still between her legs, pressed against her wet warmth, and she was holding him, tears streaming down her face. He looked up at her at last, and she saw he too had tears.

"You're the only woman I've ever tasted, Kari, the only one I've ever made love to. Just you, no one before you, no one after you, everything in between was just sex for me. It's been so long since I've made love, Kari, how about you? Have you made love since me?"

For an answer she unzipped his pants and took out his engorged flesh. Her hands wrapped around him, feeling the wetness that streamed from his tip. She spread her legs and lifted her body on tiptoe to accept him. Her eyes closed in surrender as Jon's mouth once again closed over her swollen nipple. He paused for only a second, only to say, "Tell me, Kari, have you made love since me?"

"No," she moaned, feeling the heat fill her again, "not like this, not like this, never like this." He thrust himself into her, then reclaimed her lips. She tasted her own juices and cried inside her head, *"No, Jonathan, never like this.*

When he was done, they clung to each other. Jonathan was the one to break the silence. "I love you, Kari. We're not kids anymore. Look around you at how many interracial couples there are in the world. If you leave me, it's your choice. You'll be leaving me because you want to. And I'm not coming after you again." He pulled away from her, pulled up his pants and went to his desk to get tissues for her to clean herself up.

Her hand shook as she wiped away the traces of their love-making. *Why did he have to ruin it by talking?* she thought.

"I know. I know that you're not coming after me. I came only because I didn't want you thinking you had been a cause for me, Jonathan. I loved you with all my heart."

She looked at him, a grimace of pain on her face. "I guess it was the wrong time and wrong town. I think that's what made it impossible for us to be happy."

"I think you're wrong," he answered her. "I don't think it was the town. I think it was you. I never had a problem loving you. I didn't give a damn who didn't approve. As for our child, I was praying for a little girl that looked just like you. Remember, Kari, your mother hated me also. That never once made me doubt if I would love our child. I never wondered if our child would have her features. It never mattered to me."

He watched her, his heart filling with sadness for the truth she was continuing to deny. "I think maybe I loved you more than you could ever love me. I think, Kari, Lonett is in your blood." He touched her face lightly, wondering how long it would take him to get over loving her. He probably never would.

"I'm sorry if you feel that way, Jon." Determination for what she had to do stiffened her spine. "I came here to thank you for proving to me that I had not loved you in vain. I had to tell you how sorry I am for the past and return the ring." She walked even farther away from him.

She needed to not be so close if she was ever going to get the rest of it out.

"I also had another reason for coming to see you. I'm sorry if this hurts you, but I don't want to see you again. Ever." Especially after what just happened. I want you to be happy in your life, and to be happy for me, knowing I've made the right decision."

Her answer surprised him. He had not expected such bluntness. The pain of her words sliced through him. He wished it could eradicate the love he had for her, but it couldn't. Nothing could. He would always love her, but he was done with begging her to love him.

"You don't have to worry about me returning to Chicago." His voice was cold, uncaring. *I'd make a great actor*, he thought. "There was one thing I was wondering about, though. Don't you think the man you're going to marry should know that you're still in love with me?"

"He knows, but he also knows I would never go back to what we endured."

"Was it all so terrible for you?"

"Not all of it, but enough that I never want to do it again." Her voice was firm. She had made her decision.

"Steve's one of the same people who gave us looks and stares, Kari. I saw it in his eyes. He hates me. And it's not just because I'm an old boyfriend. He's the same sort I fought so many times." He stared unflinchingly at her. "You see, Kari, I thought we were worth fighting for."

She looked away, remembering the fights. Black men who thought she'd sold out had challenged Jon. White men hadn't liked it either. She remembered the bloodied noses and the bruises. She gazed at him, the pain of what he'd endured cutting at her. She ached for him, for both of them. She cringed, "Why on earth would you ever want to go through that again, Jon?"

"Kari, I loved you. I wanted nothing more than to spend the rest of my life in your arms, surrounded by a dozen or our children. You were worth it, Kari, every punch, every bloody nose, every hateful stare your parents gave me. Our love was worth it."

He watched her, knowing no matter what he said, she would not change her mind. He wanted to stop talking and kiss her into submission as he used to do. Instead, he said, "You're marrying Steve because he can give you babies you can love, the babies you don't want with me." She was looking at him strangely, and he knew she was wondering where he was headed.

He didn't doubt that one day she would have children. "What about your kids? What happens when they grow up and fall in love with someone who happens not to be black? Are you going to disown them the same as your parents did you?"

"Of course not," came Kari's terse reply.

"What about Steven? What's he going to do?"

He watched as her eyes widened slightly, knowing his words had hit the mark. Her heavy lashes fluttered twice, then came down to cover her eyes, shutting him out.

"You're marrying your father, Kari."

"You're wrong. I'm marrying a man my father approves of. There is a difference. Steve's young, he can change. I can help him change."

A sharp pain raced through her brain. She had never thought of her children's future with Steve for a father, just her own. Behind her closed lids she conjured up the images of the brown-skinned babies she would have with Steve. She had to have those babies. She had to make it up to the other one. She would give all the love she had to those babies, and maybe she would be able to forgive herself. She would worry later about the future of her unborn babies.

She glanced at her watch. "I should go now, Jonathan."

"I'll drive you to the airport."

"You don't have to do that."

"Don't worry, it's the least I can do for an ex-girlfriend." A look passed between them. "That is all you are to me, isn't it? Just an ex-girlfriend."

Kari didn't answer him. Instead, she headed out of his office for the elevator, stopping only long enough to say goodbye to Jon's secretary.

As they waited for the elevator doors to open, Jon stood as far away from her as he could. *It almost ended on a positive note*, she thought. The tension between them still crackled with electric impulses. It was much like their passion. Only not as pleasant.

She followed him to his car without a word between them. He was asking for something she no longer wanted to give. *But oh God, it sure sounded good to hear someone tell me how much he loves me.* She shivered in her seat and leaned even closer to the door of the car. A short ride and it would all be over.

CHAPTER NINETEEN

An emotional silence filled the car until Jonathan suddenly veered off of the expressway and headed for a mall on his left. In response to the question in her eyes, he said, "I'm taking you to Peaches', for the blouse. Do you really want it or were you just being nice to Mrs. Dobis?"

"I want it. Thank you for going out of your way. I didn't expect to put you out."

Jonathan gritted his teeth at their formality. They had been through hell and back. It should have brought them closer together, yet here they were behaving like two perfect strangers, each vowing never to lay eyes on the other ever again.

He maneuvered as close as he could to Peaches's entrance. Together they walked into the store not speaking. It would have been hard for anyone to tell they were even acquainted.

Jonathan looked through the open door of the shop and spied a music store. "Listen, you take your time, I see a store I need to go into. I won't be but a minute." Without waiting for an answer he took off in the direction of the music store.

When he returned he saw Kari had found the blouse and was standing at the register. He waited. Since there were two idle employees behind the counter, Jon knew the purchase would take only a minute. He absently watched Kari, not wanting to believe he would never see her again.

When he heard her say, "Excuse me," he focused his full attention on the clerks. The male employee snapped, "Just a minute." The female didn't even acknowledged Kari.

Jon looked at his watch, wondering how much time had passed. Several minutes, he was sure.

Kari glanced toward him and he saw embarrassment in her eyes. Seven years ago she would have never stood for such blatant disrespect.

He felt angry. Angry at the world they lived in. Angry at Kari for accepting such treatment. Jon walked to the counter. "Excuse me," he barked, his voice loud, bristling with anger.

Immediately both the male and female employee turned to him. "May we help you, sir?"

Jonathan could feel the blood racing up the back of his neck. He pointed toward Kari. "This lady has been waiting here for some time. Do you ever plan to help her?"

When the cashiers looked in Kari's direction, disdain showed clearly on their faces. Several seconds passed before the woman went to Kari. She offered no apology, just took the blouse and began to ring it up.

Jon glared at Kari. "Why the hell are you still going to buy that?" He was holding her arm, preventing her from reaching into her purse.

He wanted her to demand an apology, demand to see the manager, all things she would have done seven years ago. Instead she gave him a sad wan smile.

"Jonathan, if I never bought clothes, jewelry, or cosmetics because of this kind of treatment I would buy nothing." She cocked her head. "Welcome to my world, Jon."

Before she could take out her wallet, Jonathan paid for the blouse. If she was going to have it, he'd damn well not allow her to pay for it herself. His rage was boiling over and he was tempted to throw it in their faces. But Kari was walking away toward the door, so he followed her instead.

"That's not me Kari. It never was. Leaving me, you're attempting to make me pay for crimes I never committed. Maybe you're right. Maybe we shouldn't be together. But it's you who has always had a problem with the color of my skin, not the other way around. Just you remember that."

"Jonathan, I guess I shouldn't blame you for not understanding. You're not black. You've never been denied a damn thing because of the color of your skin. You think the blouse's a big deal. It's not, Jonathan. You've never had to live with prejudice, so you wouldn't know. I'll tell you what, Jon, try being a black man, try to catch a cab. Then tell me if you're so all fired ready to take on the world."

He looked at her and made a decision. They would not leave it like this. He took the next exit off the expressway and headed away from the airport.

"Where are you going?" Kari asked.

"I'm taking you to my home. We need to talk. There's too much left unsaid."

He said nothing else until he pulled into his drive, got out and opened the door for her. "You're right, I can't pretend to know what a black man has to go through, but am I responsible for it, Kari?"

She thought of her parents, of Steve, and she knew what their answer would be. But their answer wasn't hers. She didn't blame Jon for not being black. "No, Jonathan, you're not responsible."

"Then why? Tell me why you're marrying Steve, Kari, make me understand."

"It's just easier, Jon. Steven can relate to me and I can relate to him on cultural issues you'd never understand. You take your life for granted, Jon. You go where you want, no questions asked, no one clutching their purses closer simply because you walk down the street. You can walk into a jewelry store and not be watched like a hawk. Steven's a doctor, he has plenty of money. Do you think he can do that? Do you think every time he hails a cab he gets one to stop, even in his expensive clothes? You told me to open my eyes, why don't you do the same? For all your good intentions, the world is divided, Jon, into black and white."

Jon stood for a moment looking at her, anger, then sadness, filling his veins. "What do you see when you look at me?" He walked closer to her, ripping the buttons from his shirt as he pulled it off his body.

He held his arms out in front of her. What do you see when you look at me, Kari? What do you want me to do?" His eyes fell on a small vase of pens and he reached for one, handing it to her. "Here, Kari, color me black. Will that make you happy, will you be able to love me then?"

"Jon, please," she was crying, "don't."

"Kari, I don't understand what you want from me. You say *don't*, but *don't* what? *Don't* love you, *don't* acknowledge that yes, my skin is white? So what? *Don't* ask for a reason why you can't just love me? Or is your *don't* saying, *don't* expect you to love me unconditionally, as I love you?"

She threw the pen down. Her hands went to his face and she held it. "Jonathan, I love you."

"Just not enough, right, Kari?" He turned to walk away from her but she grabbed his arm. He turned back to her, his pain evident in his eyes, twisting his features. "I would give anything to be what you want, Kari."

That was her undoing. She'd tried to be hard, to not love Jonathan with everything that was in her. She'd tried to keep her heart out of it and had failed miserably. His pain was tearing her apart. She fell in his arms, clinging to him. "I do love you, Jon. I always will." She bit her lips, wishing things could be different, knowing in her heart she was about to betray one man, just not sure which. "You made love to me, Jonathan, now let me make love to you."

"That's not all that I want from you, Kari."

"It's all that I can give, Jon. Let me love you. For right now, let me believe as you do, that our love is enough."

He wanted to protest, to tell her that with her it wasn't enough for him to simply make love to her body. But she was touching him as only she could, and she was crying. She was hurting, as much as he was. He wanted to put an end to their pain.

He lifted her in his arms and carried her to his bedroom. He closed the blinds to hide the dwindling light, sealing them in near darkness. "Is this better, Kari? Will the darkness make it easier for you to love me?"

She ignored his words, forgiving him for them the moment he spoke them, knowing he didn't mean them, that he only wanted to make her stay. "Lie back, Jon, let me love you." She trailed kisses down his belly.

"I want more," he moaned into her hair. "I want all of you." But he didn't push her away. She stroked every inch of his thighs, going between to tease, to tantalize. When she was about to take him in her mouth, he stopped her. She looked up into his eyes wondering why.

"Have you?" he asked.

"No," she replied, "you're the only man I've ever tasted. I told Steve no when he asked me to do it."

"Are you lying to me?"

"No, Jonathan." She took him in her mouth, trying to lick away the hurt as she licked away the juices that flowed from him. She felt his shudders. "I'm not done," she whispered in the darkness when he

213

tried to pull her up. "Let me finish." And she began anew to stroke him, kissing him, loving the firm hardness of him in her mouth.

She couldn't get enough of him and when he came she didn't turn away. When he was spent, he reached for her again, pulling her upward into his arms. He touched a finger to her lips, wiped away the wetness and kissed her long and deep, taking her to another world, another place.

Kari lay in Jon's arms, loving him, all of him, not wanting to leave him, not knowing if she'd have the strength, not wanting to worry about it until she had to.

"Marry me, Kari, be my wife. Let's rectify our past mistakes." She cut off his words, kissing him, crushing him to her. He noticed and allowed her her ruse.

He made love to her slowly, knowing that this had to last him the rest of his life. He kissed her tenderly, then licked her breasts in worship, his hands touching her every place at once.

He entered her, moving to match the erotic sensations, the friction of the two of them nearly sending him over the edge. He kept his eyes fastened on her face. He was home. "Kari, tell me what you're feeling right now, at this moment." He saw her close her eyes, watched as she swallowed, knowing she didn't want to answer. "Kari, tell me."

"I feel complete," she answered at last. I feel like I've been somewhere lost in a bad dream and now I'm awake, and I'm home and I'm safe. You and me, Jonathan, it feels so right. I know it, my heart knows it. But—"

He thrust into her, felt her body convulsing, her muscles tightening around him. Then it hit him with the force of a sledge hammer, his climax was rumbling up from his toes rolling through him and he wasn't ready. He pulled out of her, panting, the power of what was happening to his body claiming him still. It was going to happen without or without him being inside of her. He preferred being inside her sweet warmth.

Jon held out as long as possible, not wanting it to end, trying to make his loving her body last an eternity. His erection was so hard that it was pressing against her belly, straining to return to her moistness.

And he did. Moving slowly in her, he rose above her. In the light that filtered in through the blinds, casting shadows across her belly, he could barely make out his own hand. He wanted to see her, see her face, as he made love to her.

Jon carefully reached for the lamp switch, though there was no way in hell he would ever slide out of her. He was so swollen he could feel himself stretching her. He felt the switch and flicked the light on.

"Thanks," Kari murmured and smiled at him.

He smiled back. "I just wanted you to know that it was me making love to you."

"I know, Jon," she moaned. "You're the gift I'm giving myself. You, my love, have my heart and my soul. Always, Jon," she moaned before he thrust faster, not wanting to hear her next words.

He thrust himself in deeper, feeling her climax, her nails raking his back. She screamed out his name and still he held on, not wanting it to be over.

When he came at last, it was seven years of pent up emotions. He lifted Kari from the bed, holding her until she was almost sitting in his arms, no longer lying on the bed. He buried his lips in her neck, growling with an intensity he'd never felt before. He felt her shiver as he held her to himself. "Did I hurt you?" he asked.

"No," she answered, a smile on her face. Then she buried her head in his shoulders and he rose to immediate attention and entered her again.

"This is where you belong, Kari, here in my bed, in my arms with me buried deep inside you." He moved in circular motions, pulling back every time he sensed her getting close. The first climax had taken him by surprise with its force, this time he wanted to control it, pace it. Kari's eyes were open wide, her hips undulating, grinding against him. She was thrusting her hips with all her might, trying to get him to go deeper, faster, harder.

"We're going to enjoy this, Kari."

"Are you saying you didn't the first time?"

"Hell no," he groaned and pushed himself into her, giving her what she wanted, what they both wanted. "I just want it to last forever, that's all, baby."

"Jonathan I'm so close, I don't know how long I can hold out," she moaned.

With those words, Jonathan pumped faster, burying himself deep within her. He felt her nails digging into him as ripples of pleasure shot through Kari's torso, and her features contorted in lust. "Don't close your eyes," he whispered, "I want to watch you."

Her juices ran over him hot and wet cleansing away years of hurt, years of denial. She belonged to him and he to her. "Jonathan," she moaned.

Hearing her, he came again, the second time, more powerful than the first. He'd thought he was ready, that he was prepared. He was anything but. It felt as if his insides were pure liquid fire. Pleasure beyond anything he'd ever felt was coursing through him. As his body jerked he held tightly to Kari. Hip to hip they were locked in the all-consuming passion of their bodies. When it was over they were locked in an all-consuming passion of their hearts.

They made love until they no longer could. The two of them lay on his bed looking at each other, knowing the thoughts that were in each other's minds.

Kari turned suddenly, spooning her body into Jon's wanting to feel him everywhere. His penis now soft but still warm was pressed against her buttocks and she ground herself into him and heard him moan.

With one hand he reached around and pulled her even closer, then inserted his fingers back inside her body. Her moan came out as a laugh and she turned back to face him, wondering how on earth he'd managed to keep his fingers inside of her when she'd turned.

With Jonathan's fingers sending little waves of electrical pleasure through her, she wrapped her hand around his limp penis, neither of them wanting to break their connection.

"God, how I love you, Kari. I've missed you."

"I know, Jon." She bent her head to kiss his chest, taking his small hard nipple in her mouth, flicking her tongue back and forth, delighting in his shudders.

"I don't think I can go again," he said as his fingers moved even deeper inside her, wanting to imprint the feel of her on the tips of his fingers.

"I know, I just want to taste you so I can—"

"I know," he completed, "so you can remember." He then did as she was doing, used his tongue to store the taste of her. He licked his way from her neck to her belly, and to his surprise, he once more began to harden. He flipped over on his back, pulling Kari onto his new erection.

True to her word, she made love to him, her soul mating with his to make him whole once again. "Jonathan," she screamed out, and he moved into a sitting position, holding her buttocks firmly in place with his hands.

Spasm after spasm shook her and traveled to him. She held on, never wanting to leave him, leave his bed, his love. "Jonathan," she whispered loudly, "it's always been you." Together they fell backward to lie on the bed, both knowing no matter how much they wanted it, it would take time before they could go again.

Her face was buried in his chest, his sweat stinging her eyes. She kissed his wet chest, little butterfly kisses that were meant to convey her love. His arms were wrapped around her, binding them together.

"How are you going to be able to let him touch you after tonight? You're going to be living a lie, Kari, and even though I think he's a racist bastard, no man deserves to have a woman lying beneath him whose body craves the touch of another man.

His words brought her back to reality. She would have to leave now or she never would. She attempted to raise up but Jonathan held her in place with his hands, his eyes probing her. "Are you going to allow him to make love to you after tonight, Kari?"

She lay back against his chest, the first waves of guilt washing over her. She was what she'd accused Jon of being, a cheat. Only she didn't know who she'd cheated on.

"Jon, I won't lie to you. I wanted you from the moment I saw your name on that summons. I wanted what we had." She shivered and this time it wasn't out of desire. "I never thought I'd ever be unfaithful, that I'd cheat on the man I was going to marry."

"You didn't cheat on Steve, Kari. You cheated on me, every time you slept with him. I should be the one you're with. If you go through with this nonsense I hope every time he touches you that it's my name you moan into his ear."

"Do you really think it's going to be that easy for me, that I don't realize what I've done? Jonathan, this is harder than you'll ever know. The thought of looking into Steven's eyes, knowing what I've done... She shivered again. You cheated because you were drugged. What's my excuse? What will I use to help me live through what I've done to Steve?" This time she succeeded in rolling off Jon.

He'd loosened his hold. "Couldn't you have let me loving you be enough, Jon?"

"No, Kari, because it isn't enough. Was this enough for you?" he asked.

She didn't answer, how could she? No, it wasn't enough but it was all that she could have if she wanted those babies. And she wanted them with everything that was in her. For the first time in a long time, Kari didn't want to shower after making love. She wanted to carry the scent of Jon home with her, on her body. But that would be suicide.

"Can I use your shower?" she asked. He merely looked at her, not answering. She knew what he was thinking, that she was a coward for not following her heart. He had no way of knowing that for her, leaving him was the bravest thing she'd ever do.

For Jon, the thought of Kari leaving his life again was more than he could bear. For the first time in all those lost years, he was home. He'd always been home in Kari's arms and he didn't want to lose that. Not again.

"Do you really think washing away my scent is going to fool Steve? He's going to know you've been with me. You sure as hell don't have the energy to go again, not even to fake it."

Had he shouted at her, maybe she would have felt angry, but he was talking softly, his eyes never leaving her face. Kari was aware what he was doing. She didn't even blame him.

"Kari, what would you call a woman who went from one man's bed to another?"

His voice remained soft, but that remark hurt. She turned toward him, "If your goal is to hurt me, Jon, don't worry, you succeeded. You don't have to beat up on me, Jon. You know me, I'll do it myself."

"Kari…

"I know," she answered as she stepped into the shower. "Just stop now, okay?"

Jon stood outside the bathroom hating his cruelty. If it had worked, perhaps he'd hate himself less, but it hadn't. His words had hurt her, and he'd just ruined things. He thought of joining her in the shower, just to hold her, tell her that he was sorry, but he didn't think either of them could take it. Instead, he walked up to the shower and pressed his hands against the door.

"Kari, I'm sorry."

"I know."

"I love you, Kari."

"I know," she answered. "And I love you."

CHAPTER TWENTY

In silence they drove to the airport. There, Jonathan ignored Kari's instruction to drop her off in front of the terminal. If this was going to be the last time he was with her, he sure as hell wasn't about to drop her off as though he were a taxi driver. He aimed the car in the direction of the parking garage. They would take the airport shuttle.

"Jonathan, there's no need for you to go to so much trouble. You can't go to the gate with me. You know it's no longer allowed, not since the terrorist attack."

He waited until they were on the shuttle before he answered her. He gazed at her, feeling the heat from her body as it pressed against him in the cramped seats.

"My seeing you off, Kari, is something I need to do for myself. As for thinking of this as trouble, it's not. I love you."

He watched her, saw her swallow back more tears. She was afraid. He knew it. There was nothing he could do about that. He reached for her hand and held it, feeling the pain choking him.

When they entered the building, he turned questioningly to Kari. "Don't you have to exchange your ticket, didn't you miss your flight?" Her no, was spoken so low that if she had not also shaken her head, he would not have known for sure. She'd known all along they would make love. Why else would she have taken such a late return flight?

With a glance at Kari he proceeded to the ticket counter to buy a ticket for himself.

Kari watched him in disbelief. Jonathan was buying a ticket just in order to be allowed past the check in and the signs declaring,

ONLY TICKETED PASSENGERS BEYOND THIS AREA. She took in his profile, his stoic jaw. *Oh God*, she prayed, *give me the strength to leave this man I love.*

They walked side by side in silence to the gate. Once there, Jonathan sat across from her deliberately, so he could glare at her. His heart was about to explode with the pain. Glaring at the woman he loved was the only way he could survive her leaving him once more, and this time for good.

"Flight 532 now boarding for Chicago."

The words sounded louder to him than usual. He stood, not knowing what to do. He wanted to take her in his arms and beg her not to go but he couldn't. He had promised her. He watched her reach for her purse and the peach-colored bag from Peaches's containing her blouse. He saw her lips twitching and almost turned away. She was on the verge of tears.

How can she leave me again? She's killing me. He blinked, then closed his eyes briefly to relieve some of the anguish. She was in front of him, standing so close, her eyes brimming with pain. He shoved his hands in his pockets to keep from reaching out to her.

"I guess this is really goodbye." He tried to sound cheerful. He didn't want her to know how much he was hurting, how the mere thought of her returning home to love someone else was tearing him apart.

"I guess so," she answered, not making any move toward the plane. "Jonathan, would you mind very much telling me again that you love me?" The tears she was holding spilled over. "Steve's not very good at saying it," she confessed. "I know he loves me, but..." She looked away from Jonathan's eyes, not wanting to explain further. This was hard enough.

With her request went his last bit of strength. He drew her into his arms, kissing her lightly at first, then deeper, wanting to make the kiss last them both a lifetime.

Her tears were running faster and faster down her cheeks. He released her only to lovingly cup her face in the palms of his hands. Then he kissed her tears as he had done before.

"I love you, Kari. Telling you that is not a favor, it's a statement of fact." Once again he closed his eyes. He was about to break his promise to her. How the hell could he just let her leave again without trying to stop her? "You don't have to do this, Kari."

He watched her biting her lip, knowing she was trying to stick to her resolve to leave him. He tried again. "Kari, if you have to marry a black man, why can't you find one that's not a racist?"

Kari swallowed. She had to remain strong. She truly believed she was doing the best thing for both of them. "Jon, don't worry about me. I'm going to be fine."

"No, you're not," he answered, "not without me." He was standing so close to her about the do the one thing he'd sworn he wouldn't do. "Kari, don't leave me, please. I'm begging you, stay with me, Kari, marry me. I love you, Kari."

She pulled him to her, gave him a hug that should have broken his back, then placed a soft kiss on his lips. "Be happy, Jon." She released him and started to walk away.

"Kari." When she turned back toward him, he held out the package from the music store. "This is for you."

She took it as she wiped away her tears. "I do love you, Jonathan Steele, please believe that." She wanted to make him smile, she smiled at him. "Just think Jonathan, no more fighting anyone because you love me. If nothing else, our parents will be happy." It didn't work. He didn't find her attempt at humor amusing. "I love you, Jon." With that she ran toward the plane, not daring to look back.

Aboard the plane Kari peeped into the bag. A small cassette player with a pair of headphones was inside. She lifted the object from the bag for a closer look and saw there was a tape inside the cassette.

She placed the earphones over her head, pressed the button and listened.

Words of love, betrayal, hurt and anger came to her. At first she didn't know why Jonathan had given her that song, until she heard the words.

It was Eric Clapton proclaiming that his life was nothing without the one he loved. The song drenched her heart with memories from the first day she had met Jonathan Steele.

Different images flooded her brain in rapid fire succession: the two of them studying in the group, finding the rented house that they loved and moving in together, laughing, talking into the darkness about their future plans. She thought of their garden, the two of them planting and weeding together. Always together. And Jon climbing the trees to loosen the nuts for those awful pies he made. She was drowning in the memories of a life she wished she could return to. But it had been real! It wasn't some cruel joke, some quirk. She had loved him. He had loved her.

She continued listening to the silky voice of Eric Clapton. It was as if he had known them and had written about their life. Her heart was breaking.

She summoned up the image of her perfect circle of brown-skinned babies. And she prayed those babies would help her forget Jonathan Steele and her love for him.

Then she put on the call button and asked the flight attendant for some thing for a headache. When the woman returned, Kari had found another of the pills Steven had given her. She took it, along with the pills the flight attendant gave her. She'd betrayed two men and her was breaking-for them and for herself.

CHAPTER TWENTY-ONE

Kari spotted Steve waiting for her. For some reason she had known he would be. He'd questioned her reason for taking a late flight back. *Get it over with*, she thought as she walked toward him. She didn't try to hide the fact that she had been crying. She couldn't, even if she had wanted to. The sound of Eric Clapton reverberated through her mind over and over.

She was making the right decision. She had to believe that. Her place was with Steve. She would be happy and she would do her best to make sure he was happy too. They would build a good life together. Twice her knees buckled and she nearly fell. She wanted to think it was the pills she'd taken on the plane, or the drink after, but she knew the truth.

Her guilt was pressing down on her; it was wrong what she was about to do. She knew it with every fiber, in every membrane. Steve deserved so much better. *I'll make it up to him*, she thought, *I'll be a good wife. I promise God, just let me get through tonight and I'll be everything Steve deserves, the kind of woman he wants. I promise.*

And Jonathan, please lord give him a good life.

Steve's left eyebrow quirked upward as he eyed her coming through the door. There was a question there, the worry from before not quite receded. She pasted a smile on her face and walked toward him.

He was watching her, his eyes sharp, concentrating on her face. She gave him a light kiss on the lips, but he held her tightly, kissing the crevice of her neck, wanting it all.

"You've been drinking," he said, holding her so he could look into her eyes. "Did something happen, Kari? Is there something you need to tell me?" He looked her over. "There was no need for you to stay so many hours in Missouri. It didn't take that long to return a ring."

"I told you that Jonathan and I needed to say goodbye. We needed to talk, to understand what happened and let it go. We needed to put the past behind us. Jonathan is behind me, Steve. I came home like I promised." Her legs were trembling so hard she was surprised she could stand. *God forgive me*, she prayed silently, *please forgive me*.

She found her arms going around his neck, wanting to reassure him as much as herself that she was making the right decision. Without preamble the tears resurfaced.

Steve held her, letting her cry over another man, her head firmly planted on his chest, wetting his shirt with her tears.

For several minutes he said nothing. Then he gave her the silk handkerchief from his jacket pocket, evidently his signal to turn off the waterworks

"You know this really is for the best. It would have never worked out. We really should stick to our own kind, Kari. We'll put this out of our minds. You were young, you made a mistake."

He pushed her away then, not roughly but with an air of admonition. She waited for whatever was coming. His stance, his eyes, the placement of his hands on her forearms warned her that it would not be good.

"This is the last time I expect to see you crying over another man. I want to marry you. I think we'll be good together. But I will not put up with your cheating on me." He paused, then added, "Even if it's only in your heart."

Kari opened her mouth to answer but was silenced by Steve gently placing a finger on her lips, his eyes dark and brooding. He wasn't finished.

"This is your decision. You make your choice now. It's me or Jonathan! If it's me, I never want to hear his name again. I don't want to look in your eyes and see regret, guilt or disappointment. It's up to you. Do you want a future with me?"

"Yes," she answered. "I—"

He stopped her. Enough of being the nice guy. If she was going to be his wife, they had to set some ground rules. "Are you willing to accept my conditions?"

Kari wanted to laugh. It sounded more like a merger than a marriage, and in a way for her it would be. She bit her lips, willing the laughter to go away. Steve was in no mood for levity.

"I accept. Jonathan will never invade our lives again, in any form."

"Good." He kissed her on the forehead before taking her hand and leading her to the car.

Phase one was complete. Steven smiled to himself as he led Kari toward his car. He'd given Kari every opportunity to back out, call off the wedding.

She wasn't a stupid woman. She knew what she'd agreed to. He was the man, he would be the head of the home. What he needed in his home was an obedient wife.

Kari would be that and more. His parents would approve. She would give him babies, lots of babies. It didn't hurt either that she was beautiful and good in bed.

In that area he had plans also. He'd keep her too damn busy fulfilling his needs to leave her any time to moon over that lawyer.

He glanced down at her. Yes, she knew what he was demanding of her. She'd agreed.

♋

This is my choice, Kari thought as she followed Steven out the door. This is the life I want, no other. Steve is the man I want. This is not his decision. It's mine.

She wanted to be clear on that in her own mind. Jonathan's telling her she had changed, his disappointment in her for not standing up for herself in Peaches's still burned.

Jon doesn't understand. She held tighter to Steven's hand. Steve's right. Unless you live your life inside of this skin you can't possibly understand.

She would do as she had promised. She would push her memories and Jonathan to the farthest corner of her mind, lock them away and never examine them again.

With her resolve came a chill. She felt as if she'd just made a deal with the devil, sold her soul. The agreement she'd made with Steven was much more than the words they'd used to identify it. She could only pray that she could live up to it.

Later that night Kari lay beneath Steve's muscular brown body doing her best to reassure him of her commitment to their marriage. She ran her fingers over his skin complimenting him, admiring his physique. She had done everything but stand on her head and juggle to let him know he had pleased her. Still she could sense the doubts.

He had insisted she keep her eyes open. With every thrust he looked deeper into her eyes, as though he were capable of penetrating her very soul.

Kari was acutely aware of what he was doing. He was determined to drive thoughts of Jonathan from her heart and body. She wanted to explain that the relationship she had shared with Jonathan had transcended sex.

Oh yeah, Kari, that's just the thing your fiancé needs to hear while he's making love to you.

She had promised that she would never mention Jonathan or think about him. God, she was really trying. She wished she could accomplish that. A crazy thought came to her. Maybe she should ask Steve, get his opinion on how she should get over loving Jonathan. But she couldn't, not in a million years.

Instead, Kari clung to him, her mouth partially open, moaning as he moved around inside her. She ran her nails down his back and side, pretending nothing was wrong.

He began to move faster and faster, beating a rhythmic pattern in her body. When he grasped her head in his hands and pulled her forward she knew his mind was no longer on Jonathan but his own pleasure. His primal grunting followed by his spasmodic convulsing told her she had played her part well. She would continue to do so.

The last thing in the world Kari had wanted that night was to make love. *Hell*, she thought, *if I pull it off under these conditions, imagine what will happen when I truly forget how much I love Jonathan?*

In the following days, Kari threw herself with gusto into the last minute details of planning a large wedding. For each setback she said a prayer of thanks. Taking care of the smallest details and resolving problems gave her no chance for thinking.

The hardest task had been the counseling with the minister. After that was finished and he gave them his seal of approval, his blessing as it were, Kari walked out of the office feeling her soul convicted by the information she'd withheld from the man who was going to make her union with Steve not only legal, but holy before God.

She debated going to him privately. What if she did and he refused to marry them? And if Steve found out, he would never forgive her for telling. Her past was now supposed to be this dark mysterious secret that she had been forgiven for.

Kari knew part of her indecision came from being tired. Steven was waking her every night, three or four times, to make love. She couldn't remember the last time he had stayed in his own apartment. He was behaving as though he were a man on a mission. One night she had actually yelled out, "Mission accomplished."

She had surprised herself, but he'd liked it. He fell asleep sprawled across her, and she heard him mumble in a sleepy voice, "You're mine." She wished the words had been, "I love you." Another disappointment she would have to get over.

∞

Since Kari's visit, Jonathan had spent part of each night lying in bed awake, for the first time reliving his life without the anger. For a long time they had been happy. He would hold on to that memory and cherish having it.

At long last he took out of his wallet the one crinkled photo of Kari that he owned. He found a frame, matted it himself and stuck the picture in, sealing it behind glass. He placed the framed photograph on the nightstand beside his bed. His anger was gone.

For seven years he had lived without her, an unbearable ache always clawing at him. Whenever the wanting had threatened to erupt, he had tamped it down by remembering Kari's betrayal. But now he knew there had been no betrayal. What would he use now to make himself live without her?

He didn't dismiss Kari's fears. Hatred and prejudice were alive and well in America. He'd lived through three years of it with her. If only he could make it all go away, make color not matter. But he couldn't.

∞

Jon showered and dressed quickly, grateful to have a full work load waiting at the office. The moment he arrived he realized there was an undercurrent of excitement. People was laughing together in little groups. The only person whose demeanor had not metamorphosed was his secretary, Elizabeth Dobis.

"Good morning, Mrs. Dobis, what's going on?"

He noted the woman's hard look. At first he thought she wasn't going to answer, then her voice came out gravely. His first thought was there was something wrong with the woman, because she almost sounded as if she were in agony.

"You'll find out soon enough."

Jon started to say something more, then changed his mind. He headed instead to his office. He didn't get a chance to sit before Cassandra and Tim burst in, their faces aglow with excitement.

"What's going on?" Jon came from behind his desk and stood in front of his friends and co-counselors. "Let me in on the good news."

Tim slapped him on the back in a show of camaraderie. "You're free." He laughed hard. "You're free, man. Enjoy it."

Jon felt his fist clench involuntarily. He was a second from slugging Tim. "What the hell are you talking about?" He watched the puzzled looks exchanged between Cassandra and Tim.

Cassandra decided to take over. "We have a new lawyer. He was hired this morning."

Jon was still confused but the fingers of his right hand relaxed. They were not congratulating him on being free of Kari. *Get a grip*, he admonished himself. *They don't know about her.*

"Get to the point. What are you talking about?"

"Mrs. Dobis," both attorneys shouted at once. "You get to dump her. She's no longer your headache."

"You're free," Tim continued. "Remember? The new attorney

gets stuck with her. Now you can go to the secretarial pool and take your pick."

Tim was leering. "There are some real lookers. You should try them all, if you get my drift." He started to laugh, but the scowl on Cassandra's face stopped him.

Jonathan understood now. He could dump his disagreeable secretary on the new guy.

Jonathan, why do you treat her like that?

His head snapped to the right side to look over his shoulder. Kari's voice was so clear he thought for a moment she was there.

He glanced at his watch. "Give me ten minutes. There is something I need to take care of. Ask Mrs. Dobis to come in on your way out."

Though he managed to dismiss the pair without being obvious, he knew they would consider what he was about to do insane. But he had to do it. He had no choice.

Elizabeth Dobis walked into his office stiffer than usual. He noticed she tried to avoid even the slightest eye contact with him.

"My things are together. I'll be leaving in a couple of hours, after I show your new secretary where things are."

Jonathan looked the woman over, praying he wasn't making a mistake. "Mrs. Dobis, I didn't ask you in here to ask you to leave or to train your replacement."

"Well, then, what is it that you want with me? I have things to do."

"Mrs. Dobis, I want you to stay on. I want you as my permanent secretary." He saw the woman getting angry and wondered why.

"I don't need your pity. I've been here twenty years. I know the routine. Now if you don't mind, Mr. Steele, I would appreciate your picking a new secretary so I can train her and get my new office ready."

Jon licked his lips. The woman was making it hard for him to follow his plan. "Mrs. Dobis, this is not pity. You're a good secretary and you do a good job. I like order and routine. I think we work well together. One other thing, may I call you Liz? "

He waited for a long time. The woman didn't speak, making him uncomfortable. He had the oddest feeling that she was evaluating him, putting him on trial. It was clear that if she stayed, it would be her choice. She would control the situation.

Jon's jaw clenched. For some crazy reason, now that it appeared she might turn his offer down flat, he really wanted her to stay on. Kari had asked him to try. For her, he wanted to do so. He might not have her in his life but within himself he would know he would have her respect if she knew.

"We won't be friends."

"What?" Jonathan's thoughts were on Kari. He'd completely forgotten about Elizabeth Dobis.

"I said we won't be friends," Elizabeth repeated. "I'm not changing one thing. I stay the same as I've always been. Don't expect me to kiss your feet."

Jonathan smiled, amused and relieved. "I didn't ask you to change. But if you don't mind, I will. I'll start by apologizing to you for the way I've treated you in the past."

The woman nodded and turned to leave. "You may call me Liz," she said before she left his office. He stared after her. If nothing else, he felt good about his decision. As he gathered his papers he felt a lightness in his spirit.

He wished for a moment he could tell Kari that he had done the right thing. She had been right about that. He had changed. Now he intended to change back to the man she had known.

Jon walked out to meet Cassandra and Tim, glad that the cases they had worked on for the entire year and a half he had been at the firm were coming to an end. They had done their job well and would be rewarded in the end with a hefty bonus.

He walked past his secretary's desk, then stopped. "Mrs. Dobis, I'll see you around four. If you need me you can page me."

He tried to ignore the woman's look of shock. He had never given her permission to page him, didn't even know if she had the number. He smiled to himself before turning to smile at her. Of course she had it.

The other two-thirds of his team were rounding the corner. They stood watching Jonathan, watching his secretary looking at home with no apparent plans to move.

Jon was glad they had the decency to wait until they were out of hearing range of the woman before they began quizzing him.

Tim began. "What's going on?" He was truly puzzled. "Man, you've been given the keys to get out of hell and it looks like you've opted for a life sentence."

Cassandra stopped walking, her hand flying toward Tim. It was obvious she was trying to restrain him in his comments. Jon peered at her. He could see the wheels turning in her head. She was an analytical thinker, and he knew she was looking at more than just the surface.

"Tim." Cassandra pressed her hand against Tim's hip. "It's really none of our business if Jonathan has decided to allow Mrs. Dobis to continue with him." She turned her gaze toward Jonathan. "We're curious, though. If you want to tell us why, we wouldn't mind listening."

"I asked her to stay because she's good and I can depend on her."

Cassandra's hands went to her own hip. She stood wide-legged in the hall, amusement in her eyes. "You're not still thinking you can change her, are you, Jon?" She laughed, looking toward

Tim. "Why bother?"

"I have no plans on trying to change the woman. I plan to change myself and treat the woman fairly. You would think in a law firm we would all choose to do that." He gave the pair a hard look and started walking.

"Maybe you're right," Tim answered.

"Good luck," Cassandra shot after him.

Jon turned and studied her for a moment. She was smiling and he was aware that her smile was meant to ease the mounting tension between the three of them.

"I meant that, Jon," Cassandra said, stepping closer and touching her hand to his shoulder. "Good luck."

Jonathan returned her smile, including Tim also. He might as well practice getting along with everyone. Kari would want it that way. "Thanks," he answered.

As the three of them walked toward the bank of elevators, Jon was buoyed by his actions. Maybe he and Elizabeth Dobis would never come to the point where they actually liked each other but he would always know that he had done the right thing. For now that was enough.

CHAPTER TWENTY-TWO

Kari had made up her mind. She would tell the minister the truth. All of it. She marched to the minister's office and rapped softly on the door, biting nervously at her lips. *What if he refuses to marry us? We'll have to go to the courthouse or justice of the peace.*

She could feel the tiny beads of perspiration break out. She had tried to calm herself, had done meditation to prevent the nervousness.

"*There is no reason he needs to know.*" Those had been Steve's words when she asked him if they should tell the pastor. She didn't agree.

"Come in."

The sound of the minister's voice propelled Kari to open the door. It was now or never.

"Pastor James, do you have a few moments? I want to talk to you." The look of concern on the man's face made her smile. "Don't worry, sir, I'm not here to tell you Steve or I have changed our minds. I just didn't tell you something and I'm wondering if I should have."

Kari watched as he walked from behind his desk. He was curious and rightly so. She didn't mean to sound so mysterious, but what was she supposed to do, blurt it all out? She was grateful that he only pulled out a chair and with a smile indicated she should take it.

A few minutes later she was also grateful that he hadn't interrupted her. She had noted the time she walked in the door. Now she checked her watch again. Only five minutes had passed. It amazed her that she had been able to condense almost eleven years of her life into five minutes.

When the minister did speak, his voice was smooth, soothing as a warm cup of hot chocolate. "Kari, why did you tell me this? It wasn't necessary. Are you having second thoughts about the wedding?"

She stood up, her eyes darting around the room. "No. I have no second thoughts. I just thought you should know what's been happening in my life and I thought… Well, you told us the last time if there was anything in our past that might cause problems, we should bring it out in the open and deal with it." She looked at the minister. "I'm only following your advice."

"What if I told you that after what you've told me I can't marry you?"

"Then we'd find someone else who would. Steven and I are getting married, Pastor James. Make no mistake about that."

"Let me get this straight. You've only recently found that you're still in love with a man from your past." He scratched at his chin.

"Yet Steven is the man you want to marry because you want children with him. That is what you've just said, isn't it?"

"Yes, Pastor James." Kari looked away from him toward the door. "I can assure you my future is with Steven, if that's what's worrying you."

"Steven has to be told about this before I will marry you."

Kari laughed at the pastor's admonishment. "Steve knows about Jonathan and he's forgiven me."

"He has? Does he know about the child?"

"No."

"Aren't you worried that I'll insist on him knowing? I truly don't understand. If you're really not having second thoughts, why did you tell me? You were under no obligation to do so."

She shrugged. "I guess maybe I wanted to be forgiven."

"You know you don't need me for that, Kari. You could have asked God yourself. Haven't you done that?"

"Yes."

"Well then, Kari, you need to speak plainly. Why would you be so upset about having wished you weren't pregnant? I can understand that, if not approve. You were a young unmarried woman. As far as wishing goes, that's a natural human response." He paused. "There's more to this, isn't there?"

Kari buried her head in her hands. "Yes, Pastor James. There's more. I didn't just wish it, I prayed. I got down on my hands and knees and I prayed for God to take the baby away."

She broke down, tears scalding her cheeks. She hated what she'd done. She couldn't forgive herself. She thought she'd put it away, out of her mind, but seeing Jonathan had brought it all back.

She felt Reverend James's hands on her head, offering comfort.

"Say what it is you want, child, say it with your own mouth."

"I want God's forgiveness, pastor, for my prayer, maybe to be granted absolution or something." She looked up through her tears at him.

He smiled. "We're Baptist, you know we don't do that. If you asked for God's forgiveness, He's given that to you. I think perhaps you should ask forgiveness of this Jonathan Steele."

"I asked his forgiveness."

"And?"

"Jonathan loves me. He would forgive me anything."

The minister moved away from Kari, a look of puzzlement on his face. "Kari, I can see that you're upset, but you've got me confused here. Surely I can't be hearing you correctly. This man... Jonathan. He's forgiven you for not trusting him, for not loving him enough to have faith in his love for you. He's even forgiven you for praying such a selfish prayer to the Almighty to take away an innocent life?"

Kari cringed, but she answered him. "Yes, sir, he's forgiven me."

"And Steven, the man you're going to marry, has forgiven you, right?"

"Yes."

The minister shook his head. "I truly am at a loss. You've asked forgiveness from everyone, including God. You've been forgiven. Kari, why are you here?"

"I don't feel forgiven. I feel this ache inside. I want it to go away."

Once again the minister shook his head and moved away. This time he sat down behind his desk and scowled at Kari.

"All of this is because of the baby? You stopped trusting Jonathan because you thought he didn't want the baby, so you prayed for God to take it?"

"No, sir, that wasn't it, that's not what I said. I was afraid I wouldn't love the baby."

"Why Kari? One more time."

"Because of Jonathan's mother, I hated her," Kari screamed. "She hated me. She made my life a living hell. How could I love something that might look like her?"

"Then tell me, how could you have possibly loved Jonathan? He was her son."

"Pastor, I did love Jonathan. He was the love of my life."

"I don't think so, Kari. I think you were incapable of loving the man. All of this is evidence of it. Think about it. Your inability as a Christian to love his mother made you believe you couldn't love your own flesh and blood, your baby. It's why you doubted your love for Jonathan."

"I did love Jonathan… I mean, I do love him. When I saw him all the old feelings I thought were dead came alive again. That's the problem. I don't want to love Jonathan, not anymore. I love Steve now."

Now Kari was the one getting angry. The minister didn't know what he was talking about. "Steve said this was none of your business. I think he's right. I just thought you should know. That's the only reason I came."

The minister laughed but without mirth. "No, it's not. One more question. Tell me something, Kari, how did you decide which man you loved enough to spend the rest of your life with?"

For the first time since coming into the minister's office, Kari smiled. "That one was easy, reverend."

That was the one question she was prepared to answer. Kari licked her lips, watching the pastor, assuming he would understand and agree with her.

"Steve and I are the same, our culture, our families, our experiences." A groan of disgust escaped her. "I would never put myself through the changes I went through before."

The minister frowned. Now it was Kari's turn to become puzzled.

For heavens sake, the man was black. He knew what she was talking about. Was he living in a vacuum? He had to know that times had not changed that much, that any interracial couple trying to have a relationship still faced many hurdles.

He stared at her a long moment before he spoke. "Are you saying it's Jonathan's color that's making you marry Steve?"

Kari was offended. "I told you I love Steve."

"Yes," he answered her, "but you told me you also love this Jonathan." He smiled at her then. "You came to me, so I think I have a right to ask questions, and you have no reason to be huffy. Now, is Jonathan's skin color what's stopping you from marrying him?"

"Reverend, it's not Jon. It's the world."

"What are you talking about?"

The minister walked toward Kari and placed a thick meaty hand on her shoulder. She was aware the gesture was meant to comfort her, but she pulled away.

"You make it sound as though I'm...as if... I'm not prejudiced, sir. It's my parents, Jon's parents, Steve, my hometown. But not me."

She was up pacing the room, angry at the minister for daring to suggest such a thing. "I never was... I have lots of white friends. I love Jonathan. I lived with him for three years. How do you think I could possibly be—" She groaned inwardly. "Besides, look at me, how could I possibly be prejudiced?"

"Kari, are you by chance implying that because you're black, you can't be? Didn't you say your parents are prejudiced, that Steve is?"

"Yes, but they're not me. I've never been that way. I don't judge people. You don't know me well enough if you believe that. My life has never been about color." Her voice was now haughty and she knew it. "I don't care what you say, I'm not prejudiced. I can't be. I wouldn't have lived with Jonathan if I were."

"And you think you should be praised for that? Is that the best reason you can come up with? Kari, we all have some degree of bias in us."

Pastor James slapped his palm hard against his forehead. "That is the silliest misconception. I can't believe the number of people who believe that very thing.

You think your entire town, including your parents and friends, was affected by this and you escaped it?"

She watched as the minister searched for an example. Her first thought was to question him about his all black congregation, but she held her tongue and decided to listen. Maybe she needed to hear what he had to say. He waggled his fat finger in her face before beginning.

"Some women won't look at a man they consider fat. And don't let one be short. They won't even give him the time of day.

"As for color, I can't tell you, Kari, how many black people judge each other because of the color of their skin. Men and women alike think that the lighter you are, the better, so don't get me started on prejudice, Kari"

He hit his head again. "Yes, it's possible for you to be prejudiced. Not only is it possible, you are. You let Jonathan go because of the color of his skin. I don't care how much you try and deny it."

"You're wrong, pastor. I left Jonathan because I thought he was in love with another woman."

"Hogwash. The woman was white. That was your proof that the man didn't love you. Flimsy, flimsy excuse. You were too afraid to fight for him. Too afraid of being hurt. And yes, Kari, I think color was behind it."

"That wasn't the reason. But even if it were, it was the right decision. Jonathan's life is a success, so's mine. We both did better in our own worlds."

For a moment the room was silent. Only the grunting sounds the minister made deep in his throat alerted Kari that he was disgusted with her. Well, so what? She was disgusted with herself.

"This kind of thinking is stupid and you're not a stupid woman. It seems Jonathan was right. You are the one with the problem."

Kari felt angry. "You didn't live my life," she yelled. "My parents disowned me and his did the same to him. Reverend James, you're not listening to me. You weren't there, reverend, you don't know. I tried. For three years I tried. You have no idea of the names we were called, of the hate mail, the stares.

"No one is going to tell me I didn't love Jonathan. I did love him. I loved him to the exclusion of everyone else. I had no one but Jonathan." She shivered with the memory of finding him with

Sharon. "When I thought Jonathan didn't love me, that he never had, it nearly killed me." Kari's eyes closed with her remembered pain.

"When it was over, when we were done, I had my family again. I moved here to Chicago. No one knew about my past except my friend Jackie. I didn't have to worry about being shunned, having people whisper about me behind my back. I had a new circle of friends. I was no longer alone. I like it like that, Pastor. I like not being shunned."

She sat down in the chair, a lump forming in her throat. "When Steve first found out, he wouldn't even touch me. He couldn't look at me. He thought I was dirty. He's just like my father on that matter." She attempted a laugh. "No race mixing."

"That's not a very Christian attitude."

"Christian? Let me tell you something, reverend, Christians are the worst people to expect Christian charity from, and for the worst place to go looking for it, try church. Last Sunday Steve and I went to a friend's church and we decided to take communion. The priest looked at us both with such contempt."

"What did you do?"

"What do you think? I stared him down and took communion. I almost had to pry the cup from the man's hand. Do you know how hard it was for me to drink from that cup? I hate drinking behind people in the first place, and to drink behind hundreds, ugh," she shivered.

She stopped and saw that he was watching her. "What's wrong? Why are you staring at me like that?"

"I'm wondering why you drank," he said.

"Because no one can tell me I can't take the Lord's Supper, plus I did it since he didn't want me to."

She was feeling smug. She had proven her point. "Now do you think that was Christian?"

"No, I don't. But I wonder why you'll fight to take communion at a church you're not even a member of, but won't fight for the right to be with the man you love. To think you wouldn't love a child because it might resemble someone you hated... That isn't a very Christian attitude. Kari, you're not only a bigot, you're a hypocrite!"

Kari shot out of the chair sputtering, trying to pull her words together into a cohesive thought. She was in church and she was talking to her pastor. If not, she would have been tempted to tell him to go to hell.

Kari finally shrugged and decided to ignore his comment. "Reverend, I am marrying the man I want to marry. If you have problems with it, then maybe we should just go to city hall."

As he considered the matter, she was trying to figure out what she would tell Steve about ruining their lavishly planned wedding if he refused.

"No, Kari. If you and Steve have no problems with this, then morally there is no reason for me not to marry the two of you in the eyes of God. I just want you to think over what I've said. If you have any concerns, don't hesitate to call on me."

She stuck out her hand. The minister gripped it in a firm hand-shake and held on while he probed her with his eyes.

"Did your skin ever make any difference to Jonathan? Did he treat you disrespectfully?"

"Of course not." She was indignant. "You don't know Jonathan, he loved me." She lowered her voice. "With him there was no hiding, no compromises, and no fear. He stood up to both our parents." She frowned slightly. "He even stood up to me in the beginning, when I wanted to end it, when I wanted to stop fighting."

"Kari, I think you're right. Both you and Jonathan are proba-bly better off with others. He deserves a woman who loves him as much as he loves her and evidently you're not that woman.

"There is one other thing I want you to know before you leave this room. God didn't answer a foolish, selfish prayer like that. God didn't take the child because you didn't want it, thinking you couldn't love it. What kind of a God do you think we serve?"

His voice rose higher and Kari thought any moment he might start to preach. She attempted to wring her hand from the man's firm grip but he refused to let go.

The reverend continued. "I want you to let go of that guilt and forgive yourself. That's really why you came here, Kari. You want me to give you something that I can't. It's your own forgiveness you seek. That's why you still carry the burden in your heart, why you don't feel forgiven. You haven't forgiven yourself.

"If this helps, Kari, I will tell you truthfully that your wishes and prayers did not cause the death of that baby."

He looked at her sadly. "I pray that God gives you and Steve perfect babies 'cause Lord help them if they happen to be born with an infirmity." With that he released her hand and turned away in sadness and what she thought looked close to disgust.

Kari moved slowly toward the door. When her fingers were within inches of touching the knob, she turned back. "Pastor James, it is for the best. Steve and I will live a very happy life and in a few years when you're immersing our children in the baptismal pool, you'll realize that."

"I hope I'll be able to teach them the true meaning of Christian love. It doesn't seem either of the prospective parents really knows the meaning. Good day, Kari."

With that he moved back to his desk and she walked out the door, the sting of his words as cutting as a knife blade.

He's wrong, I am not a bigot. I'm just rectifying a mistake I made in my youth.

She walked out of the church, the clicking of her heels resounding throughout the quiet sanctuary.

CHAPTER TWENTY-THREE

Three weeks had passed since Jonathan had asked Elizabeth Dobis to stay on. Despite her promise not to change, he had noticed in subtle ways that she had, just as he had.

He'd started with little things, a couple of dozen doughnuts dropped on her desk with him telling her they were for the office. Then there were also the mornings when she came in and gave him a surprised look when she discovered that he had started up the coffee. On two occasions she had actually gone to lunch with some of the other employees, something he had never seen her do.

To top it off, he swore that once she almost smiled at him before catching herself and stopping.

The entire office staff seemed to have improved their various relationship with the Elizabeth. He had not heard a soul giggling about her behind her back, or making comments.

Even Tim and Cassandra had come around and were courteous to her, appearing not to be as put off by her combative behavior.

Jonathan checked his calendar every day. He would be relieved when the two weeks were past. Every day he took Kari's stolen wedding invitation from his drawer and looked at it. The pain sometimes ran so deep that he thought it might actually be a physical problem.

At work he did his best to camouflage the pain, but the moment he stepped into his car for his journey home, the mask came off. He no longer attempted to soothe himself with the physical comfort of a soft feminine body. There was only one woman for him and he would have to wait it out. It would take time before he could even start to heal.

One day he sat alone in his office, dejected, going over case folders, anything to keep his mind occupied, when a knock came at his door. It was a welcome sound. He looked up and smiled at Liz when she came into his office. The woman was eyeing him strangely, her mouth twisting. He sensed she was debating with herself, so he waited until she decided to speak.

"You're in love with her, aren't you?"

"With who?"

"With Kari Thomas, the client you sued."

Jon's bottom lip dropped about an inch. He was cautious, wondering if the new cease-fire was over, if she might be planning to blackmail him or something. He waited, not saying anything, allowing her rope enough to hang herself if that was her game.

"I know it's none of my business, but you've changed since she was here. I saw you looking at her. It was in your eyes that you love her."

"Am I that obvious?" She did smile at him then. There was no mistaking it.

"Yes," she answered him. "It's that obvious, even more so since she went back to Chicago. You're more thoughtful, but your eyes are so sad. I can see the hurt there."

"How, Mrs. Dobis?" He slipped back into his former habit of formality with her. "Tell me how can you tell I'm hurting?" She looked away from him but he sat patiently watching her.

"I've been there," she finally said. "I didn't marry the man I loved and I'm afraid I've been trying to make the world pay for it ever since."

"Was he black?" Jon hated asking, but he wondered if that's why the woman was confiding in him.

"No, he was white." She sought his eyes and held them. "He was a widower with three small children. My family had a fit. They wanted me to be with someone with no responsibilities."

Jonathan was curious. "But you were married, right, or do you just use the title?"

"Oh I married." She frowned. "A young man, my age, no children. He worked for my father and saw dollar signs when he looked at me. He never loved me, and he abused me. I stayed married to him for fifteen years, just because my parents approved of him."

Jon didn't interrupt. She was twisting her hands and pacing around the room. He could tell the memory haunted her still.

"After my divorce I looked up the man I had loved. It was too late. He was married and happy. He and his new wife had had two more children." This time she brought her eyes up to meet Jonathan's. "She was a real nice woman. We could have been friends under other circumstances. I left and moved here. I couldn't live in the same city with him, knowing I had made the biggest mistake of my life. I still love him," she said sadly, "but there is nothing I can do about it. You can, Mr. Steele."

"I'm afraid it's too late for me also," he answered her. "She's getting married."

"But she's not married yet. She won't be for another two weeks."

"How do you know that?" He stopped. Of course, she had been in his desk, had gone through his things, had seen the invitation. Knowing she risked losing her job for what she had divulged, she had come to him anyway. "She asked me not to interfere. She said if I loved her I would let her go, and let her be happy."

"She loves you too."

"Yeah, maybe." He turned toward the wall. "Just not enough. She can't deal with the color of my skin. I guess I'm the color of trouble." He tried to laugh, but it sounded more like a sick bull's call.

"Thanks for your help, Liz, but there is nothing I can do. She's afraid. She said loving me wasn't worth the pain involved. I would love to promise her that we would never have a single problem, that I would never let pain touch her again, but that would be a lie. I won't lie to her."

Elizabeth Dobis started to leave. "I'm sorry, Mr. Steele. I really liked her. You know, she might think she's going to be happy with the other man, but she doesn't truly know. And neither do you. The way the two of you looked at each other, it's obvious you were meant to be together."

"I'm all for that." He ran his hand through his thick dark blonde hair. "Maybe you should go to Chicago and tell her. She won't listen to me."

For several moments the two of them faced each other, each with their own heartache, each accepting the other's pain. Elizabeth was the first to speak.

"I just thought if there was a chance for the two of you to be happy you should take it. I would hate to see either of you end up like me."

"There could be someone else out there for both of us to love." Jon twisted his neck, stretching, trying to get the knots of tension to leave. "We have to hope, Liz."

"You could be right," she answered him. "I'm sure we could both find someone to marry, but will we find another soul mate? I doubt it. It's rare to find them in the first place. So I choose to be alone. You don't have to be." She opened the door and stepped out. "You can try again. She's not married yet." The last she said as she closed the door.

Jonathan went to his desk and removed the invitation for the second time that day. The embossed lettering and the black couple facing him were mocking him.

Steven Anderson wins by default because he happened to be born with a little more melanin in his skin. How ironic. This was one time when being considered a member of the majority was a handicap.

He kept the invitation out on his desk. He had to face up to what was about to happen. Keeping the card hidden away would not stop the inevitable.

He thought of the movies where the hero always got the woman he loved. The hero would stop the wedding if need be, declaring his love for the bride.

And the bride, ahhh yes, the bride would run down the aisle and throw herself into the hero's arms.

Jon glanced again at the card. What would Kari do if he showed up? *It doesn't matter*, he thought. *I told her that I loved her. Stopping her wedding won't help.*

What the hell am I thinking? It's that damn Liz turning mushy and romantic. I am not going to Chicago and I'm certainly not going to go and watch Kari take wedding vows with another man.

What are you afraid of?

The question startled him. It was loud, as if someone had spoken it. Hell, he would be glad when Kari married Steve. Then he could stop hearing her voice and whoever the hell had just spoken.

He looked again at the couple on the invitation, then took a white piece of note paper and covered the man.

"There that's better." He'd have to watch that. He was beginning to talk out loud.

ॐ

After her talk with her pastor, Kari had done her best to avoid him. After church services she would always rush away.

Steve had glanced at her as he moved in the line to shake the pastor's hand. He had questioned her once about her seeming aversion to the man who was going to marry them.

She had replied that was not the case, that she was busy and only wanted to get home. The man was known to be long-winded so Steven had no problems believing her.

Now if she could make herself stop playing that damn tape she would be fine. She had at last gotten through crying every time she heard the words. Eric was wrong and so was Jonathan. She was not lost in her own fears. She was not marrying Steve out of fear.

CB

Kari kept herself busy working on every detail, not leaving one thing undone. Her interest in her wedding plans made Steve happy as well as her parents. They all had been eyeing her, waiting for her to show some telltale sign of weakness.

What they didn't know was that she was the strongest she had ever been in her entire life. She had to be to walk away from Jonathan, putting what he meant to her in the back of her mind for a safe and secure future.

If she were weak she would have remained in Kansas City, Missouri, with the man who held her soul and spirit. No, this she did for herself and for her unborn babies.

The only thing that puzzled Kari was her lack of emotion. That, she had to fake. Since the day she'd last seen Jonathan and felt the chill around her heart, she'd ceased feeling any emotion about what was going on around her.

The mother of one of her dear friends had died unexpectedly, a very nice woman that Kari cared about. She felt nothing.

She went through the motions of comforting her friend's family, saying the right words, doing the right things. But inside she felt dead.

Her heart was encased in ice. She knew that, had felt it happen. Since then she'd been like an actor playing a part. That worried her a little, but not much. Her heart was too frozen to really care.

03

Jonathan had managed to get through the remaining days by ignoring the looks Liz often threw his way. Now it didn't matter any more. It was Friday. In less than twenty-four hours Kari Thomas would become Mrs. Steven Anderson.

Jon worked way into the night, staying in his office listening to the sounds of people leaving for home. He would have to leave soon. It was only so long that he could put off the inevitable. Eventually it would be morning, then afternoon, and his chance for happiness with the woman he loved would be gone forever.

His desk was clear. There was not another thing he could even pretend to do. So he turned off the lights and walked out of his office. Elizabeth Dobis sitting at her desk startled him. He'd thought he was the only one left in the building.

"Liz, what are you doing here? I thought you were gone."

"I was waiting for you. I wanted to give you something." She extended her hand.

He knew immediately what it was. Jon looked at the bulky envelope, the airline tickets peeking out. Biting on his lip, he closed his eyes, trying to swallow the sudden lump in his throat. He looked again at the proffered envelope, noting five different tickets.

Elizabeth Dobis, had taken it on herself to buy him five tickets to Chicago. He was touched.

"I can't."

Liz shrugged. "It's your decision, Mr. Steele." She rose and came toward him, pushing the envelope insistently toward him.

"If you change your mind, you won't have to kick yourself for not having a way to get there in time."

He glanced at Liz as he once again looked at the bulky envelope and the array of tickets, a question in his eyes.

Liz shrugged. "I wanted to cover every flight that would get you there in time."

The lump was still in Jon's throat, making it difficult for him to answer. He swallowed several times before speaking. "I thought you weren't going to change?"

"I thought I wasn't either. It just goes to show you never know what can happen. Good night, Mr. Steele."

"Liz, I'll pay for the tickets." She smiled, giving him the feeling he already had. She walked toward the elevator. "Good luck," she murmured low.

Jon stared after her. "Thank you," he managed in a low voice. He looked over his shoulder toward his office.

Damn, I must be crazy. He pushed open the door and reached for the invitation. Not looking at it, he shoved it into his jacket pocket.

Just in case, he thought, *just in case."*

Jonathan's drive home was the loneliest of his life. He dreaded going into his empty home and brooding. But the thought of going out, of talking with people, was too much for him to handle. He would spend the night in mourning, have a wake for true love.

He had barely entered the apartment when he spied the unopened bottle of bourbon he had received several months ago as a gift. "Now that's a plan," he shouted at the walls. He poured a full glass and took a healthy swig. The burn that started in his throat and worked its way down into his stomach didn't stop him from polishing off the whole glass.

He glanced at the bottle. *I should drink the entire thing, maybe pass out. Then I won't have to make a decision. I'll be in a drunken stupor. When I wake up it'll be Sunday and it will all be over.*

But for now he knew he had to get through the night and the next day. The whiskey would never offer the comfort he needed. A primal ache filled his body, racing through his blood and capturing every single cell with its intensity.

He sat on the couch in the dark with no sounds except his own breathing. He fell asleep at last and when he awoke, it was almost eleven. Only four more hours to go. Kari would be married at three.

Jon walked to where he had carelessly tossed the envelope the night before. He pulled out the tickets and checked the time. Three had already gone. The next plane left in under two hours. If he was going to do it, it was now or never.

He pictured Steve's hate-filled face and he remembered Kari asking him to tell her that he loved her. How the hell could he stay in Missouri when the woman he loved was about to make the biggest mistake of her life? He couldn't.

He dialed Mark, his friend in Chicago, the same friend who had drawn up the papers for the bogus lawsuit. At the sound of Mark's voice, Jon blurted out that he needed a ride from the airport and to the church.

"Are you planning on stopping the wedding?"

"God, I sure hope that's not my plan."

"Didn't you say Kari asked you not to come? You told me she said she didn't want to see you. Ever."

"I know."

"Then why?"

"I love her."

"Are you a masochist? What if she has you thrown out on your ass?"

"I've hired guards to keep out uninvited guests." Steve's words came back to Jonathan.

"That might happen, but I have to go. Mark, I love her. I can't let go of her until I see for myself that she really is married to that jerk."

"That sure as hell sounds masochistic to me."

"I'm not a masochist, just the opposite. If I don't actually see her getting married and hear her saying the words for myself, I might not believe she went through with it. I don't want to live the rest of my life not knowing."

Jon sighed. "Listen, I'm wasting time. I have to shower and change and make it to the airport in under an hour. Just say you'll be there for me."

"I'll be there. I think you're crazy but I'll be there."

Jon tapped on the phone with his fingers for luck. He was thinking the same thing, he was crazy. "Thanks for your help. I owe you one."

"No, you owe me two." His friend laughed, referring to the phony case Jon had coerced him to file.

"You're right. How about if we make it three?" Jon asked his other favor, ignoring Mark's protest that it was impossible, that it was Saturday and couldn't be done.

"Just do it, Mark. I'm counting on you." With that he gave Mark the address of the church and ended the call.

Smiling to himself, Jonathan dialed the operator for a number and waited impatiently for his call to be answered.

"Mrs. Dobis, Liz, this is Jonathan Steele. I was wondering if it would be possible for you to give me a lift to the airport." He heard the laughter in the woman's voice and continued. "I barely have time for a shower. I'm just afraid if I drive myself or take a taxi I'll be late."

"How soon do you want me there?" Liz asked.

"Fifteen minutes too soon for you?" Jon answered.

"Don't worry, Mr. Steele, I'll be there. Good luck."

Jon gave his secretary, now his new friend, his address and ran for the shower, dropping his clothes along the way. He had a plane to catch.

CHAPTER TWENTY-FOUR

For Kari Friday night was filled with tension. She nearly pushed Steven out of her home, along with her father. Both men were getting on her nerves. She felt as if they had appointed themselves to guard her virtue.

It would have been perfect if she could have thought of a way to get rid of her mother but there was no tactful way to do it. Her mother would probably have to be blown out with dynamite. There was no way she was going to allow Kari to stop her from being there to help her dress.

What does it matter? Kari thought as she kissed Steve goodbye. Her parents were glowing, happy that she was going to be safely married within a few short hours.

For the first night since returning from Missouri she did not listen to Eric Clapton. Her ties with her past would have to be severed permanently now. She might as well start with the song.

Wondering how she would ever sleep, she remembered the pills Steven had given her a few months earlier when her life had been torn apart. She popped one of the remaining pills in her mouth and lay in bed waiting for it to work its magic. She needed one dreamless night.

She wanted to pray for that but was a little leery of the power of her own prayers. So she lay there trying to make her mind a blank, waiting for the lightness that accompanied taking the pill.

Although she couldn't believe it, she must have slept. The next thing she knew her mother was shouting at her, shaking her shoulder and telling her to hurry. Steve was on the phone. For some reason his deep sexy voice annoyed her.

Had he said, "I love you," or even "I miss you," she might have forgiven the intrusion, but what he said was, "It's time to get dressed."

"I am aware of that," she snapped, then saw her mother was wearing a look of concern.

"I'm sorry that I snapped at you, Steve. Don't worry, I have plenty of time."

The image of a prisoner being marched toward his execution and the clang of metal bars intruded on her subconscious. A shiver passed through her body followed by an electric jolt. Kari shook her head several times to dislodge the image. *Now why would I think a thing like that*? When her mother pointed at the clock, she dismissed the image. She had a wedding to go to.

"Kari, it's for the best."

Kari stopped what she was doing and looked at her mother. "Mom, do you really believe that?"

"Yes. Steve's a good man. He'll make you happy."

Kari smiled at her mother, not saying anything. Not saying that once she'd had a good man who'd made her happy. What good would it do?

"Kari?"

Her mother turned away from her, that alone telling Kari her mother wanted to talk about Jonathan. She couldn't remember when her mother had ever been at a loss for words.

"We saw that boy, Kari, at your house a few weeks back. He said you'd had an abortion."

Kari waited, wondering why her mother could never just call Jonathan by name instead of referring to him as "that boy," even now that he was a man.

"If that's true, if you did that, I just want to tell you how proud of you I am."

"Proud of me?"

She must not be hearing right. Maybe she was still under the effects of the pill she'd taken. "Why would you be proud of me, Mom, if I killed my baby?"

"You didn't need a half-white baby, Kari. Look what happened with that boy. You'd be raising the baby all alone."

"No, Mom, that would have never happened. Jonathan loved me as much as I loved him. He would have been there for me."

"Well, none of that matters now, Kari. You don't have his baby. Now you're free to have babies with Steve, lots of babies that you can be proud of. Your father and I can't wait to be grandparents."

"And will you and Dad help us to raise them to be good, loving Christians?"

"Of course we will," her mother answered, either ignoring or not accepting the sarcasm. She kissed Kari's forehead, offering her a cup of tea.

Kari wanted to scream, to be angry. Instead, what she felt was disgust. And in that moment she realized Reverend James was right. Jonathan was right.

Oh God, please no, she prayed. She was exactly like her mother and father. She was the perfect woman for Steve, she was what she'd never thought she was, what she'd accused Steven and the entire town of Lonett, Alabama, of being. She was a bigot.

Filled with remorse, she prayed. Change me, Lord. Change my heart. I don't want to be this way. Please thaw the ice around my heart.

ᘓ

The house filled quickly with bridesmaids, the photographer

and several people she didn't recognize. Kari moved as though in an assembly line, every person in the house having to tuck, pull or straighten something on her.

"Kari, you're looking kind of strange. Are you going to be okay?"

Kari barely glanced at her maid of honor. She was tired of fighting with Jackie over her decision to marry Steve. She wished she'd never confided to her that she still loved Jon. "Jackie, I'm fine," she answered at last. "All brides are nervous on their wedding day."

"This has nothing to do with nerves and you know it," Jackie answered her. "I'm not a fool, we've been friends too long. I know you slept with Jonathan when you went to Missouri. Steve's not crazy, he has to know it. Kari, this obedient robot act isn't fooling me. How long do you think you can keep it up?"

"Why are you doing this now? Leave me alone."

"I'm trying to help you, you're not thinking clearly. You think because what happened with you and Jonathan before it's going to be easier with Steve because he's black."

"Jackie, marriage is hard with any man, I know that. I'm not fooling myself about that and I'm also not fooling myself about being a good wife to Steve. I will be. I'll do everything in my power to make him happy."

"And what about Jonathan?"

"Jonathan is my past. Now would you please leave me alone?"

"I would if I believed you, but I don't. How can you marry Steve knowing that you've cheated on him? Don't tell me you told him because he would have kicked your ass but good. He's that kind of man."

Kari covered her eyes with her hands. She was doing her best not to retch, thankful that she had nothing in her stomach. "Jackie, why are you doing this? You don't even like Steve. Why are you being his champion?"

"Because it's not right."

Kari whirled around, "I know what I did and I know I'm being a hypocrite. My God, Jackie, I'm not stupid. I know what I've done. It's killing me inside, but I'm going to make it up to Steve. I love him, I truly do. I'm going to be a good wife to him, you'll see. I really will make it up to him.

"How? By being his meek little, subservient, dutiful wife the rest of your life?"

"If that's what it takes. Now Jackie, Please, leave me alone. If you no longer want to be my maid of honor, just leave. It's your choice to make just as it's mine to make as to who I want to marry."

❧

At last Kari stood before the full-length mirror and sucked in her breath. If she had to say so herself, the gown was breathtaking, seed pearls everywhere and the veil shimmering with tiny pearls interspersed with sapphire and garnet stones, just as she'd designed it.

As the time grew closer, a low rumble began in her stomach. She gave her tummy a pat; she felt butterflies rioting there. Her mother had tried on several occasions to get her to at least eat some crackers and drink a cup of tea, but she'd refused. There was no way she would dare put anything in there with the butterflies.

❧

Jonathan was on the plane before he had a chance to talk himself out of the foolishness he was about to embark on. He ignored the flight attendant asking if he wanted a cup of juice. There was something happening in the pit of his gut. If he dared a drink he would puke.

Sweat was pouring from his armpits and down his sides causing his shirt to cling to him. His silk suit, usually cool, was hotter than hell. Jon knew the source of his maladies. A five foot, three, honey-brown woman with chocolate drops for eyes.

His heart was pounding, and he couldn't believe what he was about to do. He glanced at his watch, hoping for once the plane would land early. He thought of Kari. Elizabeth Dobis was right. Kari wasn't married yet. He didn't believe she would be able to go through with it. *But what if she did?*

He licked his lips. They were dry and his mouth didn't even have the small amount of saliva it would take to moisten them. It was as though every bit of moisture had been sucked out of him. He was amazed that he still maintained the function of breathing.

Within moments after the plane landed, Jonathan was out of his seat and running down the aisle, bumping into people and shouting, "Sorry, emergency, sorry." People sat back down making way for him. "Thank you," he yelled over his shoulder several times as he darted off the plane.

A quick check of the time told him it was almost two. He continued running until he passed through the automatic doors and hit the hot air outside. He cast his eyes about looking for Mark, hoping the Chicago police had not chased him away.

It was then a well-dressed black man caught his eye. He was frantically trying to wave down a cab or a limo. No one would stop for him. *"Jonathan, your skin gives you a free pass. Do you know how many black men are unable to get a cab to stop for them?"* Kari's words slammed into him. She was right. His color did give him an advantage. He couldn't change the world, but he knew right now, there was something he could change. Without thinking,

Jonathan thrust his hand in the air for a cab.

Almost immediately he heard the squeal of brakes as the car slowed for him. He opened the door, maintaining a tight grip, and beckoned for the black man. The man came over, looked at him suspiciously before climbing in and muttering thank you, obviously ashamed and angry that something so simple was denied him because of the color of his skin.

Jonathan glared at the driver and growled, "You know what you're doing is illegal."

When he heard the honking of a horn, he started toward the sound without even checking to see if it was Mark. Lucky for him it was.

The two men looked at each other. "Did you get it?" Jonathan asked, as he climbed in.

"I got it," Mark answered. "And I owe half the city of Chicago a favor for it." He passed the envelope over to Jonathan, who deposited it in the inside pocket of his suit coat.

"Thanks, Mark. I owe you big for this."

"If you get to use that, consider all debts paid." Mark smiled at Jonathan.

For an answer Jonathan merely pointed at the steering wheel, indicating he wanted Mark to stop talking and start driving.

Mark did just that, not asking any questions or giving any unwanted comments. He pulled up in front of the church with eighteen minutes to spare.

At the top of the cement stairs stood two big burly men. They each wore a tux but something about the physique of each man alerted Jonathan that Steven had not been kidding about security. They sat in the car for several moments watching the men check each guest invitation.

"What are you going to do now?" Mark questioned.

Jon turned toward Mark. "I have an invitation."

He saw his friend's eyebrows arch and a questioning look come into his eyes.

"All right, I stole it." Jon continued watching, noting that small groups were not detained as long as single white males who were carefully scrutinized.

He got an idea. He looked up and down the street. He instructed Mark to head for the adjacent parking lot.

Jon got out of the car and waited until a car pulled up with four women and one man, all white. He smiled at Mark. "Bingo," he said, and gave Mark a wave.

When they got out, Jon walked straight to them. "Excuse me," he smiled, "are you by any chance going to the wedding?"

"Yes," the redhead answered.

"Would you mind if I tag along? You see, I'm by myself and I feel…well, you know, out of place."

This time the group laughed. Jon had known it would work, that they would band together to take in one of their own. He would use that to his advantage.

As they walked the short distance, Jon joked with them, making them laugh harder each time. When they reached the security guards he passed in with the group.

How ironic, he thought, as they were seated on the groom's side.

As Jon looked around he saw a man with a flowing black robe trimmed in velvet making his way toward the back where Jonathan was seated. He was shaking hands and conversing with everybody. Jonathan guessed it was the minister.

He stirred uneasily, not wanting the man to come to him, fearing somehow he would know him for who he was. At last the man stood at his row, shook hands with others, then smiled and reached for Jonathan's hand.

Jonathan felt sick to his stomach. He tried to smile as the minister took his hand. Though the minister had given only an obligatory shake to most people, he imprisoned Jon's hand in his own while his eyes searched Jon's face.

Jon noticed the man had a strange look on his face as though he knew him. Could it be Steve had planned this, had given the minister a picture of him? He licked at his lips nervously, then gave a quick glance around the church, what he hoped would be a signal to the man to let go. Still the minister held on.

How it had come about, Jon didn't know. But it was clear the minister knew who he was. He didn't say a word but something in his manner gave him away. His eyes held pity and that made Jon want to run out of the church. But he had come too far to give up now. After what seemed forever, the minister released his hand and moved on.

When the choir began singing, Jon joined in the clapping but would have been hard pressed to say what they sang. A side door opened at the front of the church across from the pulpit and Steven stepped through with his best man.

The soloist sang and Jon felt tremendous stabbing pains. He knew what was coming next. After a brief interlude the organist began the wedding march and the entire congregation stood for the arrival of the bride. He saw Kari hesitate at the door, then look around. For a moment he thought she knew he was there. He ducked his head only seconds before she looked at his row.

My God, she looks so beautiful. For a brief moment, Jon had forgotten what she was about to do, then it hit home. *No no,* Jonathan screamed silently in his mind. *Kari, don't do this please. I love you. You're marrying the wrong man.*

☙

As Kari walked down the aisle on her father's arm, she kept her eyes fixed on Steve standing at the front, waiting for her.

Kari, I love you. You're marrying the wrong man. It was Jonathan's voice she heard in her mind. She was sure of it. She felt her smile waning as she let go of her father's arm and looked to her left and right. With an act of will she brought her attention back to the front of the church, to Steve who was waiting for her. It would be over soon.

Oh God, she moaned inwardly. *Oh God.*

ɞ

Steve stood at the front of the church smiling as he watched Kari come up the aisle to him. When he saw her hesitate and glance around, he froze. Then she sought him out. He smiled. Everything was as it should be. He'd won. She was his. In a matter of minutes, this beautiful woman would be his wife. After that, Jonathan Steele could rot in hell.

ɞ

Kari reached for her father's arm that she'd dropped only moments before. *The tension must be getting to me*, she thought. *That couldn't have been Jonathan's voice. He's in Missouri.*

She caught a glimpse of her mother's tear-streaked face as, a little shaky, she arrived at the altar. Kari was determined to stay focused, refusing to allow her mind a chance to wander. Her father placed her hand in Steven's, then kissed her forehead through the veil.

Steve kissed her hand. She smiled up at him. She should be feeling something. She wanted to feel something.

Here she was about to get married and she felt nothing.

She was dead inside. She had to be, she was so cold. She felt her body begin to shiver. If only something could happen to make her feel warm again.

And then she heard the voice again, louder, more insistent. *Kari, I love you. You know you love me too. This is wrong, Kari, you can't marry Steve. He's the wrong man. Don't be afraid, fight for us, Kari. Fight for us.*

Not now God, she pleaded inwardly.

But you love him, Kari. He's the one you should be marrying, not Steve, came the answer.

But I want babies, she answered the voice. *I have to make it up to the other one*, she thought, as she clung tightly to Steven's hand. *I want babies*. She forced herself to concentrate on Steven Anderson, her black knight. The man who could give her the babies she wanted.

As long as she kept looking at Steve, everything would be as it should be. She gazed deep into his eyes, longing for the picture of the babies she always got when she wanted to be sure.

There, she had it. There was her circle of beautiful brown-skinned babies with dark eyes and tight curly hair. She smiled briefly, enjoying a sense of peace. That peace quickly evaporated as the babies began to waver and change.

Kari felt a stirring deep inside of her, as though something was clawing to get out. She could barely stand being in her own skin.

Then there was a feeling of being shocked by a high voltage of electricity. It ran from the top of her head, curled through her spine and flowed out her toes. But it didn't stop. It continued until Kari's entire body felt electrified.

This had never happened before. Always before when she conjured up her babies she felt only peace and joy. Now something strange was happening.

The babies continued to change. Their skin tones now ranged from pale gold to dark chocolate, and their hair was a mixture of curls highlighted with blonde streaks. A chubby baby appeared in the center with skin so light, and eyes so blue, they could only belong to one other person. The baby lifted its chubby arms toward her. She reached out in return. She knew the child. It was hers.

A pop burst around her heart. The ice was melting. She was finally beginning to feel warm. As Steven's arm encircled her waist, her mouth gaped, but no words came out.

She stared at Steven and tried to focus on his face, desperately trying to conjure up the circle of dark-skinned babies, but it no longer worked.

The only picture she saw was of infants of varying shades. A sense of rightness coursed through her as love for the chubby baby with the blue eyes overwhelmed her.

"My God, I was so wrong," she murmured in a voice that was barely more than a whisper. "Forgive me. I'm so sorry. I do love you. I'll do whatever it takes to have you. I'll fight for you, I promise," she said to the chubby baby. At last she was able to focus on Steven. She couldn't go through with it.

ଓ

Steve's stomach churned like crazy as he looked at Kari. Something was wrong with her. Kari was standing before him like a zombie, talking to herself. "Kari," he called as loud as he dared.

He felt a shudder of disgust rip through his body as she reached her hand out trying to take hold of an imaginary something only she could see.

She was making a fool of herself and a laughing stock out of him. Their entire wedding was being ruined.

"Kari." He called her name again before circling her wrist. He applied as much pressure as he dared to the hand that he was holding. "Kari, snap out of it."

She looked first at Steve, then at her pastor. "I can't, Steve." She reached up and touched his cheek with her free hand. "My God, I'm so sorry. I thought I could, but I can't. I love Jonathan."

"Don't do this, Kari, not now. You're just nervous. You probably have low blood sugar from not eating all day."

"I don't think that's it." She looked again at the minister. "Reverend, stop this please."

Steve applied even more pressure, enough to force Kari to whimper in pain. Her eyes went down to her hand that Steven Anderson, her supposed black knight, was squeezing.

She glared at him and wrenched free. "That's the last time you will ever touch me, Steve. I'm not your property, and I'm not marrying you."

She spotted the door across from the pulpit, the same one Steven had walked through only minutes before. With her head held high, ignoring the gasps of surprise that flew quickly throughout the church, she walked out.

Steve followed right behind her. He grabbed her elbow, just as her father called to her.

"Kari, come back here, what do you think you're doing?"

"Don't worry," Steve said. "I'll handle it."

She stopped before reaching the door. "No, Steve, you won't handle it. I will." She knew what she had to do.

God, why couldn't you have given me this revelation a little sooner?

☙

At the back of the church, Jon realized something was wrong with Kari. She had gone from smiling at Steve to being in a seeming trance. He saw her stumble and reach out her hand and he rose automatically to go to her.

The minister stared back at him, shaking his head no. As he slid back down into the pew he saw Steven lean down and whisper something to Kari. Suddenly he felt hope. *Fight, Kari, fight*, he whispered silently. *I love you.*

When he saw Kari's hand touch Steven's face in a gesture of consolation, he knew she wasn't going to marry Steve. His heart felt as if it suddenly had wings. He wondered if anyone else was aware of what was happening.

What the hell? Jonathan stared in shocked horror. Even from where he sat in the back, he could tell Steve was squeezing Kari's hand, hurting her.

Jonathan rose, determined to kick the crap out of Steven, never mind that they were in church. There was no way he would tolerate seeing anyone hurt the woman he loved. He realized suddenly that the minister with those all- knowing eyes was watching him. The moment he slipped into the aisle, two ushers took hold of him, urging him to return to his seat. One of the men placed a note in Jonathan's hand and whispered, "Pastor James wants you to read this."

Jonathan's eyes went to the tiny slip of paper. "Wait. Kari needs to handle this herself." Just as he lifted his eyes he saw Kari suddenly exit through the door, her parents running wildly behind her shouting. Jonathan closed his eyes and offered up a prayer of thanks.

The minister asked the soloist to sing but it was no use. The woman's voice was no match for hundreds of people gossiping behind their hands. They were curious. Who wouldn't be?

CHAPTER TWENTY-FIVE

Twenty minutes passed before the door opened again. As Kari walked out alone, the crowd fell into an expectant silence. Jon searched her face for signs that she was hurting, but instead he saw a strength in her that he had not seen since the first year they were together. The smile she wore was wide and dazzling, not the look of a distressed bride. She held her back straight and had an air of confidence. She was happy.

"Thank you, God," Jonathan muttered aloud. He continued watching as Kari whispered something to the minister, then walked toward the microphone. Jon's right hand clutched at the pew in front of him. He was doing his best to remain seated. His heart wanted to run to her but he would have to wait. He sat still and listened

ଔ

Kari glanced around the church filled with her friends and family, Steve's family and co-workers. She felt a surge of love reaching out to her, causing her to close her eyes and whisper loud enough for those close to her to hear, "Jonathan, I love you."

Then she took a deep breath to steel her resolve and spoke into the microphone. "I want to tell you all that Steven and I appreciate your coming here today. I know you're all wondering what happened. Before the rumors start, I would like to fill you in."

Kari looked toward her parents, then back at her guests. "None of this has anything to do with Steven. This debacle is all my fault. I'm in love with someone else, someone who just happens to be white. I've denied loving him even to myself." She paused, then glanced again at her parents.

"I was wrong. I only recently realized that because of bigotry, my own as well as that of others, I almost made an irreparable error. I almost gave up the only man that could ever make me happy, my soul mate.

"I truly thought if I fell in love with a black man enough to marry him, it would ease the ache of not being with the man I really love. But it hasn't eased, and I know now that it won't. I'm meant for one man only, and his name is Jonathan Steele. I don't care that Jonathan's skin isn't black. He's the right color for me."

Kari licked at her lips and looked at her parents. "Mom, Dad. Be happy for me, please." Her voice was quavering, filled with her raw emotions. She turned back to the audience. "I will personally make sure that all of your wedding gifts are returned.

"The hall has been paid for, so I'm asking that you go and enjoy the party." She smiled then. "You've all been so supportive, so I'm asking that you continue to support Steve."

She turned from the audience walked toward her parents. She no longer cared about their approval.

"I'm going to Missouri. I'm going to beg Jonathan Steele to forgive me. If he still loves me, I'm going to spend the rest of my life proving I deserve him. I want to spend the rest of my life loving him and our babies.

As she walked toward the minister's office, her parents blocked her way. "We will disown you again," her father growled through gritted teeth.

Kari smiled sadly at them. "I feel so sorry for you. You're missing out on being loved by your future grandchildren's father."

"We're not kidding, Kari. Marry that boy and you're out of our lives for good. Just think what kind of life you're letting yourself in for. You're always going to have to fight prejudice, Kari."

That sounded so funny coming from her mother. She couldn't possibly realize what she was saying.

"Prejudice cuts two ways, not just one. Bigotry is a habit, Mom. A learned habit, one I plan on breaking. That's something Jonathan told me a long time ago. He was right. I love him. Can't you be happy for me?"

"You go looking for him, you marry him, and we want nothing to do with you. Ever," her father growled.

"I don't care," Kari answered as she kissed them both. She smiled, a smile so big it lit up her face. "I also don't have time for this now. I'm going to catch the first plane I can get heading for Missouri. I'm going to find him."

She glanced at her bridal party and ran over to hug them. When she came to Jackie, she stopped. The tears in her friend's eyes and the smile on her face told her she approved of her decision. "Wish me luck," Kari whispered as she kissed her best friend.

"You don't need luck." Jackie answered her. Jonathan always loved you."

Kari ran through the door to the minister's study. She felt lighter than she had in seven years. She waited for Reverend James to come, knowing she had left him to clean up her mess. She stood with her back to the door waiting for him, the phone in her hand. She was getting on the first plane out of Chicago and heading to Kansas City, Missouri.

When the door opened, she felt shivers go up and down her spine. Then a current of electricity coursed through her. She didn't have to turn. She knew he was there. Maybe she'd known it all along, why she'd felt something combining with her own strength; his strength, making her stronger.

"Jonathan," she said without turning.

"Did you mean it?"

At the sound of his voice she turned. "Were you there the entire time?"

"Yes."

"Were you going to let me go through with it?"

"Yes, if that's what you wanted."

"Then why did you come?"

"I was hoping you would change your mind but if you didn't, I had to see it for myself in order to go on."

She looked at him, the love in his eyes telling her what she needed to know.

"Jonathan, you're lying. You were not going to sit there and just let me marry Steve. Were you?

He smiled back at her, knowing he'd been caught. "Hell no," he growled playfully. "I let you get away once, but not again."

"Does this mean…" She looked down and away, her cheeks hurting because her smile was so wide.

"What do you think?" He held his arms open and she went into them. He crushed her to him, not believing what had happened, not believing she was in his arms, that their seven years of hell were over.

Jonathan held Kari a little away from him and brought her hand upwards so he could examine it. "Did he hurt you?" he asked as he kissed each hand in turn.

"Not really," Kari answered.

"Why did you ever become involved with a man like that? Didn't you see that hate in him?"

"I saw it. I pretended I didn't. I was looking for a man that was the exact opposite of you. Steven was exactly that. Jonathan, I'm so sorry. Can you ever forgive me for being…for being a bigot? I didn't know I was. I'm just like the rest of them."

"No, you're not, Kari, and of course I forgive you, my love."

"How can you say that I'm not like them? God, I hate feeling like this. I hate myself for it."

"That, baby, is the reason you're not like them. You don't want to be, and you've chosen not to be."

"God, how I love you, Jonathan," Kari said, kissing him all over his face. For the first time in more than seven years she was whole. She was home, in the arms of the man she loved. Together the two of them could conquer anything, even hate.

The door to the minister's study opened and the pastor entered.

"So I take it this is Jonathan?"

Jonathan stuck out his hand again. "How did you know?"

"That was easy," the minister answered him. "You looked as though you were in great pain. Everyone else was filled with joy. I saw the burden in your face. You looked as if you had lost something precious, something irreplaceable. I knew."

"I thought I had." Jon turned to Kari. "I love you. Will you marry me?"

"Yes. When?"

"Now. You're dressed for it."

He turned to the minister. "Is it legal for you to marry us now? I mean, is there some waiting period or a morals clause?" He watched the man smile at him.

"You have to have a license."

Both Kari and Reverend James watched as Jonathan pulled a document from his pocket. No explanation was needed. He had come prepared. Jon passed the paper to Kari to sign, grinning as she noted his signature already on the document.

Jon turned toward the minister. "Well, sir, how about it?"

"Usually I wouldn't do it in this type of situation," the minister chuckled, "but I believe this was Divine Intervention."

He looked at the puzzled couple so obviously in love. "I've been praying since Kari told me about you that the Lord would lift her confusion and allow her to see clearly. I think she came to me for that reason.

"You see, Kari, you're not the only one who believes in the power of prayer."

"Thanks, Reverend James," Kari answered smiling. "I wish you had prayed for better timing."

"God's never late, Kari. He's always right on time."

"Just barely," Jonathan teased. "Just barely, padre."

Reverend James beamed at the couple. "Kari, are you ready? The world hasn't changed all that much in seven years. You're still going to have to fight some battles."

"I know, sir." Kari smiled at him before turning her smile on Jonathan. "I'll work on my own prejudice first. If Jonathan's willing to forgive me for my own bigotry, I think I can wait for the world to come around. And if it doesn't, I still have the only man I will ever love. Believe me, he's worth fighting for."

"Good, you're ready." Pastor James smiled and began the ceremony.

Kari was too busy accepting Jonathan's kisses to hear much of what the minister said. Jonathan pulled the ring from his pocket, the one he'd bought for her years before.

As Jon placed it on her finger, she heard Reverend James say, "I now pronounce Jonathan Steele and Kari Thomas husband and wife." It was then she believed it was for real. Finally, it was for real.

Her heart was bursting with love for her new husband, the way it was meant to be. Warmth flooded her body and electrical impulses shot between them. The ice that had encompassed her heart had melted completely away.

"I love you, Mrs. Steele."

"And I love you, Mr. Steele. For ever and always.

Jon kissed his wife before lifting her in his arms and walking through the church with a triumphant grin, ignoring the stunned smattering of guests still remaining. He deposited his bride in the car of a waiting and surprised Mark.

"Mark, I'd like to introduce you to Mrs. Jonathan Steele, my wife." Jon grinned like an idiot. "All debts are paid. I used the license you got for me."

THE END

EXCERPT FROM UPCOMING TITLE,
A LARK ON THE WING,
BY PHYLLIS HAMILTON

"You know, I've been looking forward to seeing you every since we tied up two weeks ago." Smiling he added, "I thought you knew that."

No longer able to maintain her angry front, Austin's words were like a sweet balm. Beaming, she reached up to give him a kiss. "Austin, I..., Achoo! Achoo!" Unable to control a barrage of sneezes, she began to noticeably shiver.

Quickly handing her his handkerchief, he realized that not only was she soaking wet, but cold as well. In a manner that was both attentive and loving, he draped the jacket that he had been carrying across her hunched shoulders. "Here take this, it's no wonder you're sneezing. Not only are you soaking wet, you're freezing. If you're not careful, you are going to find yourself in bed as my patient."

Gratefully snuggling into the deep folds of his jacket, Sedona remained silent as she enjoyed a warm rush imagining how it would feel to be under Austin's attentive care.

Oblivious of her thoughts, Austin suggested, "Since the rain isn't showing any signs of letting up, why don't we head on over to the coffee shop. While you warm up, we can sit, do some catching up and listen for your name over the intercom."

"Ok, but first I want to stop by the ladies room and try to make myself a bit more presentable."

Smiling down at her, Austin gave a wink and pointed across the terminal. "Don't be too long. I'll head across the way, over to the restaurant." Watching her retreating figure, it was obvious where his thoughts were heading.

Looking in the mirror, Sedona grimaced at her reflection. What was once a very flattering mid thigh turquoise sarong, now looked no better than an expensive silk washcloth. No wonder Austin couldn't help but laugh, she looked as if she had rolled right out of the gutter. Not only had the water spotted the dress, but also in some places, the fabric was almost transparent. Every inch clung to her frame as if it had melted. Desperate to fix herself up, she turned on an electric hand dryer and directed its nozzle first towards her dress, then her hair. The difference the effort made was negligible, not even a fresh application of lipstick helped.

Giving up, she reached for Austin's jacket and placed the cotton fabric up to her face. The warm sandalwood scent that still clung to its' fibers immediately conjured emotions so strong, that they literally left her weak in the knees. She couldn't wait until she had him alone. Even though he mentioned staying at a hotel instead of her place – some 'gobbly-gook' about wanting her to know that his visit was about more than just the physical aspect of their relationship, Feminine intuition assured her that she could change his mind. That was the easy part. After all, despite his pragmatic mind, he was still a man. She knew all too well that his cool exterior was just a protective cover for simmering emotions - not to mention the practical point that he had had just spent six months out at sea. Austin James was just as warm blooded as the next man, this she knew for a fact. What she had to figure out was much harder. She had to get under his skin, in his head and capture his heart. A week or two of pleasure would be wonderful in the short run, but what she wanted was Austin, in toto.

2003 Publication Schedule

January	Twist of Fate	Ebony Butterfly II
	Beverly Clark	Delilah Dawson
	1-58571-084-9	1-58571-086-5
February	Fragment in the Sand	Fate
	Annetta P. Lee	Pamela Leigh Starr
	1-58571-097-0	1-58571-115-2
March	One Day At A Time	Unbreak my Heart
	Bella McFarland	Dar Tomlinson
	1-58571-099-7	1-58571-101-2
April	At Last	Brown Sugar Diaries & Other Sexy Tales
	Lisa G. Riley	Delores Bundy & Cole Riley
	1-58571-093-8	1-58571-091-1
May	Three Wishes	Acquisitions
	Seressia Glass	Kimberley White
	1-58571-092-X	1-58571-095-4
June	When Dreams A Float	Revelations
	Dorothy Elizabeth Love	Cheris F. Hodges
	1-58571-104-7	1-58571-085-7
July	The Color of Trouble	Someone To Love
	Dyanne Davis	Alicia Wiggins
	1-58571-096-2	1-58571-098-9
August	Object Of His Desire	Hart & Soul
	A. C. Arthur	Angie Daniels
	1-58571-094-6	1-58571-087-3
September	Erotic Anthology	A Lark on the Wing
	Assorted	Phyliss Hamilton
	1-58571-113-6	1-58571-105-5

THE COLOR OF TROUBLE

Other Genesis Press, Inc. Titles

A Dangerous Deception	J.M. Jeffries	$8.95
A Dangerous Love	J.M. Jeffries	$8.95
After the Vows	Leslie Esdaile	$10.95
(Summer Anthology)	T.T. Henderson	
	Jacqueline Thomas	
Again My Love	Kayla Perrin	$10.95
Against the Wind	Gwynne Forster	$8.95
A Lighter Shade of Brown	Vicki Andrews	$8.95
All I Ask	Barbara Keaton	$8.95
A Love to Cherish	Beverly Clark	$8.95
Ambrosia	T.T. Henderson	$8.95
And Then Came You	Dorothy Elizabeth Love	$8.95
A Risk of Rain	Dar Tomlinson	$8.95
Best of Friends	Natalie Dunbar	$8.95
Bound by Love	Beverly Clark	$8.95
Breeze	Robin Hampton Allen	$10.95
Cajun Heat	Charlene Berry	$8.95
Careless Whispers	Rochelle Alers	$8.95
Caught in a Trap	Andre Michelle	$8.95
Chances	Pamela Leigh Starr	$8.95
Dark Embrace	Crystal Wilson Harris	$8.95
Dark Storm Rising	Chinelu Moore	$10.95
Designer Passion	Dar Tomlinson	$8.95
Eve's Prescription	Edwina Martin Arnold	$8.95
Everlastin' Love	Gay G. Gunn	$8.95
Fate	Pamela Leigh Starr	$8.95
Forbidden Quest	Dar Tomlinson	$10.95
From the Ashes	Kathleen Suzanne	$8.95
	Jeanne Sumerix	
Gentle Yearning	Rochelle Alers	$10.95

Glory of Love	Sinclair LeBeau	$10.95
Heartbeat	Stephanie Bedwell-Grime	$8.95
Illusions	Pamela Leigh Starr	$8.95
Indiscretions	Donna Hill	$8.95
Interlude	Donna Hill	$8.95
Intimate Intentions	Angie Daniels	$8.95
Kiss or Keep	Debra Phillips	$8.95
Love Always	Mildred E. Riley	$10.95
Love Unveiled	Gloria Greene	$10.95
Love's Deception	Charlene Berry	$10.95
Mae's Promise	Melody Walcott	$8.95
Meant to Be	Jeanne Sumerix	$8.95
Midnight Clear	Leslie Esdaile	$10.95
(Anthology)	Gwynne Forster	
	Carmen Green	
	Monica Jackson	
Midnight Magic	Gwynne Forster	$8.95
Midnight Peril	Vicki Andrews	$10.95
My Buffalo Soldier	Barbara B. K. Reeves	$8.95
Naked Soul	Gwynne Forster	$8.95
No Regrets	Mildred E. Riley	$8.95
Nowhere to Run	Gay G. Gunn	$10.95
Passion	T.T. Henderson	$10.95
Past Promises	Jahmel West	$8.95
Path of Fire	T.T. Henderson	$8.95
Picture Perfect	Reon Carter	$8.95
Pride & Joi	Gay G. Gunn	$8.95
Quiet Storm	Donna Hill	$8.95
Reckless Surrender	Rochelle Alers	$8.95
Rendezvous with Fate	Jeanne Sumerix	$8.95
Rivers of the Soul	Leslie Esdaile	$8.95

Rooms of the Heart	Donna Hill	$8.95
Shades of Desire	Monica White	$8.95
Sin	Crystal Rhodes	$8.95
So Amazing	Sinclair LeBeau	$8.95
Somebody's Someone	Sinclair LeBeau	$8.95
Soul to Soul	Donna Hill	$8.95
Still Waters Run Deep	Leslie Esdaile	$8.95
Subtle Secrets	Wanda Y. Thomas	$8.95
Sweet Tomorrows	Kimberly White	$8.95
The Price of Love	Sinclair LeBeau	$8.95
The Reluctant Captive	Joyce Jackson	$8.95
The Missing Link	Charlyne Dickerson	$8.95
Tomorrow's Promise	Leslie Esdaile	$8.95
Truly Inseperable	Wanda Y. Thomas	$8.95
Unconditional Love	Alicia Wiggins	$8.95
Whispers in the Night	Dorothy Elizabeth Love	$8.95
Whispers in the Sand	LaFlorya Gauthier	$10.95
Yesterday is Gone	Beverly Clark	$8.95
Yesterday's Dreams, Tomorrow's Promises	Reon Laudat	$8.95
Your Precious Love	Sinclair LeBeau	$8.95

Dyanne was born in a small town in Alabama. She then moved to Chicago when she was eleven, with her mother and sister, where she remained. She's happily married to William Davis, her newest critique partner. They live in a nearby Chicago Suburb with their only child, William Davis, Jr.